Praise for the TREE OF LIFE Series

"*In the Cradle Lies* hooked me with its intriguing premise and fully delivered on it. Newport masterfully weaves together past and present storylines that left me eager to turn the next page."
—Lindsay Harrel, author of *The Secrets of Paper and Ink*

"With a delightful mixture of ancestral discovery and small-town charm, the characters come alive in their devotion to family roots, warmhearted kindness for their neighbors, and gentle faith. A must-read for anyone who loves exploring family origins!"
—Jaime Jo Wright, Daphne du Maurier and Christy Award-Winning author of *The House on Foster Hill*

"Newport smartly differentiates herself in the popular 'time slip' genre by rooting her story in the art of genealogy. Anyone who has ever wondered how the patches of their histories are sewn into the fabric of their lives will feel completely at home."
—Rachel McMillan, author of *Murder in the City of Liberty*

TREE OF LIFE • BOOK 2

IN THE CRADLE LIES

Olivia Newport

SHILOH RUN PRESS
An Imprint of Barbour Publishing, Inc.

© 2019 by Olivia Newport

Print ISBN 978-1-68322-995-7

eBook Editions:
Adobe Digital Edition (.epub) 978-1-64352-395-8
Kindle and MobiPocket Edition (.prc) 978-1-64352-396-5

Cover design: Faceout Studio, www.faceoutstudio.com

Published by Shiloh Run Press, an imprint of Barbour Publishing, Inc., 1810 Barbour Drive, Uhrichsville, Ohio 44683, www.shilohrunpress.com

Our mission is to inspire the world with the life-changing message of the Bible.

 Member of the
Evangelical Christian
Publishers Association

Printed in Canada.

DEDICATION

For my children, Caleb and Cana, who stand in the stream of our family's story, and Mike, whom we've welcomed to the story.

CHAPTER ONE

J illian Parisi-Duffy was of firm enough character to defend her choice regardless of the criticism, and she had faced plenty.

First, from her father before she left the house that morning. "If you plan to spend most of your time sitting in the lodge with a book, at least take a novel."

"Bye, Dad," was all she said as she shoved her choice in her bag and went out the front door to meet Kristina Bryant in her idling sedan.

Then there was Kris. "That's the book you brought to read while I ski?"

"It's been at the top of my pile for weeks. I can finally dig in."

Then other guests in the lodge, coming and going to warm up between runs and plopping down beside her on the sofa in front of the massive fire with their hot chocolate. "What are you reading?"

She'd shown them the cover and watched their predictable expressions.

"That's a mouthful," they said, or "Not exactly leisure reading," or "Is somebody making you read that?"

"How's the skiing?" she replied every time. They'd chatter about snowpack and powder for a few minutes and then be ready to go back out.

Jillian had been out on the lodge's deck a few times to stretch her legs, inhale the bracing mountain air, and try to spot Kris's purple ski jacket and leggings on the slopes against the cerulean sky and sprays of glimmering alabaster powder. But most of the time she remained camped in front of the stone fireplace with one of a progression of steaming beverages, hot chocolate piled with whipped cream, rich caramel latte, and finally dark hot chocolate with hazelnut syrup. Once she interrupted the flow of beverages with the simple sandwich and chips fare the lodge offered, because her father would later ask if she'd eaten anything all day. With a turn of her head in either direction, she could gaze out floor-to-ceiling windows at the luminous Colorado day and the ski lifts moving people to the tops of the runs. The day was stunning, no question.

But so was her book. She didn't have her laptop with her and hadn't even brought a yellow legal pad for notes, so technically this wasn't work. It was recreational reading that happened to be of an academic nature and coincidentally intersected with her profession as a genealogist. With her hands free of hot beverage and food, at least temporarily, Jillian slipped her feet out of her low-cut, fur-lined boots and folded them under her legs on the deep, thick-cushioned leather sofa. Then she began a new chapter, letting the sounds of the lodge fade into the background.

"How's the book?"

"Fantabulous." She knew the voice and angled her head toward the inquirer. "How's the skiing?"

"Astonishing!" Kris unzipped her jacket and shrugged out of it as she dropped onto the sofa beside Jillian.

"What's so astonishing?" Jillian moved her bookmark, closed the volume, and twisted toward her best friend. "You've skied here dozens of times."

"Of course I am always an astonishing skier." Kris tugged off her cap and tucked it into the helmet in her lap.

"And humble," Jillian said.

"There is a dude out there you would not believe. You know how you always say that the way I ski is one of the biggest arguments for why you *don't* ski?"

"It is. You're a maniac daredevil."

"You would reconsider that description if you saw this guy."

"Who is he?"

Kris shook her head. "Not a clue. But I've never seen a more audacious skier."

"That's saying a lot."

"And I mean it. If you hear sirens for the ski patrol, they will be for him. He's going to kill himself."

"Come on, Kris. This is a family-friendly ski business."

"Tell that to him. He's looking for danger. When I do the double-black runs here, I don't usually have much company. Not many people have the skills. But he didn't even take a minute at the top to see where the path down was. He just got off the lift at the top and pushed off without a breath or a beat."

"Well, is he as good as he thinks he is?"

Kris shrugged. "His turns are pretty tight, I'll give him that. But he's scary fast and doesn't seem to believe in stops."

"Maybe he's a competitive skier."

"Then why ski here?"

"Don't know. Hey, why did you come in? Hungry? Cold?"

"Grr. The buckles on one boot are not holding properly. I'm spending half my time stopping to adjust them, and even still I feel my heel moving too much for good turns. I'm not going to take chances. I have to call it a day and have Leif Mueller look at it back in town."

"You've been out there for hours." Jillian put her feet back in her boots. "Have something to eat first. I'll start putting stuff in the car."

The day still blazed resplendent on the drive back to Canyon Mines, which was within easy driving distance of half a dozen ski locations. It wasn't often that Kris could get away from Ore the Mountain, her ice cream parlor on Main Street, for an extended day excursion, but January—especially the lull just after Christmas—was a better time than most to leave the shop in the hands of a part-time employee. Though there might be ski season foot traffic through town, freezing mountain temperatures did not put ice cream at the top of tourists' lists, and the Canary Cage coffee shop just down the block sold hot beverages that Kris could not compete with. Hot chocolate was the only exception, because her secret ingredient was hand-tempered chocolate supplied by Carolyn, who ran Digger's Delight, the candy shop that shared the building with Ore the Mountain.

"So Veronica and Luke are having their usual winter party soon," Kris said as she turned her car toward the town limits. "Are you and your dad going?"

"With sleigh bells on," Jillian said.

"As usual, the theme is hush-hush. Have you heard any leaks?"

"Not yet."

"And if you did?"

Jillian smiled. She could keep a secret. "Nia said Meri promised to come back for a weekend at the Inn after she's settled at grad school in Denver."

"You all did a good thing for her, helping her sort out her genealogy—and her family."

"I don't always get to see the difference genealogy searches make quite so dramatically." Jillian pointed out the windshield. "It's starting to snow again."

"Fresh powder."

"You're already thinking about getting back out on the slopes."

"Sure, if I get my boots fixed. Will your dad cut back his days working in Denver?"

"Just January and February. Two days a week instead of three. If we have a mild stretch, he can always change his mind." Nolan Duffy's home office was upstairs while Jillian's was downstairs. He worked part of the week in Denver and part in Canyon Mines, and she worked full-time out of the house. Their arrangement had worked for years. Nolan's practice as a family law attorney and mediator was brisk, and Jillian's work creating family trees for individuals or looking for missing people for insurance or law firms, along with speaking at genealogy conferences and writing for journals, produced a steady stream of requests for her expertise. Since losing her mom when she was fourteen, Jillian and her dad had created their own rhythms of companionable living.

"I heard Clark Addison is threatening to remodel the Canary Cage," Kris said.

"He'd better not get rid of our couch."

"You got that right. We might have to stage a sit-in."

"How's Carolyn's daughter?"

"Getting close to delivering, I think. Carolyn's going to close the candy store for a month when the baby comes and go to Golden to help out."

"Makes sense. Business is slower than in the summer."

"People still buy more candy in the winter than they do ice cream. Without her next door, I could go days without selling a scoop," Kris said.

"Close up and take a real vacation. Go someplace you've always wanted to ski."

"Hey, do you mind if we go straight to the ski shop? I might as well find out what Leif thinks about my boot and whether I have anything to ski with."

They drove past the conjoined ice cream and candy shops, past Veronica and Luke O'Reilly's Victorium Emporium, past the Canary Cage, and detoured off Main Street to Catch Air, the shop Leif Mueller had been running for the last twelve years to take advantage of the town's proximity to Colorado ski country. Kris took both boots from the trunk and carried them through the door.

Just inside, she elbowed Jillian and whispered. "There he is."

"Who?"

"The guy from the double blacks." Kris pointed by tilting her head. "How did he get here so fast?"

"He drives the way he skis?"

The man was older than Jillian's twenty-eight years, in his mid-thirties, tall. The pockets of his radiant green ski jacket overflowed with a yellow hat and gloves. At least he took the precaution of being visible on the slopes during his daring downward flights. Jillian didn't have to be wealthy or a skier to recognize that this man had invested some serious money in outfitting himself, and he wasn't shopping the clearance rack now. Over one shoulder, in stark contrast to the high-end garb that covered him head-to-toe, hung a drab, gray cloth backpack well past its best days.

Leif looked up. "Can I help you ladies—or at least the one of you who skis and is not afraid of tripping over herself?"

"Ha." Jillian grimaced. Having the shop owners in a small town know you had a downside. When the weather improved, she'd get back to regular running—and she rarely tripped.

Kris deposited both boots on the counter, and she and Leif entered a conversation about the technicalities. Jillian hadn't been in Leif's shop many times and began to wander. Even nonskiers could find warm winter gear here. Her dad's latest winter jacket had come from this shop, and it was easy to recognize the vivid hats and gloves around town. The daredevil skier Kris had seen on the slopes was browsing a rack of goggles and had two pairs in his hands with the grip of intent to purchase.

"Are you sure?" Kris's pitch rose. "That's pretty pricey."

Jillian shuffled back toward the front of the store.

Leif tilted his head and shrugged one shoulder. "You asked my opinion. Your main problem is the power strap. Yes, I can try changing that for you, but the other buckles are not in great shape either. We'll have to do them all, and they might never snap the way someone of your caliber deserves. You've had these boots forever, Kris. At the level of skier that you are, I really think you'd be happier in the long term if you started looking at a new pair."

Kris threw her head back and stared at the ceiling.

Jillian put one hand on her friend's shoulder. "You'll figure something out."

The man with the goggles put both pairs on the counter. "Give her whatever she needs and put it on my bill."

Kris's head snapped back into position and spun toward him. "What? No, of course you can't do that, Leif."

"Why not?" the man said. "Leif here says you need new boots. I saw you skiing today. You clearly warrant an excellent pair."

Kris colored. "No. Definitely no."

He extended his hand. "Tucker."

She took it. "Kris. My friend Jillian."

Jillian nodded.

"Knowing your first name does not mean you should buy me a pair of ski boots," Kris said.

"Pay it forward," Tucker said. "Isn't that what it's called?"

"This is not a Starbucks drive-through," Kris said. "This is a different animal altogether."

Even Jillian knew that the quality boots a skier like Kris needed would cost hundreds of dollars.

"I insist." Tucker looked at Leif. "What boot do you recommend for Kris?"

"I can suggest something," Leif said.

Tucker opened his wallet and laid down six crisp hundred dollar bills. "Will this cover it?"

Kris gripped Jillian's arm, gulping. "No. . .Tucker. That's very generous, but I cannot accept."

"The thing about generosity is it's a gift. Freely given." Tucker looked at Jillian. "What could you use?"

"Nothing, thank you. I don't ski."

"A new jacket?" He opened his bulging wallet again. "I hear it's going to be a cold winter."

"No, really, I'm fine." Her jacket was only two years old and perfectly warm. Why was he carrying so much cash? Hadn't the man heard of credit cards?

"A new hat, at least?"

Jillian pointed to the blue knit cap with its red stripe that contained her mane of black hair.

"Some decent sunglasses then." He grabbed a designer pair off the nearest rack and set them on the counter with another two hundred dollars.

"Please, that's not necessary." Jillian shook her head at Leif. Why was this complete stranger determined to give away so much money? Skied like crazy, drove like crazy, and apparently spent like crazy. Cash. Who did that?

"None of it is necessary," Kris said. "I'm sorry if I sounded like I was whining. It's a thing I do. React sometimes without thinking. I'll sort out the boot dilemma." She slid the stack of bills so new they looked like they'd come straight from the Federal Reserve toward the end of the counter, away from Leif and toward Tucker.

Tucker picked up the money and deposited it directly into Leif's hands. "Fit her for the boots she obviously needs, and the sunglasses go home with her friend. If this is not enough, you know where to find me. Try not to have any left over."

He picked up the goggles and left the store.

CHAPTER TWO

Don't you dare, Leif," Jillian said. She wouldn't be caught dead in a pair of sunglasses that cost more than her weekly grocery bill. By a lot. That just wasn't her style. Most days she wrangled her mass of black curly hair behind her neck and tried to make sure her shirt didn't come out of the laundry with visible stains. Designer sunglasses. This Tucker guy did not know her.

"I will be back to talk to you about the boots," Kris said to Leif, "on my own terms."

"What am I supposed to do with, um, eight hundred dollars minus the cost of two goggles?" Leif said.

"That's your problem."

"He said you knew where to find him," Jillian said.

Kristina scooped up her deficient boots. "Let's go, Jillian. I have to think about this."

"I can walk home from here," Jillian said. "I just need to grab my bag from your car."

"I'll take you. But first I just want to pop by the shop and make sure there's been no catastrophe."

"Lindy would have called."

"I guess, but I should check. I'll give you a quart or two of double chocolate chip cookie dough to take home, since there probably haven't been any customers anyway."

"Stop being such a pessimist. But I'm not saying no to that offer."

At the Victorium Emporium, Luke was in the front window, on a ladder, unrolling a large poster of a winter scene in a Victorian village.

"I'm a fan of winter," Kris said, "because I love to ski, but those two go overboard."

"Marketing," Jillian said. "The tourists will eat it up. Veronica will sell woodcrafts with a nice little tag saying they are handmade by Leo

Dunston out at the Inn at Hidden Run, and maybe next time they'll book at the Inn. Then the tourists will wander up and down the street poking into every shop. It's good for everybody."

"In the summer, I agree with you. At this time of year, the theory is sketchy."

"There's a lot of ski season left."

Kris's shop was next door to the Emporium, but she had to overshoot it to find an open parking spot on the street. Jillian held her tongue and did not point out that the lack of parking should be an indication of brisk business on Main Street despite the weather. They got out and turned back toward Ore the Mountain.

"You and Carolyn should cook up more ideas for selling frozen treats made from her candy," Jillian said. "More than just the hot chocolate."

"Maybe."

"Kris, look."

Tucker, with his tattered backpack over his shoulder, exited the ice cream parlor with a cone.

"Looks like you had at least one customer today," Jillian said.

"That's freaky. He can't have known that was my store."

"I doubt it."

"Where's he going now?"

"What difference does it make? He'll browse like all the tourists do."

"Except he has serious money to spend. Let's follow him."

"Hello, what?" Jillian grabbed Kris's wrist.

Tucker paused outside Ore the Mountain briefly and turned his head in both directions.

Kris threw an arm out and imprisoned Jillian up against the brick wall of the art gallery.

"Hey!"

"I don't want him to see us," Kris said.

"What are we doing, Kris?"

"Aren't you curious?"

"What happened at Catch Air was out of the ordinary, but that doesn't mean I want to take up spying."

"It's not spying."

"You're right. It's *bad* spying."

"Don't give me that I-don't-care attitude, Jillian. Your entire profession hangs on dogged curiosity."

"And if Tucker Whatshisname hires me, I will be doggedly curious on his behalf. Right now I'm curious about the quart of ice cream you promised me." It couldn't have been more than twenty degrees. Just the thought of eating ice cream outdoors made Jillian's teeth chatter, but it would taste delicious in the warmth of her home.

Tucker moved on to the Emporium window and waved at Luke.

"Do you think they know each other?" Jillian said.

"See, I knew I was not alone in this curious quest."

Tucker sauntered on to the used bookstore, making rapid progress on his ice cream. Across the street were a specialties teas shop, a men's clothing store, a Colorado home decor store, Ben's Bakery, and Canary Cage. Any minute now Tucker would be free to go inside establishments up and down Main Street without being scowled at because he had sticky, dripping food in his hands.

Jillian and Kris were in front of the building Kris shared with Digger's Delight. They glanced into the ice cream parlor.

"Looks like there's a family inside," Jillian said.

"Good. Maybe I made enough today to pay Lindy for looking after the place."

Tucker walked past the bookstore without going in.

"Somehow I don't see him going in the cards and candles shop," Jillian said.

"Maybe he loves his mother," Kris said.

"Boo."

They both jumped at the sound of the male voice behind them.

Jillian put her hand to her chest. "Leif, what are you doing?"

"Making deliveries. The big one is for you." He put the large sack in Kris's hands. "And the baby bag is for you." He handed the tiny one to Jillian.

"We told you, Leif, no." Kris tried to shove the bulky sack back at him, but Leif stepped away.

"I spoke to my paying customer, and I'm following his instructions. Come into the shop with your skis, and we'll do a proper fitting on the buckles before you ski again. But I'm warning you both, there are no returns on this merchandise, so you may as well receive the gift."

"No returns?" Jillian said. "Since when?"

"New policy. On select merchandise."

"You're impossible," Kris said.

But Leif was ten feet away and waving at them with the back of his hand.

"Now what?" Kris said.

"You could always sell the boots on eBay if you don't want them. Give the money to the homeless shelter. Or donate the boots to the ski club at the high school, like an equipment scholarship."

"And your fancy shades?"

Jillian blew out her breath. She must know someone who would want them. Maybe Nia or Veronica.

They peered down the street at Tucker, who turned and waved—at them.

"Oh great," Jillian said. "Just great."

Her father stepped out of the Emporium. "Well, two lovely ladies fresh from snow heaven."

"Hi, Dad. What are you doing here? Finished working?"

"I might ask what you are doing," Nolan Duffy said. "Skulking down Main Street? Meeting for secret handoffs?"

"Skulking? We're just walking."

"Might as well tell him, Jillian," Kris said. "He gets the truth out of everyone eventually."

Nolan feigned a diabolical laugh.

Jillian was all business. "See that guy up there, Dad? With the green jacket and the backpack? He was out at the ski resort today, and Kris says he was living dangerously. Then he was in the ski shop throwing money around trying to buy us stuff. Expensive stuff. With cash. We don't even know who he is or why he's here."

"Looks like he succeeded in buying you expensive stuff."

"He sent Leif chasing after us. He spent *hundreds* of dollars on ski boots for Kris. That is not our doing, Dad."

"Surely not. But I can help you with your questions. No need to pretend you're with the CIA."

They both stared at him.

"Dad, you know that guy?"

"Not technically. I haven't had the pleasure of meeting him. But I know his name is Tucker Kintzler, and he's from Missouri, possibly St. Louis. He's staying at the Inn at Hidden Run. The word on the street is he intends to live up to the Inn's name by skiing the old abandoned run the Inn is named after."

"If you know that much without talking to him," Kris said, "I'll be very impressed by what you find out when you do talk to him."

"He was in the Emporium before I was. Luke chats. If Nia and Leo invite me to the Inn and he happens to be there, it would be rude not to speak to him, don't you think?" Nolan wiggled an eyebrow. "Otherwise, I'm on my own to run into him in town."

Jillian had no doubt her father would manage to do this.

"Hidden Run—the ski slope—isn't that dangerous?" Jillian said.

"Very." Nolan dug in his pockets for his gloves and pulled them on. "It's in poor condition—hasn't been maintained."

"Where exactly is it?" Kris asked. "In all my years skiing everything around Canyon Mines, I've never actually been there."

"A few old maps show it," Nolan said. "But it's aptly named. It was only open to the public for about seven years in the 1930s, and even then it wasn't easy to get to and the run itself was hard to discern for all the trees. People pulled themselves up the mountain on a rope to find the top of the run. There was a rugged warming hut, but the hut burned down, the rope kept breaking, and the run itself was too difficult to have any real commercial possibility."

"Double black," Jillian said.

"Way worse than that. Maybe you'd call it triple black." Nolan's cell phone rang, and he pulled it from his jacket pocket, glanced at it, silenced it, and shoved it back in.

"Doesn't sound like something anyone should try to ski then," Jillian said.

"I don't imagine any modern ski authorities would be enthused at the prospect."

"Wouldn't he need a permit or something?"

"First he has to find it," Kris said. "It might even be on private property."

Nolan nodded.

"But maybe he's not a permit kind of guy."

"Maybe not," Nolan said. "But the smartest thing is for him not to attempt it in the first place. I suggest we take a vote about who should talk to him."

"Be serious, Dad." Jillian was starting to wonder if there wasn't someplace warmer to have this discussion.

"I am." His phone rang again, and again he silenced it without more than a casual look.

"None of us knows him, Dad."

"I nominate Nolan," Kris said. "His qualifications are that he can make friends with anyone and he is incredibly persuasive."

"Duly noted," Nolan said. "I nominate Kris, on the grounds that as a fellow expert skier, she can identify with Tucker's thirst for adventure while also moderating it with common sense about the particular adventure he has in mind. Plus, he did just buy her new boots, so she has a natural in for more conversation. A personal thank-you will open doors like nothing else."

When Nolan's phone rang this time, he didn't even remove it from his pocket before silencing the call, instead merely pushing a hand in.

"This works out well for me," Jillian said. "You've nominated each other, and I have no compelling qualifications to be of any help. Mr. Kintzler doesn't seem to need a family tree. I'm freezing. Dad, did you bring your truck into town or walk?"

"It's across the street at the Cage."

"Don't you want your ice cream?" Kris asked.

"I scream, you scream, we all scream for ice cream! Rah! Rah! Rah!" Nolan bellowed. "Tuesdays, Mondays, we all scream for sundaes! Sis-boom-bah!"

"Dad, please. I can't feel my feet." Jillian rolled her eyes. He knew her rule about extemporaneous singing in public. "You two are going to have to work out what to do about the ski demon later. I need to thaw out."

"I didn't promise I'm going to do anything!" Kris said.

"Let's all just get warm and discuss this another time," Jillian said.

"The vote is officially tabled." Kris pivoted back toward her shop.

Jillian and Nolan crossed the street toward the Canary Cage coffee shop. Tucker had crossed ahead of them and now pulled an item out of a yellow Victorium Emporium bag.

"I know what that is," Nolan said.

"What?"

"A topographical map of the old mines and ski runs in the areas. Luke sells them at the Emporium. I have a lithograph of the same map hanging in my office at home. You've seen it."

"With all the little squiggly lines and numbers? I never paid attention to what it was."

"Now you know."

Nolan's phone rang for the fourth time just as they reached the curb outside the Cage, and this time Jillian lurched toward him and thrust her hand into his jacket pocket. It was unlike her father to ignore calls, especially when someone was this persistent.

"What's going on, Dad?"

The caller ID said PADDY. That had been her great-grandfather's name. Pop Paddy. But he had passed years ago, when she was a baby. The only other person in her father's contact list who might be listed by that nickname was her Uncle Patrick, whom she'd only seen a handful of times in her entire life.

Just before the call rolled to voice mail, she answered. "Uncle Patrick?"

"Jillian? Is that you?"

"It is!"

"It's lovely to hear your voice."

"Likewise. How is everyone?"

"We're all fine. I was looking for your dad."

Nolan was half a block ahead of her now, unlocking his truck.

"He's not available right now," Jillian said. "I thought it might be important when you kept calling, so I decided to answer."

"That was thoughtful, Jillian, but I need to talk to Nolan. I've been trying for days."

"I didn't know."

"Just tell him he should call."

"I will."

"He'll know why."

Patrick ended the call, and Jillian hustled to catch up with Nolan.

He was close to his eldest brother, Seamus, and the rest of his family who still lived in northern Colorado. But the brother he never saw called repeatedly, and Nolan dodged his calls? What kind of genealogist was she that she didn't know the story under her own nose?

CHAPTER THREE

Near St. Louis, Missouri, 1936

He smiled. He even cupped the back of Mattie's head and answered the questions of the grinning lady.

"Just turned four."

"Wouldn't go anywhere without that wooden horse."

"Matthew likes our little trips to see a bit of the world. Don't you, son?"

Mattie nodded. It wasn't true, but it was the right answer. He angled his gaze upward and to the side, reading the falsehood in his father's face. At home it was Mama who read Mattie stories and tucked him in and knew what his favorite toys were. Papa went on trips alone, or he sat in the parlor looking so glum Mattie knew not to bother him. And why would he bother him? Playing in his room was much more pleasant.

"He is so adorable," the ladies said. "I remember the day you first brought him with you on a sales call. Alyce was a beaming mother."

Mattie's parents' gazes arched toward each other over his head.

"She still is," Papa said. "She's doing a wonderful job with him."

"I suppose you ought to get down to business," Mama said. "After all, that's why we're here. Hospital central supplies."

"Of course," the lady said. "I'll let Mr. Anderson know you're ready to meet."

"Mattie and I will be in the outer waiting area, as usual." Mama took his hand and led him away.

"Are we going to play now?" Mattie asked.

"I'm afraid we have to wait just a little while longer," Mama said.

"But we've been waiting a long time today." Mattie twirled the horse in his hand, imagining he had all the horses in his corral with him. Papa already had three meetings before this one. Mama smiled at the ladies, and Papa met with the men while Mattie had to be still or play without making noise. Sometimes Papa went down the hall for a special meeting, and Mama's face turned a funny color.

"I know," Mama said. "But this is the last meeting for today."

"I want to go home and play with Jackson."

"You won't be able to see Jackson today, Mattie."

"But I want to. Why do we have to come on these dumb trips?"

"Mattie," Mama said. "You know better."

"Sorry."

"This is your father's work. Sometimes he likes my company. Besides, it's nice to be together since he travels so much. You'll be six and in school soon enough, and then we won't be able to come with him at all."

Good. Mattie galloped his horse through the air. At home Mama was regular Mama. On trips she was nervous Mama, sweaty Mama. It wasn't at all nice that they traveled with Papa.

"This chair wiggles," he said.

"They are very old chairs."

"Grandpa Ted could fix them. He could bring something from his hardware section. They just need some new screws."

"What a clever boy you are."

"Grandpa Ted says things like that all the time." Mattie wriggled in the chair and listened to the squeaking that resulted. "He knows how to fix things."

"Indeed he does. But perhaps you ought not to squirm so much unless you have some screws and a screwdriver in your pocket."

"Can I sit on the floor then?"

Mama inspected. The tile floors were as clean as the chairs as far as Mattie could tell. Hospitals were supposed to be very clean.

"All right," she said.

Mattie rubbed his nose. "It tickles, and it smells funny. Like flowers."

"It's how they keep the hospital clean. Your papa sells them the cleaner! But please keep your hands off your face."

"I'm thirsty," Mattie said. "It's hot."

Mama checked her watch. "You haven't had anything to drink in hours. You stay right there. I'm going to let someone know I'm running down the hall for a cup of water and to be mindful of you."

Mattie nodded.

Mama was back in a moment. "Mrs. Gibson was away from her desk, but I spoke to your father. He assured me he is almost finished and will be out in a moment. I'll be right back with some water. And where will you be?"

"Right here." Mattie thumped a chair.

"That's my good Mattie."

Mama's steps clicked out of the waiting area and down the hall.

All day long, one horse was all Mattie had to play with. He'd cantered and galloped and neighed and jumped fences. There was only so much one horse could do, and this one had reached its limit. Mattie laid it down and tugged at his collar. At home he would not have to wear a tight shirt around his neck and be this hot. And bored. And thirsty. Mama was taking a long time.

Mattie placed both hands on the polished floor—probably with cleaner that Papa sold to hospitals—and pushed himself up. It would be all right just to look into the hall and see if Mama was on the way back with water yet.

At the wide opening of the waiting area, there was no real door, just a broad wooden frame like the one in the church hall where Mama sometimes served food with the ladies. Mattie lined up his toes at the edge of the tile squares that met the frame and leaned his head out into the hall. Which way was the water fountain? It didn't matter, because he didn't see Mama in either direction. It was a quiet hallway. He'd been here before, on another trip, and Mama had explained it was where the hospital offices were, not where the patients were.

Mama must have had to go a long way to look for water, or maybe she needed the ladies' room too. The only people in this hall were a nurse carrying a baby at one end and a man at the other. They walked toward each other, not slow, but not running either. They knew the rule about no running indoors, and of course when you are holding a baby you want to be careful. Mattie knew that from watching all the ladies at church and the gentle way they handed new babies around and cooed and made goofy faces.

Mattie hugged the wall and watched. In the quiet hallway, without even stopping, the nurse put the baby in the man's open arms and then pivoted to walk alongside him.

A blue blanket slid between them to the floor as they passed him.

Mattie waited for one of them to stop and pick it up. Because it was the baby's, they would want to wash it after it had been on the floor, but it was important not to lose it.

They kept walking.

Toward an outside door.

Mattie stepped into the hall. "Wait!"

They didn't look back.

"You dropped something!" Mattie picked up the blanket.

They were near the door to the outside now. The nurse glanced at Mattie as he held up the blanket. But she only turned away to hold the door open for the man. He left with the baby, and she went around a corner in the hall and disappeared.

Mattie fingered the blanket. It had letters on it. Mama said she was going to teach him to read before he went to school, but they hadn't started yet. He only knew his letters. A big *J*, like his father's name, Judd. And a big *A*, like his mother's name, Alyce. And some others that didn't matter. They must be the baby's name though. Someone made the blanket and put the baby's name on it when he was born, so they would be looking for it. He could give the blanket to Mama when she got back. Or Papa. Or Mrs. Gibson. A grown-up would know what to do with it so the man could come back and find it.

Whenever Mama wanted him to fold his clothes neatly, Mattie didn't do a very good job. She wouldn't think he did a good job with the blanket either, but he tried before he took it back into the waiting area.

Papa was there. "Where were you?"

"Just in the hall."

"You were not supposed to be anywhere but right here."

"I saw somebody—"

"You were not supposed to be in the hall." Papa snatched the blanket from Mattie's hands. "Where did you get this?"

"Someone dropped it. You could—"

"Did you see who?"

"Yes, sir. You could—"

"You shouldn't have been in the hall."

"I'm sorry, sir. You could still—"

"Sit down, Matthew."

Mattie sat in a wiggly chair and didn't try to explain again. He only pictured the man with the baby getting farther and farther from the hospital without knowing he had dropped the blanket. The real Papa was here, the one who didn't let Mattie finish sentences. He could still go out those doors at the end of the hall and catch the man with the baby and give him the blanket so the baby would have it. If he was the baby's father, who had come to take the baby home from the hospital, he would want the blanket. But Mattie couldn't explain that to real Papa.

"Why are you speaking to Mattie that way?" Mama sat down next to Mattie and offered him the promised cup of water.

"Where did you go?" Papa said.

"I told you I was stepping out for water. It's stifling in here. You did say you were almost finished."

"What took so long?" Mattie said.

"The water fountain was broken. I had to go over to the next hall." Mama stroked Mattie's head. "What are you holding, Judd? Is that. . . ?"

Papa dipped his head once.

"How did you get that?"

"The boy found it."

Mama tugged at one corner. "It's hand-embroidered, Judd."

Papa was silent. Mattie drained his water cup.

"Somebody cared about that child." Mama's voice was like she had a sore throat.

"It's done," Papa said.

"What's done?" Mattie handed his empty cup to Mama.

"Nothing you need to worry about." Mama thrust the blanket back at Papa. "I only stepped out for five minutes, Judd, to take care of *our* child. This is a problem."

"I'll take care of it."

"I'm taking Mattie outside," Mama said. "At least there will be some fresh air. We'll find a bench out front and wait for you. My parents are expecting us for supper. We can still get to St. Charles on time."

Mama took Mattie's hand and led him through the hallways, which felt like the harvest maze they went to with his grandparents, where the walls were made out of hay and made Mattie sneeze. Finally, they were out the front door, and Mattie yanked at his collar, wishing it were unbuttoned. Only when they were alone on a bench under an oak tree did he dare speak.

"Why did the nurse drop the blanket and leave it on the floor when she gave the baby to the man?"

"I don't know, sweetie." Mama opened two buttons on his shirt.

Mattie wondered what Papa would do with the blanket now, but he couldn't ask that question.

"Why did the nurse give the baby to the man? Don't they give babies to the mamas?"

"Perhaps there were special circumstances," Mama said. "Nurses do what they think is best."

"Jackson said he was born at home, not in a hospital."

"Yes, many babies are born at home. Most babies, I suppose."

"Unless there are special circumstances?" Mattie tried out the big words.

"That's right."

"Jackson says only rich people go to the hospital to get babies."

"Jackson is only four years old, just the same as you. There is a lot he does not know. Different mothers have different needs. Different babies have different needs."

"Special circumstances."

"That's right."

"Do you think that baby was all right? The one the nurse gave the man?"

"Goodness, Mattie, you are full of questions."

"Sorry."

"No need to apologize. I've always known you are a curious child."

"Maybe the baby was in the hospital because he was sick. Maybe he wasn't just born."

"Yes, that could well be."

"Or maybe the baby's mama died, so they gave the baby to the daddy. That would be a special circumstance, wouldn't it?"

"Yes, it would. A very sad special circumstance, but sometimes it happens."

"Then we should pray for the family with the special circumstance, shouldn't we?"

Mama's shoulders lifted. "That's my good Mattie."

"Was *I* born in a hospital, Mama?" If he was, Mattie hoped the nurse gave him to Mama and not Papa.

"Look, here comes Papa." Mama stood up. "We can find the car and be at Grandpa Ted and Grandma Bea's in time for supper. You can tell Grandpa Ted all about the loose screws in the wiggly chairs. We'll stay the night. Maybe Uncle Alan can take you fishing in the morning. Won't that be fun?"

CHAPTER FOUR

Nolan filled his lungs and held the air as long as he could. Immaculate mountain air, free of Denver traffic and city smells and anything smacking of congestion. This is why he and Bella had come to Canyon Mines twenty-six years ago, when Jillian was just two, and spent nearly every penny of their joint net worth on rehabbing the old house.

He let out his breath with a burst and a gasp and a cough. The air was not only clean but once again frigid. The meteorologist promised sun would warm the Saturday air, but it was still the first weekend in January and early in the day. Nolan wore shoes with thick tread to tramp through the residue of snow still on the sidewalks between the house he shared with his daughter, who was working on a Saturday to make up for playing hooky on Friday, and the downtown stretch of shops that were a twenty-minute walk from home. He and Jillian kept their property shoveled—most of the time—but some of their older neighbors could use help. Nolan resolved to attack the task later in the afternoon.

His target today was the hardware store over on Second Street for some lightbulbs. Jillian didn't trust him to buy appropriate groceries, but it never occurred to her to buy lightbulbs or vacuum bags. While he was on the right block, maybe he'd mosey into Catch Air and get the story on those expensive boots straight from Leif.

"Well, I'll be." When no one was within earshot, Nolan considered it perfectly acceptable to speak aloud to himself. He was good company, after all.

In the next block, Tucker Kintzler was trotting in Nolan's direction with a yellow and green striped blanket in one arm. It was simple to see his aim. Harv Reicker was readying to cross the street with his granddaughter, a firm grip on her hand while her eager feet itched to leave the curb.

"Harv!" Nolan called.

Harv turned his head. "Morning, Nolan."

Nolan quickened his pace. "How did you manage such a lovely Saturday morning date?"

"Better than I deserve, that's for sure." Harv beamed at the little girl.

"Is she three now?" Nolan glanced at Tucker, who was almost there.

"Just last week."

"Princess party?"

Harv laughed. "Star Wars."

"Of course! What was I thinking? Forgive my gender stereotyping!"

Tucker was slowing enough to catch his breath. "Excuse me, sir."

Harv pivoted his attention to the new voice. "Oh my goodness. The blankie. I didn't even realize we'd dropped it."

"I was hoping it was yours. I didn't see anyone else with a child."

"That's mine!" the little girl said.

"Then I want you to have it." Tucker handed it to her.

"I'm Nolan Duffy." Nolan offered a handshake.

Tucker accepted it. "Tucker Kintzler."

"Harv Reicker." Harv pumped Tucker's hand. "She may think she's a Star Wars Jedi, but if I took her home without her blankie, I would never hear the end of it."

Tucker squatted in front of the child. "Now I know everybody's name except yours."

"Trillia."

"Hello, Trillia. Meeting you is the best part of my day so far, and I don't think anyone else can make me smile as much as you have." Tucker produced a huge, ridiculous grin.

Trillia pointed at him. "You're silly."

"That's the best way to have fun."

"Thank you again, Tucker," Harv said. "You rescued my whole family from sleep time trauma."

Harv led Trillia across the street.

"You have a way with the little ones," Nolan said.

"It's nothing," Tucker said. "Just comes from being around them."

"Do you have children?"

"Me? No."

"Others in your family?"

"Somehow my grandfather seemed to attract them. Or seek them out, actually. He loved to have a group of them around." Tucker shrugged and grinned. "It rubbed off."

"I was about to visit Canary Cage for coffee," Nolan said. "Care to join me?"

"I should let you get on with your day."

Nolan smiled. Serendipitously running into Tucker was a perfect excuse for revamping his morning's agenda. "I always have time for coffee with a gentleman running with a blankie."

"I did have two cups at the B&B, but that just gets me started," Tucker said. "My treat."

They fell into step and walked the final half block to the Cage.

"Coffee doesn't wind you up?" Nolan said.

"Never. 'Keep it coming' is my motto."

"A man after my own heart," Nolan said, "though I admit the older I get the more I have to cut myself off at some point in the day."

It was Jillian who lived on coffee to the point of forgetting to eat some days. Her mother had done the same thing.

Inside, Clark Addison was behind the counter, his gray hair in a hygienic braid out of the way of his work. "Morning, Nolan. Two large Colombian coffees coming right up. You two are peas in a pod—except for the milk in his."

Nolan glanced at Tucker. "You've been here before."

"I might have been a time or two," Tucker said.

"Are you eating this morning?" Clark asked.

"I think we both ate," Nolan said. "Just the coffee."

They took their coffee to a table by the window where they could watch the street.

"That was a sweet thing you did for Harv," Nolan said.

"It was nothing. I saw right away that it must be the little girl's and she was out with her grandfather. Maybe a Saturday morning breakfast."

"You're probably right about that. Most likely at Ben's Bakery down the street. Harv has a sweet tooth when it comes to breakfast."

"He seems like a nice guy. Reminds me a little of my grandfather."

"Did you go out to Saturday breakfast together?"

Tucker nodded. "We did a lot of things together. I used to love spending time with Grandpa Matt."

"Did he indulge you behind your mother's back?"

Tucker laughed. "When he could get away with it. Isn't that what grandparents do?"

"I'm pretty sure it's part of the job description."

"I wish I could remember more from when I was as young as Trillia. The solid memories don't kick in until I was a little older."

"That's normal. We moved here when my daughter was two, but her earliest memory is about age four."

"That's what Grandpa Matt said."

"Did he tell you what it was?"

"Just vaguely. A day trip with his parents while his father worked. But I adored him. In my earliest memories, he's always there."

"Same with me," Nolan said.

"Where did you grow up?" Tucker swished the last few drops of his coffee.

"North of here. My parents and oldest brother still live up there. My Pop Paddy's family were an Irish immigrant mining family back in the day. The Irish were desperately poor, so they did a lot of the scut work in the mines or the really dangerous jobs and hoped for a big payoff. A lot of them died young of black lung or accidental explosions. Somehow Paddy's father survived. Half deaf most of his life though. Paddy always said they did a lot of yelling when he was around, but they had a good time."

"That's a great story," Tucker said.

"Stay right there," Nolan said. "I could use another cup of coffee. How about you?"

Tucker nodded. Nolan refilled their cups from the ready-made coffee urn at the end of the counter, making a guess at the amount of milk Tucker liked, and returned quickly. The more he kept the coffee coming, the more the stories would flow.

"What about your family?" Nolan set the cups on the table. "Any interesting stories?"

"Nothing like that." Tucker picked up his coffee and sipped carefully. "I didn't know my father. He left when I was two. My grandfather was the only father figure that mattered."

"I'm sorry," Nolan said. "About your father. But I'm glad you had your

Grandpa Matt. Is he still around?"

Tucker shook his head but didn't elaborate.

Nolan switched gears. "I think you met my daughter yesterday."

Tucker's eyes flicked up. "Kris?"

"No, the other one. Jillian."

"Oh. The friend. She doesn't ski. Who lives in the Colorado mountains and doesn't ski?"

"You'd be surprised," Nolan said. "Jillian just never wanted to learn. We lost her mom when she was young, and she developed other, more unique interests."

"Sorry for your loss," Tucker muttered.

Nolan sipped his coffee, which was still scalding hot. "She became a genealogist. She's very good. I couldn't be prouder."

Tucker set down his coffee and pushed it a few inches away.

"It's too hot to drink, isn't it?" Nolan's tongue was burned.

"It's not that," Tucker said.

Nolan cocked his head. "Something. . .about your family story?"

"It's nothing." He glanced out the front window. "The snowpack was pretty solid where I was yesterday though I thought they needed to make some artificial powder to top it off. I suppose the pack would be about the same everywhere around here?"

"I guess so," Nolan said. "I confess these days I don't have a much better record than my daughter. I haven't skied in years, so I don't keep up with the ski reports."

"I guess you take it for granted if you live here. But I'm from Missouri. Skiing is the thing I came to do."

"And you're here alone?"

Tucker nodded. "Needed space to think about some decisions."

"Nothing like mountain air to clear the cobwebs," Nolan said.

"I'm counting on it."

Hidden Run wasn't just skiing. It was breakneck, madcap temerity— and a decision to be intercepted.

"Have you ever taught anyone to ski?" The words left Nolan's mouth without premeditation.

"Me, a ski instructor? No, never."

"Let me rephrase," Nolan said. "As I said, I haven't skied in years. I've never made a conscious decision not to ski again. Time just got away from me. At this point the common sense thing is to undertake some remedial recreational refreshment."

Tucker chortled. "Remedial recreational refreshment?"

"Right. Go out with somebody I can have a little fun with who can remind me of the basics at the same time. Just a few outings to get my legs under me again."

Tucker rubbed his chin, considering. "Sure, why not? I can help you out and still get in the kind of skiing I came to do. I'm in no hurry to go home."

"Work is not waiting for you?"

Tucker waved a hand. "It's a family business that practically runs itself. Do you want to go today?"

"How about tomorrow?" Nolan countered. "I'll be all yours as soon as church is out. You can come if you want—to church."

Tucker shook his head. "Let's just stick to the skiing."

"Then I'll pick you up at the B&B, we'll grab lunch, and try not to break anything."

Nolan hustled home and clomped down the stairs to the basement. His equipment was there somewhere. Another set of steps on the stairs made him look up from the pile of bins.

"Hello, Jilly."

"What are you looking for, Dad? You never come down here." Jillian sat on the third step from the bottom.

"My skis. Boots. Poles. You know. Everything."

"What?"

"I'm going skiing tomorrow."

"Dad, you haven't skied since I was—I don't know, eighteen or nineteen."

"So, nine years. That's not so long."

"Long enough."

"I'm not an old man, Jillian."

"I didn't mean that."

"I'm in good shape."

"I know you are."

"It's not as if I've never skied before. Just because you chose to grow up in the mountains and not ski doesn't mean I'm not capable of refreshing my skills."

"Dad, what is this about?"

"Tucker Kintzler is going to give me lessons."

He watched her face. Her eyes bulged. "See? You wanted to delegate this dilemma to Kris and me. This is what it takes."

"First of all, I didn't delegate anything. You two nominated each other. Second, the idea was for someone to *talk* to him."

"And what better way to earn that right than to enter his world? I just had coffee with him, and we're going skiing tomorrow afternoon."

She blew out her breath. "I can sort of see that point."

Nolan opened a long low tub. "Here we are. Poles and helmet. The boots can't be far."

"I think the skis are under the stairs. With a lot of stuff in front of them."

"And by the way, I smell something in Tucker's family story." Nolan patted Jillian's knee and circled around to look under the stairs. "Don't think you're off the hook."

"What does that mean?"

"Genealogy, of course. He adored his grandfather but doesn't want to tell me much of anything."

"Kind of like you and Uncle Patrick, Dad?" Jillian stood up and followed Nolan.

Nolan pulled his ski boots from a box. "That's for another day."

"When, Dad?"

"Just not today." He grinned at her. "Do you want to come skiing with us? We could rent your equipment."

"No thanks! Someone will have to take care of you when you break your leg."

"Thanks for the vote of confidence."

"I have work to do."

"I'm going to take this equipment down to Leif to check out, just to be sure."

"Dad?"

"Yes?"

"Uncle Patrick. I do want to know."

"One thing at a time."

"Sure, Dad." Jillian climbed a couple of steps. "Remember the lightbulbs."

CHAPTER FIVE

Midfifties was not old, but Jillian had assumed that after nine years of letting his ski equipment gather dust, her father had given up skiing. He hadn't skied that often to begin with. It was her mother who could hardly stay off the slopes and came home from every outing with a pink in her cheeks that seemed to linger for days and infect her demeanor with contentment. She could ski circles around her husband and let everyone know it. Nolan went skiing primarily to witness Bella's joy—and he let everyone know *that*. In the five years between her mother's death and the last time Jillian could remember her father taking his skis out, he'd gone perhaps three times at the invitation of friends.

He'd better stay on the bunny hill. That's all she had to say about it. Except she couldn't actually say that to him. At least he had the good sense to make sure his old equipment was safe, and maybe he'd find a way to get right to the point with Tucker Kintzler and short-circuit this dangerous nonsense about skiing Hidden Run.

Being away from her desk most of Friday meant Jillian had some catching up to do. She had four active projects right now. One client whose parents were both immigrants from different continents had an especially challenging family tree to sort out. An insurance company who gave her steady work always seemed to be trying to track down somebody named in a policy, or verify that the person they'd found was actually related to the deceased policy holder. This time Jillian thought they'd gotten it wrong, and she was trying to find the right person with an incredibly common name. And the morgue in Denver had an unidentified homeless man who carried no outright ID but assorted other interesting papers they hoped she could make sense of to help them find someone to notify.

Somehow the mess on Jillian's desk had gotten out of hand. If she accomplished nothing else on a Saturday morning, she'd get a grip on her workspace and be ready for a clean, organized start on Monday. Paper would go into folders, and folders into racks or drawers. On her computer, the files she tended to stash on her desktop would get sorted and properly tucked away in client folders. Her calendar and to-do list would be updated, with stars beside the priority tasks for the coming week. Jillian Parisi-Duffy, genealogist, researcher, speaker, and writer would be ready for a fresh burst of productivity.

Jillian glanced up at the antique clock on the bookcase. She'd always loved it as a child, and when she was twelve, her mother gave it to her and allowed her to keep it in her bedroom. It had come from the Parisis, the Italian side of her own genealogy. It didn't keep exact time very well and required consistent TLC to remain in working condition at all, but true time wasn't why Jillian kept it around. For that she had plenty of twenty-first-century gadgets. This clock, dating to a hundred thirty years ago, reminded her of why the work she did mattered.

The rap outside her office didn't startle her. It only made her smile. Only Kris Bryant ever came to the exterior door on that side of the house. Long ago the Victorian home had been two cottages with a shared wall, and now the heavy door on the other side of the house served as the main entrance. This one, far simpler in design, led to a porch where Jillian could take a few steps and work outside in nice weather and feast on mountain views. She got up and welcomed Kris into the house, pointing to a rug where she could stamp snow off her feet.

Kris paused to pull off her boots and drop them on the rug. "You must have some coffee in this joint."

"Your wish is my command." Jillian led the way to the kitchen.

"I'm in the mood for a hazelnut latte." Kris padded behind her in thick socks.

"I can do that." Jillian didn't require many accoutrements, but she had invested in coffee machines that would never leave her grumbling about the quality of what she consumed. A gleaming café barista-quality espresso and cappuccino system and a single-serve machine with a built-in frother kept wide options at her fingertips day and night despite her father's penchant for straight black coffee. "What brings you here?"

"You have to come skiing with me."

Jillian took a wide green mug from a cabinet for Kris and rinsed out her own favorite taupe mug with the maroon swirl around the bottom edge. "Didn't we just do that yesterday—as close as I ever come to skiing?"

"This is different." Kris sat on a stool at the granite breakfast bar and spun it toward the coffee machines. "I talked to Tucker."

"You too?"

Kris's eyes widened. "You mean you saw him?"

"Not me. My dad. They're going skiing tomorrow."

Kris whooped.

"Be polite, Kris." Jillian jabbed a couple of buttons on a machine and put the mug in place.

"Sorry. But I've seen Tucker ski. And Nolan? The two of them together?"

"Forget that image. You said you talked to Tucker. Did you warn him off Hidden Run?"

"Not exactly. How would he even know that I knew he was planning to ski Hidden Run? That I heard from a friend of a friend? This isn't junior high."

The machine whizzed and whirred. Jillian moved to the fridge for milk. "Explain."

"He came by Ore the Mountain and ordered a massive amount of ice cream."

"He what?"

Kris nodded. "He wanted me to sit with him and eat it. No one else was there. It was awkward, but what could I do?"

Jillian spoke over the steamer now. "So you ate banana splits with him?"

"Jillian, it was. . .I mean. . .I had a nice time."

Swallowing, Jillian poured warm milk over the espresso. "Well, that's good, isn't it? If he finds you friendly, he'll listen to you about Hidden Run."

"Maybe."

Jillian set the finished beverage on the breakfast bar and herself on a stool beside Kris. "What does this have to do with the two of us going skiing?"

"Actually, it would be the three of us."

Jillian narrowed her eyes. "You, me—and Tucker Kintzler?"

Kris nodded. "A night ski! He wants to take me tonight, and I want you to come along."

"Why?"

"I just do."

"Kris, is this a date?"

Kris hesitated a beat. "It's hard to say. It's been so long since I had one."
Jillian knew her friend well enough to just wait.

Kris wrapped both hands around the latte cup. "No, it's not. Of course it's not. It's the first step in getting to know him well enough to say Hidden Run is a bad idea. But I don't really know him, right?"

"Right."

"Tucker said he found a great hill to ski informally. We hardly even have to leave town." Kris tucked loose strands of her red hair behind her left ear. "It's clear of trees, and steep enough to be exciting but not so steep that it's dangerous in the dark. The sky is supposed to be clear tonight, and there's a decent moon. It'll be beautiful, Jills. Who else will I ever get a chance to do this with?"

"I don't know, Kris. It sounds like the influence factor is going in the wrong direction."

"Don't be like that. Please."

"Sorry. Really I am. What do you want me to do, Kris? There won't be a lodge for me to hang out in with a book."

"Drive me up there. It'll be a chance for you to get to know Tucker too. You can bring lights if that will make you feel better about things. If you get a bad vibe—about Tucker, I mean—you don't have to leave me alone with him."

"And if there is no bad vibe?"

Kris shrugged. "You can always say you have things to do."

"So like a date with an out if you need it."

"Maybe. I don't know."

"What exactly did you talk about?" Jillian hadn't even had lunch yet, and Tucker and Kris had filled up on ice cream by the middle of the day.

"Stuff. He ate a lot of ice cream. I couldn't keep up. But I can keep up on skis. If I'm ever going to talk him out of Hidden Run, I'll have to ski with him at some point."

"Funny, that's the same thing my dad said."

"As quirky as your dad is, he has good instincts."

"Do you have to do it at night? Isn't it unsafe?"

"Please, Jills."

Jillian thumped both hands on the breakfast bar three times. Kris would go with or without her. "Where do I meet you?"

In January they didn't have to wait for the evening to grow late before it was plenty dark. Jillian and Kris rode in Jillian's small SUV to the designated meeting place, where Tucker was already waiting for them. She knew the hill. She'd hiked it with her father on several occasions for the sake of the vista it provided in broad daylight. Tucker's assessment was accurate. Once they left the roadside, there was little chance either of them would collide with a tree on the way down, the path was wide enough for them to push off side by side, and the untouched snow would give them a good ride down.

"Glad you came, Jillian." Tucker lifted Kris's gear from the vehicle. "Maybe once I get your dad up and going on his skis again, we'll persuade you to try."

"I don't think so," Jillian said, "but I can see how this would be exciting for the two of you."

Kris was sitting under the open hatch of Jillian's car, getting into her boots—the brand-new ones Tucker had bought. In a familiar way, Tucker was fiddling with the buckles.

"Are you feeling good about the way we worked on getting everything to fit this afternoon?" he asked. "I want to be sure these are on good and safe."

Jillian tried to catch Kris's eye, but Kris was focused on Tucker. And it wasn't just about the boots.

"Where's your car, Tucker?" Jillian asked.

"Glad you asked," he said. "I left it down at the bottom of the hill and hiked up by the road. We'll need it when we get down there. No point in stranding it up here in the dark."

That made sense.

"Kris tells me you have some reservations about whether this is safe," Tucker said.

So they'd been talking. Had there been more ice cream involved in the afternoon?

"I have a high-beam battery lamp." Tucker moved away from the car and hefted a light Jillian hadn't noticed sitting beside a tree along with his shabby backpack. "You can take this with you and drive down. My rental is a gray pickup with Wyoming plates. When you see it, you'll know you're in the right place. You can park there, find the base of this path down, and shine the light up. That will give us something to aim for, and everyone can feel more at ease."

Scenario one, he'd listened to her concerns and was being incredibly transparent and kind. Scenario two, this was a big setup and there was no gray pickup rental with Wyoming plates and Jillian would be abandoning her friend to a sociopath.

"Where exactly are you parked?" Jillian asked.

"There's a restaurant," Tucker said. "A big sign about buffalo burgers in blue letters. The back side of their lot was the closest I could get to where I think this hill comes out."

For someone who had arrived in Canyon Mines only a few days ago, his description was incredibly accurate. Jillian waffled about finding that creepy or smart.

"You know the place," Kris said. "We ate there a couple of months ago."

Jillian nodded.

"You'll have to hike up a little from the parking lot to see us, I would imagine," Kris said.

Tucker laughed. "We're not going to ski right onto the asphalt."

Kris and Tucker looked at each other, eyes meeting and catching moonlight. Jillian might as well have been in the next county.

"Well then," Jillian said, "good thing I have a great light."

"Right." Tucker gripped his backpack. "I promise we won't push off until we see the beam."

Jillian looked at her friend's face, which clearly said, *You can go now*, and imagined herself describing to a police officer the last place she had seen Kristina Bryant alive. And why in the world she would have left her there.

But she had to admit, even to herself, that she didn't have a bad vibe about Tucker. Nevertheless, she would hurry.

"Okay then." Jillian tugged on her blue knit cap. "It shouldn't take me more than fifteen minutes to get down there."

Down the highway, around the curve, into the parking lot, park alongside the gray pickup, lock the car. She made her way toward the base of the wide trail by the light of her phone, with the stars and moon, waiting to turn on Tucker's high-beam lamp until she was in place. Twelve minutes total.

Jillian could see them at the top of the hill, which wasn't such a high elevation when she put things in perspective. The night was clear, and Kris obviously was elated for a night ski with someone whose skills matched her own and away from the crowds of a commercial resort. Why shouldn't Tucker turn out to be a perfectly nice man who could be well suited to Kristina? It wouldn't hurt for Jillian to ratchet down her suspicions a notch or two. Just because she'd hadn't found the right man in the right place at the right time didn't mean Kris wouldn't. Jillian had thought she'd been there once. They'd even looked at rings together before it all fell apart. But, as her friends tried to convince her, it was not meant to be.

Kris and Tucker pushed off in perfect tandem, but from there it was a race to the bottom, with every lean and turn swishing up snow. Kris got there first and wedged her skis in an impeccable stop smack in front of Jillian. By the time Tucker got there, Kris had her helmet and goggles off and was laughing.

"That was a blast!" Kris's breath was short and fast. "I don't know anyone else who would do something like that with me."

"You're a speed demon." Tucker yanked off his helmet. "I can see I'm going to have to work to keep you challenged."

"Bring it on."

"Count on it," Tucker said. "I've got my eye set on Hidden Run. You know it?"

Jillian caught Kris's eye.

"Yes, I know of it," Kris said. "I've never skied it. Never even been there."

"I ordered special backcountry skis with climbing skins," Tucker said. "I'm just waiting for Leif to tell me they're in."

"You can't ski Hidden Run alone," Kris said.

"I'll get you some skis then. Another few days waiting won't matter."

Jillian cleared her throat.

"That's not what I meant," Kris said. "It's too dangerous for anyone to ski."

"I disagree. You just have to plan. Why does it matter, anyway? You only live once."

"What about your work? Aren't you on a schedule?" Jillian asked. Surely Kris was not seriously considering skiing Hidden Run with Tucker. Who even owned the land? Would it be legal? Would that matter to Tucker?

"Have internet, can work," he said.

Jillian couldn't argue. That's how she ran her business.

"Still," Jillian said, "Hidden Run is something to reconsider. For safety's sake. You have a company to think about." If it was a family business, there must be family of some sort.

"People who are afraid to learn to ski always think skiing is reckless. It's a sport like any other." Tucker indulged her with a patronizing smile. "I assure you I know what I'm doing."

Jillian turned her eyes to Kris in appeal.

But Kris gave Jillian a smile that said, *Get lost now.*

CHAPTER SIX

Maple Turn, Missouri, 1940

They never raised their voices. The tidy home on the curved lane in Maple Turn, Missouri, was as civil as any story Matthew ever read in school illustrating proper social manners. But this year his teacher had begun asking the class, "What do you think this character might be feeling?" The answer was rarely found in words suggesting the volume of dialogue. Matthew could hear Miss Lampier's voice in his head now as he listened to the murmurings of his parents in the room below his bedroom, certain they were unaware of the unpredictable ways sound carried through the old house.

His mother never called him Mattie anymore. Once he started school, his father insisted on his proper name, Matthew.

Matthew Judd Ryder.

If only his middle name wasn't Judd.

The only person who still called him Mattie was his friend Jackson, and only when no one else was around.

Matthew blew out his breath, wide awake. No one could make a person sleep just by saying it was time for bed. It wasn't even really time for bed. His mother only said that because his father was home between sales trips, and giving Matthew an earlier bedtime than usual seemed easier than explaining—again—that he had outgrown his old bedtime and ought at least to be allowed to read quietly in his room while his parents caught up on their days apart. Mama could talk to his father all she wanted, but why did Matthew have to lie in the dark?

The house was old and simple, a relic of the last century. *Relic* had been on a school vocabulary list only last month. Matthew liked the sound of it. Downstairs at the front of the house were a parlor and a room Judd used as an office. Matthew thought of him that way. Judd. Not Papa. Out of respect for his mother, though, he accommodated expectations when he spoke of his father and called him Papa to everyone else. At the rear of the house were a dining room and the kitchen. Upstairs were three bedrooms, none of them large, and a space that had been sacrificed to modernize with an indoor bathroom at some point before his family moved in. The family rarely traveled together on Judd's sales trips to hospital central supply administrators anymore, which suited Matthew. If Judd wanted his wife with him on a trip during the school summer vacation, Matthew pleaded to be allowed to stay with Grandpa Ted and Grandma Bea.

The age of the Ryder home meant any efforts to heat it efficiently were unsuccessful, a matter that plastered a scowl on Judd's face every fall when he took delivery of the oil he hoped would see them through the winter if they were sparing with the radiators and generous with sweaters and quilts. Installation of the radiator system had left gaping holes that had never been properly sealed, one of the reasons sound carried as well as it did from the kitchen beneath Matthew's bedroom. Three years ago, he was five when he discovered that the sounds he heard during the night were not in his dreams, and if he got out of bed and peered down through the hole, he could see as well as hear. His mother hadn't moved the position of the small kitchen table for at least as long as Matthew had been present in the home, and his parents hadn't changed their habit of lingering at that table with coffee cups in the evenings. It was the warmest room in the house during the winter. Irresistible yellow light climbed alongside the iron pipe into his bedroom.

Matthew eased out of bed now, counted four steps, stepped across the board he knew would squeak under the braided rug, and raised one hand to judge the temperature of the radiating heat.

Not too strong. It hardly ever was.

He knew just how to squat next to the fixture, tilt his head, and get a good look.

"I only want you to make something of yourself," Mama said. "Be in a position to make a contribution to the community. Isn't that what you want? You used to talk about your dreams. I didn't think it was. . .this."

"I need capital, Alyce. You know that. I'm doing all of this for us."

"But the way you're getting the capital, Judd."

"It's how I'm going to get what we need. It's the same way you got what you wanted. You didn't complain then."

Mama's breath drew sharp.

What was he talking about? Mama never wanted anything but a home and a family, and she had that. Matthew's head bumped his bookcase in a sharp jerk.

He froze.

The conversation below stopped.

"Is the boy up?" Judd said.

"Perhaps for the bathroom," Mama said.

"I'll check on him."

Matthew jumped on tiptoes over the squeaky board and dove back into bed. His heart was still pounding when Judd opened the bedroom door, but his eyes were closed and he was tucked in.

"Matthew?"

Matthew waited a few seconds and didn't open his eyes. "Mmm?"

"You all right?"

"Mmm." He couldn't say he thought he was getting a lump on his head.

Matthew peeked out through one partially opened eye. In the glow of light coming up through the pipe, Judd picked up a couple of books that had fallen from the bookcase.

"Matthew," Judd said.

Matthew stirred and rubbed his eyes. "Sir?"

"You need to take better care of your things."

"Yes, sir."

Judd replaced the books in the case. "Go back to sleep."

"Yes, sir." Matthew rolled over.

Judd closed the door behind him. Matthew counted the seconds as his father descended the stairs and returned to the kitchen. A chubbier child would not have been able to get out of bed and return to the radiator with the practiced stealth Matthew possessed.

"He's all right?" his mother asked.

"A couple of books fell. He probably didn't put them away properly."

"He's usually so careful."

"What were we talking about?" Judd's interest in Matthew had already dispersed.

"I don't want to quarrel, Judd." She reached across the table.

Judd took her hand. "I do want to make you proud. Surely you know that. A business of my own would set us on solid footing, and I would know that you would be taken care of if something happens to me."

"Nothing is going to happen to you."

"I hope not. I want us to live into our dotage together, Alyce. Nothing would give me greater joy."

"And we have Matthew to think of."

"Yes, I suppose you will want him to have an education."

Matthew's stomach hardened.

"Don't you?" his mother said.

"If that is what will make you happy, then that is what will make me happy," Judd said. "But it costs money to send a young man to college. I didn't get to go."

"Surely if you could start a business, by the time he is old enough, it would be flourishing. My father always said he could have managed to send Alan if he had wanted to go."

"He's already eight. College is only ten years away."

"Maybe it would be safer to stay in sales after all." Disappointment dripped from his mother's words.

"No," Judd said. "Selling into the hospitals for the supply company has given me connections. The hospitals are crawling with nurses and social workers who would help—for the good of the children."

What children?

Matthew held his breath as long as he could, hoping his mother's silence would not outlast his ability.

"How long do you suppose it would take?" she finally said.

"I'm not sure. It depends on what kind of business I settle on and how ambitious we want to be."

"Surely you will have a bank loan. Don't all businesses do that?"

"It would be suspicious not to. But I have to have some money down, and the house is already mortgaged."

"A second mortgage?"

"We don't have enough equity. And the debt ratio to the starting revenue, no matter the business, would be unbearable without sufficient starting capital."

They were using words Matthew didn't understand, but he could look them up in the dictionary tomorrow. *Equity. Capital. Ratio. Revenue.*

"I'm afraid the house doesn't have enough value on its own, Alyce.

You are as thrifty a wife as any man could hope for, and you do a wonderful job running the household, but our rate of savings on my sales earnings alone is too slow."

"I understand."

"You do want me to make something of myself. You've said that so many times."

"Perhaps I am wrong to put so much pressure on you."

"You only mean to encourage me. You must trust me," Judd said. "I can take care of you."

"I do trust you."

She was giving up. Every objection she had to whatever Judd's scheme was—Matthew didn't know what it was—melted under the heat of his words.

Grandpa Ted always talked about having made something of himself. He took Matthew fishing and told him stories of having come of age just when the depression of 1893 hit the country, yet he managed to start a business and support a family. He had done well for himself, he thought. His family never wanted for anything. Even when the stock market crashed in 1929, before Matthew was born, and the Great Depression strangled the country, his business survived because it was built on a solid foundation. He might have made more money if the Great Depression hadn't happened, but he'd always looked after his family. A man just needs some ambition and cleverness. That's what he always said. Ambition and cleverness. He wasn't rich, but he did all right. He made something of himself.

Grandpa Ted had a better house. It was bigger and closer to St. Louis and had a large yard on a hill where Matthew could roll in the grass in the summer and play in the snow in the winter. If Judd made something of himself, maybe Matthew's mother could live in a nicer house again. She could go in the dress store and buy the green dress she liked so much instead of only looking at it in the window.

"Perhaps my father could help," his mother said downstairs.

Matthew startled. Sometimes it seemed as if his mother was reading his mind, but never before had it happened when they were not in the same room.

"No." Judd's denial was immediate and carried that tone that meant no arguing. "I am going to do this on my own. Either you trust me or you don't. Despite all his big talk, Ted will have to work until the day he dies. His general store does just enough business to take in your brother, but Alyce, we must be realistic. He will have nothing to leave you when he is gone. As it is, Alan will take on debt unless he wants to go bankrupt."

"I certainly hope that doesn't happen."

"Then it's up to me to do this my way. Someday the tables may turn, and your family may need me to help look after them. Wouldn't you like me to be in a position to do that?"

Matthew squeezed his eyes shut. He didn't understand everything his father said, but he did know his mother was wilting. If she wanted Judd to make something of himself, she had to say yes.

Did it matter? He would do it anyway, whatever it was.

Matthew opened his eyes and leaned over the hole again, ignoring the crick developing in his neck. Judd stood and took Mama's hand, pulling her to her feet.

"I can't stand the thought that you would ever want for anything," he said, wrapping his arms around her and settling his head on the top of her head. "You deserve so much more than you have."

She fastened her arms around his waist. "I married a man with a good mind and good heart. I know I did."

"You married one who will love you to the end of the earth and to the end of time."

Mushy. Matthew and Jackson had been to moving pictures where people said things like that, so he knew it was a way grown-ups said they loved each other.

Jackson's father poked him in the tummy and said, "Love you, buddy."

Judd loved Alyce, and Alyce loved Matthew. That was as much as Matthew could hope for from his father.

"Will you be home for church this weekend?" Mama asked.

"I should be. I suspect the pastor wants to talk to me about joining the deacon board."

"Judd, do you really think you should?"

"What I do helps families, Alyce. Isn't that what deacons do? Help the orphans?"

Now they were kissing.

Matthew stepped over the squeaky board again and got back into bed.

CHAPTER SEVEN

Nolan's truck was new the last time he skied, so it had an outrageous number of miles on it now. But he kept up the maintenance faithfully, and the engine had never given him anything to worry about. After church and a quick change of clothes, he stowed his gear in the back and headed a few blocks down Main Street and turned left on Double Jack Street. The Inn at Hidden Run filled the second short block with its imposing expanse. He parked in front and went in the main entrance to fetch his ski instructor.

"Leo, my friend." In the parlor, Nolan slapped his palm into the open hand of the innkeeper. "Missed you at church."

"My week for the duty," Leo said. "Somebody has to look after the guests at the Inn on Sunday mornings."

"Nia did an exceptionally fine job with the children's sermon today."

Nia came into the parlor from the dining room, tossing her long, dark braid over one shoulder. "Are you talking about me?"

"What if we are?" Leo asked. "We only say the good parts."

"It's Sunday, and I'm feeling the glow of the Lord," Nia said, "so I'll let pass the suggestion that there are less good parts. Hello, Nolan."

"Jillian tells me the two of you are in cahoots to spend the afternoon together."

"We are. And I nearly dropped the entire breakfast tray this morning when Tucker Kintzler said he was going to teach you to ski."

"He's not going to teach me to ski. I know how."

"Of course. I believe the phrase was 'remedial recreational refreshment.' Which could only have come from you."

Nolan wagged a finger at her. "Be careful, young lady, or I may never hire you to babysit my daughter again."

"I'm pretty sure you never paid me for the last time."

Leo howled. "Pay up, Nolan. With compound interest. Nia has her eye on a new sewing machine. Let's see. She last babysat when Jillian was twelve. That's sixteen years. Let's be generous and just calculate on the basis of three percent interest."

"Oh, stop it, Leo." Nia pointed toward the library across the hall. "He's in there."

"What time did he get in last night?" Nolan asked.

Nia's eyebrows pushed up. "We don't have a curfew for our guests."

"In other words, you know exactly when he came in."

"It was late," she said. "He had his skis with him. He makes a hobby out of taking care of those things."

"Remedial recreational refreshment," Leo said. "That's a good one."

"Always happy to entertain." Nolan pivoted and went across the hall. Tucker sat in one of the twin champagne-colored tufted armchairs.

When he saw Nolan, he set his book on the round mahogany side table and stood. "Ready?"

"What are you reading?"

"Just some Colorado ski history. Leo has collected some interesting books."

Nolan glanced at the book's title. It looked harmless, not something that would focus on lost ski resorts.

"Let me help you with your gear." Nolan scooped up the skis and poles. "Impressive!"

"They do the job." Tucker pushed his arms into his luminous green ski jacket, picked up his backpack, and grabbed his boots and helmet.

"Did you bring these on a plane or ship them ahead?" Nolan maneuvered toward the front door.

"Checked them on the plane. I don't like to break the chain of custody any more than I have to."

"I don't blame you, with beauties like these."

"They're fast too. Wait till you see."

"Remedial, remember?"

"It'll come back to you before you know it."

They arranged Tucker's equipment beside Nolan's, which was far less fancy but had been deemed safe by Leif. If Nolan broke anything today, it would not be because of the age of his skis or even his boots. Nolan made sure the topper on the back of the truck was secured and motioned for

Tucker to go around to the passenger side. Once they were buckled in, he pulled away from the curb and headed out on Main Street, west toward where he could pick up the highway into the mountains.

"Do you think Leo and Nia realize how much sound carries through the heating system in that old house?" Tucker settled in comfortably.

"What do you mean?" Nolan said. "They updated everything when they remodeled."

"The rooms are toasty," Tucker said. "I have no doubt they have a modern, energy-efficient system now. But the old, empty channels are there, and they still carry sound."

"You may have a point. I'm not sure what they did about the old radiator pipes during the renovation."

"Who's Meri?"

Nolan glanced over at Tucker. "Were they talking about her?"

"Yep. Nothing bad. In fact, they seem to like her a lot."

"We all do. She worked at the Inn for a few months—right up until about a month ago, actually."

"What happened?"

"Happy ending," Nolan said. "Jillian did her genealogist thing and helped Meri's family understand their history better. Meri decided to go to graduate school in Denver."

"So Joelle is new?"

"Very—at the Inn. She's lived in Canyon Mines a few years. She's enamored of old Victorian houses, so she loves it here."

"The old pipes remind me of my grandfather saying he used to be able to hear his parents talk in the kitchen from his bedroom on the second story."

"That sounds like a sneaky little secret. Did they ever know?"

"He never said. It just came up one time when I was thinking of buying an old house to rehab. He thought it was a bad investment for several reasons, and I didn't do it. We never talked about it again. He mentioned just one time that he used to get out of bed and put his ear to the hole where the radiator pipe came up. It wasn't sealed very well."

"Seems like the kind of thing a boy might keep to himself as a child but confess later for everyone's amusement." Nolan accelerated onto the highway.

Tucker shook his head. "Grandpa Matt never talked about his father much. I knew Great-grandma Alyce though. She lived to a ripe old age. He was very tender toward her. I had the feeling he thought I might break her or something."

"Probably just protecting her from a rambunctious little boy."

"Probably."

"Are you an only child?"

"I am," Tucker said. "You said you have a brother north of Denver? Is that your only sibling?"

"There's another brother between us." Patrick. Whom he hadn't called back. Yet. "We were a noisy Irish household, on both sides, with seventeen cousins total. We all lived near enough to see each other a lot. Somehow we had more than our fifty-fifty share of boys, and we got into a peck of trouble, but we had a lot of fun."

Until that last bit with Patrick.

"I have cousins," Tucker said. "But I was the first grandchild, and I always knew I was Grandpa Matt's favorite."

Nolan laughed softly. "There's always one, I suppose."

"Did your grandfather have a favorite?"

Paddy. Nolan would have to dissolve the thickening in his throat before he could answer. He tried a soft cough and clearing.

"Patrick. My other brother. He was named for Pop Paddy. My mother always said Paddy took a shine to Patrick from the day he was born. Pop Paddy claimed Patrick was his spitting image, even though no one else saw the resemblance."

"Sometimes we see what we want to see," Tucker said.

Nolan nodded. The thickening was back.

His phone buzzed in his jacket pocket.

"Do you want me to help you get that out?" Tucker said.

"No thanks. It'll keep." Nolan knew who it was. *Not today.*

They drove the rest of the way to the ski resort speaking only intermittently. It was a lost opportunity. With a captive audience, Nolan was usually more efficient at drawing out the information he was after, but this grandfather business was hitting too close to home.

As they changed into their boots and unloaded the rest of their gear, Nolan checked his phone.

WHY ARE YOU AVOIDING ME? the text said. IT'S TIME.

"Everything all right?" Tucker asked.

"Absolutely." Nolan zipped his phone into a secure pocket. "Let's have some fun."

"Almost ready."

Tucker removed his jacket, hung his mostly limp backpack over his shoulders, and donned his jacket again. Nolan tried not to watch too closely, even though it was peculiar.

"We could lock that in the truck if you like," he said. With the topper on the bed of the truck, anything they left in it would be out of sight.

"No thanks. I'm good." Tucker picked up his skis and poles and began striding toward the slopes.

At the top of the bunny hill, Nolan stabbed his poles into the snow, dropped his skis, and got ready to snap his boots into the bindings.

"Since this is a remedial course," Tucker said, "I'm going to assume there may be lapses in your muscle memory and watch you closely in the beginning."

"Fair enough." Nine years was a long time to remember just how the bindings should sound or feel as they grabbed the boots, and Nolan would never hear the end of it if he did something foolish. Meanwhile, a child who could not have been more than seven pushed off and skied with impressive competency to the bottom of the hill.

"Maybe we can set you up with a race partner before the day is over," Tucker said.

"Very funny."

"If you're a very good boy, I'll let you watch me ski the grown-up hill."

"Ha ha."

Tucker looked around and raised his voice. "Who would like to show my friend here the proper way to come to a stop on his skis?"

Sly smiles broke out on faces of several skiers in the under-twelve bracket as they started demonstrating the proper angle for the tips of their skis and where to place their poles. Behind them, assorted parents chuckled.

"Very good, class!" Tucker grinned. "And now, who can tell us what happens to your boot if you fall and start spinning around?"

Tucker's impromptu giggling students explained the function that allowed bindings to release boots and save legs from fractures.

"Finally, who wants to tell me about the first time you ever skied all the way down the hill without falling? What advice do you have for our friend?"

By this time, Nolan was practically in stitches. Parents and other adults who were beginning skiers were certainly eavesdropping, and the amusement factor was running high.

"My friend Nolan hasn't skied since before some of you were even born," Tucker said. "Shall we watch him ski down the hill and give him a big cheering applause if he gets all the way down without his skis coming off?"

"Yes!" The shout of a dozen kids was unanimous.

"I think I need a new teacher," Nolan muttered.

"Too late. You're prepaid for the entire course." Tucker turned to the kids. "Let's count down for Nolan. Three! Two! One! Go!"

Nolan pushed off. Within a few yards he was confident his hips and knees and ankles were remembering what to do, how to adapt to the slight variations in the landscape without toppling. It was a short, wide bunny hill. When he reached the bottom, he made a perfect wedge stop before turning to pump a victorious fist in the air and watch the children clap and whoop in joy on his behalf.

Tucker swiftly skied down. "Congratulations."

"My, you had a good time."

"I did, actually."

Most of Nolan's pleasure had come from watching Tucker with the children. First Trillia on Main Street yesterday, and now a dozen kids on the bunny hill. Tucker Kintzler went out of his way to make children happy. "A lot of people could learn a thing or two from you about interacting with kids."

"I used to go out with my grandfather. He always had pet projects around the area to help children."

"He taught you well."

"I think you're ready to move on," Tucker said. "Your skills are still there. But you have to listen."

"Of course."

"Let's find the next hill."

As they traipsed toward a lift, Nolan took his phone from his pocket.

Three more texts from Patrick.

"Watch out," Tucker said. "There are some kids in line for this hill who aren't much older than the bunny hill bunch."

"I was skiing blue hills before you were born." Nolan jammed his phone back in his pocket. "You don't scare me."

"Don't overrepresent yourself," Tucker said. "I'm a businessman. I see through that."

"I'm a lawyer. I smell fraud."

Tucker laughed. "So this is how it's going to be?"

They rode the lift, and at the top of the blue hill, Tucker sobered with advice. It wasn't a complicated hill, but it wasn't a bunny hill. Nolan needed to pay attention to every detail of his body and his skis and the snow. They skied it three times, including practicing turn techniques, and each run was smoother than the one before. By then, the resort, which had no lights for night skiing, was about to close. They headed back to the car.

"How did I do?" Nolan asked.

"Pretty well—for a remedial student! We definitely have some mechanics we can work on if you're serious about getting back on the slopes. You sit a little too far back, for instance, and we can practice turning some more."

"I'd like to go out with you again." Whether Nolan would ever ski again after they successfully discouraged Tucker from Hidden Run remained to be seen, but in the meantime, further lessons seemed prudent.

In the truck he checked his phone again, just to be sure Jillian wasn't trying to reach him. When he saw the voice mail from Patrick, he almost ignored it, but Tucker was still outside the truck, and Patrick's points of contact were becoming more intense, not less.

He clicked play and listened to a voice he hadn't heard in years.

"You owe me, Nolan. Just call. You can do that much, can't you?"

CHAPTER EIGHT

D avid Miller. A name didn't get plainer than that. Even with a likely place of birth and an approximate age, unless David Miller lived in a very small town, he wouldn't be the only David Miller to show up in phone records, birth announcements, or obituaries in area newspaper archives, marriage and divorce records, private property transactions, or a half dozen other forms of public records Jillian could easily get her hands on. That his father's name was John wasn't especially helpful, considering how common that name was as well. The insurance company that retained her believed the mother of the David Miller they were looking for, deceased, had been Lucille. Jillian's investigation suggested that was a middle name the bearer preferred, and the real David Miller the company needed to find had a mother whose legal first name was entirely different. The policy payout in question was not large, but it ought to go to the proper next of kin, whoever it was.

Jillian had a couple of Monday morning queries out to confirm her suspicions and typed an email to Raúl, her contact at the insurance company, summarizing her working theory. By lunchtime it seemed reasonable to take a break.

Normally she didn't take breaks.

Her father might push her out the door for some fresh air occasionally.

Nia might turn up and drag her—without much resistance—down to the Cage for coffee and a gab session with Kris and Veronica.

She might face the necessity of grocery shopping or some other errand.

Kristina had already spirited her away for an entire day on Friday. And Saturday evening.

But Kris was the reason she needed another break now. Jillian had heard crickets from Kris since leaving her at the bottom of the hill after the night ski on Saturday evening. No call. Not one text message. The silence was distracting. If Jillian was going to get anything done that afternoon, she had to see Kris's face for herself. Garbed in warm boots to slog through the snow that seemed to melt slightly and refreeze with each cycle of the sun without completely disappearing, and her perfectly warm jacket of two years, she set off for the walk down Main Street and a visit to Ore the Mountain. Tucker Kintzler wasn't the only one who could eat ice cream in the middle of the day. Chocolate chip cookie dough ice cream, double-dipped in a hard shell and served in a waffle cone could also be called *lunch* as long as the room was warm.

She pulled open the door to the ice cream parlor. Perfect. Not a customer in the place.

"Hey you," Jillian said. At least she didn't have to report Kris missing, a thought that had flitted through her mind.

"Hey yourself." Behind the counter, Kris had a laptop open on the counter and looked up. "Just trying to decide if it's worth ordering any supplies or whether to hold off another week for the sake of cash flow."

"That's what you're leading with?"

"It's a bona fide business decision."

Jillian extended one finger and pushed the laptop cover closed. "The last time I saw you, approximately forty hours ago, you were slightly indecisive about talking Tucker out of skiing Hidden Run while completely decisive about wanting me to scram."

Kris blushed.

"Spill," Jillian said.

"Would you like some ice cream?"

"Yes. But you still have to talk."

Kris picked up a cone and sidestepped to the chocolate chip cookie dough. "I thought your father was on Team Tucker too."

"He is, but somehow I think he's not quite as close to the target as you are."

"It's not like that."

"No?"

Kris dipped the cone, twisted it, and dipped it again before lifting it upright. By the time it was in Jillian's hand, the chocolate shell had hardened. Jillian grabbed two paper napkins against the inevitability of drips once her teeth broke the shell.

"As a matter of fact," Kris said, coming around the counter, "I have successfully used Saturday night's excursion as a launching point to talk about Hidden Run."

"So he sees sense?"

"I'm afraid not. I saw him last evening—after he got back from giving your dad a lesson, which he thought was hilarious—for pie and coffee. And he was just here a few minutes ago."

"Did you ply him with midday ice cream again as well?"

"Not today. We ran over to the Cage for a late breakfast. I didn't have anyone in here anyway."

Jillian bit into her cone and sat at a table expectantly.

"He remains committed to the goal," Kris said. "He's not easily scared off. On the contrary. He understands the history of Hidden Run and finds it fascinating. So do I, actually. His careful preparation is very impressive."

"It's still dangerous."

"I agree. But that's not a reason Tucker won't do it."

"Then what would be a reason?"

Kris turned up both palms. "That's what we don't know. But I'm not giving up. Tucker is opening up to me."

"What does that mean?"

"We talk."

"What does that mean?" Jillian said again before taking another bite.

"It means we talk. Normal conversation. He's easy to talk to, and I think he finds me easy to talk to as well."

Normal conversation. Easy to talk to. Kristina's shoulders relaxed when she said these things. She was forming an attachment.

"That sounds nice." Jillian licked a drip on her cone.

"It is nice. His middle name is for his grandfather, Grandpa Matt. He used to run the family business, Ryder Manufacturing."

So he didn't bear the family name. His mother must have been a Ryder.

"We discovered our birthdays are only three days apart," Kris said. "Can you believe that? He's older than I am, of course, but what are the odds?"

"Don't let Mr. Green from our high school statistics class know that we don't know how to calculate that question," Jillian said.

Kris laughed. "Sworn to secrecy. Especially since it was AP stats. Those skis are brand-new. His mother gave them to him for Christmas. He has four other pairs. Can you *imagine?*"

"And he ordered backcountry skis for Hidden Run," Jillian said.

"Yeah. I'm going to keep working on that. I'm closing early this afternoon, and we're driving down to Genesee for dinner."

Jillian busied her mouth with the cone and tried not to raise her eyebrows. Middle names. Birthdays. Christmas presents. They'd been lingering over coffee and *talking*. And Kris, who rarely left the shop, had already hung the CLOSED sign once during business hours and now was going to close early to drive to another town with a man she didn't know three days ago.

"Genesee?" Jillian said.

"He wants a good steak, and I'd like to relax without setting tongues wagging. Having coffee with a tourist is one thing. Dinner is another."

"Um. . .yes. I see your point."

"I thought my sapphire dress," Kris said. "I haven't worn it that much. It's not too dowdy, is it?"

"Dowdy? Not at all." That dress wrapped Kris liked a second skin. Definitely an emotional attachment. Jillian crunched the last of the waffle cone in her mouth and wiped her lips with a napkin. "Keep me posted."

"Dinner out of town will give us a longer chance to talk," Kristina said. "The technicalities of skiing and all."

Jillian waved a hand over her head. "Whoosh. Things I know not of."

"Hopefully between your dad and me, we'll get this handled."

"The sooner the better—before Leif gets those backcountry skis in."

"Right."

Jillian trudged home at a slower pace. She was happy for Kris. She hadn't seen her care so much about which dress she wore since—ever. Lingering conversations over coffee, dessert, and steak certainly had appeal, and someone who was her match on skis would add a missing factor to Kris's life. But Jillian also didn't want Tucker to hurt her.

The thought was irrational. Why would Kris get hurt? Other than throwing money around like candy at a Fourth of July parade, Tucker seemed perfectly wonderful. Even Jillian's dad found him charming.

Nevertheless, back in her office Jillian pushed aside her paid projects for a few minutes to do what she was sure Kris hadn't.

Google Tucker Kintzler and Ryder Manufacturing.

The information was ordinary. The company had always been family held, and though it had been prosperous, leadership had made no move to take it public or expand to other locations. Matthew Ryder had led the company for decades. His obituary, from not so long ago, listed Tucker as one of many survivors. His mother's name was there, along with those of her siblings, and Tucker's grandmother's nee name. Out of habit, Jillian began plopping the tidbits of information into a program that would build a family tree. The obituary led to a trail of archived articles about the philanthropic spirit of the company, under the leadership of Matthew Ryder. Jillian copied links into a file and scanned a series of articles. She couldn't read everything right then. She'd have to come back to more of them later. Ryder Manufacturing seemed to get regular press for accomplishments such as Best Place to Work in the county, creative employee incentives, community engagement, philanthropic matches, environmental protection upgrades, and profiles of leaders in business publications. Matthew Ryder's name came up again and again.

Tucker seemed to be an upstanding guy from an upstanding family running an upstanding company in a cozy town outside St. Louis.

Nothing hinted at why Tucker would do something so dangerous as skiing Hidden Run—or throw cash around like water from a broken pipe when he came from a tradition of supporting established charitable causes.

If lingering conversations about personal details led to something more between Tucker and Kristina, they would make a lovely how-we-met story someday. Maybe they would even include "How she saved me from doing something stupid."

But why did he want to ski Hidden Run in the first place? Was it the same as wanting to climb Mount Everest despite the legacy of frozen bodies of people who never made it home? Or exploring the South Pole? Or circumnavigating the globe for the first time? Or leaving families behind to go into space with the possibility of never coming home?

"Am I being too judgmental because I don't even have the courage to ski?" Jillian said aloud.

"Did you say something, Silly Jilly?"

Jillian sank against the back of her chair. "Dad, how long have you been home?"

"Just got here," Nolan said. "My late afternoon meeting was canceled, and I decided I couldn't sit upright in a desk chair any longer."

Jillian's effort to squelch her laughter was unsuccessful. "A bit sore today, are we?"

"Your Honor, let the record show that I did not fall yesterday." Nolan rubbed a knee. "I just twisted and turned in ways I haven't for a long time."

"Counselor, I also make note that you were younger then."

"Don't make me send you to your room without supper."

"You never did that."

"There's always a first time."

Nolan eased into a chair across from Jillian's desk. "Enough about me. Why were you muttering to yourself?"

"I talked to Kris today. Tucker is still determined to ski Hidden Run."

"I know."

"People have done crazier things. Did we really *need* to put a man on the moon? Kris says he's well informed and planning carefully."

"Even if he could avoid all the trees—which I doubt—he can't change the underlying topography, Jillian. He doesn't have a team of scientists planning and training for every eventuality, and even the space shuttle blew up because of an ordinary O-ring."

"Do you really think you'll be able to stop him?"

"I don't think we should stop trying to figure out why it's so important to him. That's key."

"I agree." Jillian gestured toward her computer. "I was just trying to find out something about his family. I don't have much to dig for yet, but so far nothing seems off. He's running a family business, exactly as he claims to be. It's public record."

"He was very attached to his grandfather," Nolan said. "We swapped a few stories yesterday."

"Grandpa Matt," Jillian said.

"Yes, that's right. How did you know?"

"Kris."

"Is she getting somewhere?"

Jillian scratched the back of her neck. "Well, they're talking."

"I have to say," Nolan said, "he seems to have a way with families with children that's unusual for a single young man in the business world. I've seen it here in town and out on the slopes."

"You think that's something?"

"I'd like to find out."

CHAPTER NINE

"Was it supposed to be this bad?" Veronica stared into Jillian's eyes as if she knew the answer.

"Genealogist." Jillian pointed to her own chest and then waved a finger back and forth. "Not meteorologist."

Nia scooted forward on the couch that brought them together at the Canary Cage and picked up the last pecan and cream cheese muffin, baked at Ben's Bakery, from the low table. "They said one to three inches for the whole day."

Kristina scoffed. "We already have at least five, and it's not even noon and still coming down."

"It's wicked out there," Veronica said. "We might as well shut down Main Street. I love winter, but from a business standpoint, this is ridiculous."

"It's not that bad." Jillian sipped her frothy butterscotch caramel latte. "It'll blow through. Tomorrow will be fine."

"I don't doubt that. But business has already been slow with the after–New Year's lull," Veronica said. "Holiday spending is over. Christmas break ski vacations are over. It's not even the weekend. It's a lousy Tuesday. When I-70 closes or gets icy, people can't even get out here for a day trip. If they're looking at the weather forecast from anywhere on the Front Range, they're making other plans now."

"You're not wrong," Nia said. "We already had two cancellations at the Inn, which basically leaves us with one paying guest this entire week."

That would be Tucker Kintzler. Jillian eyed Kristina.

"I only scooped one cone yesterday," Kris said, "and the person who ate it didn't even pay for it."

"Hey!" Jillian said. "I'm good for it."

The others laughed.

"Seriously, look around," Veronica said. "The four of us are the only ones in the Cage, other than Clark. Doesn't that say something?"

"It says we're hardy," Kris said, "and we can have all the coffee and pastries we want."

"Well, there you have it." Nia wiped cream cheese off her chin.

"It reminds me of being in school on snowy days," Jillian said. "My mom would want to keep me home because she was just sure the school district was going to decide to close after she went to all the trouble to get me there when there wouldn't be enough kids to have real lessons anyway. But I always made her take me. I loved those days."

"Me too," Kris said. "There would be three or four kids in a class. Teachers had to get creative. We did the most fun things."

"And it was a win for the school district because it counted as an in-session day," Nia said.

"But this is not that." Veronica stuffed her napkin in her empty coffee cup. "When I get back to the store, I'm telling Luke we're closing up. I've got too much to do at home plus planning for the winter party to spend the next seven hours coddling four customers who might stroll through just to prove they're tough enough for a blizzard and not spend a penny."

"What's the party theme?" Kris asked.

"Oh no, no." Veronica wagged a finger. "You know how it works. No early clues."

"But how will we know how to dress?" Jillian deadpanned.

"Anything between a bathing suit and a parka is acceptable attire," Veronica said. "But my list of things to do is three miles long."

"Well, there you have it," Nia said. "Joelle slid into work today to finish up the weekend's laundry. I suppose I should send her home."

"It's the merciful thing," Veronica said.

"Think about all the people who get snow days," Jillian said. "My clients don't care about the weather in Colorado."

"They know you work at home." Nia flicked muffin crumbs at Jillian. "They don't know you're slacking off at the coffee shop."

The door opened with a blast.

"Close the door!" the foursome said in unison.

Tucker obliged and then grinned, stomping his boots. "What a great day!"

"Colombian with milk coming right up," Clark said from behind the counter.

Tucker waved him off. "No time for coffee."

Clark rolled his eyes and went back to his magazine.

"Kristina!" Tucker said. "Let's go skiing."

Kris jumped up. "In the middle of a snowstorm?"

"It'll be perfect, I promise."

Jillian tugged at Kris's wrist. "What about visibility?"

"You're the one who said it would blow through," Kris said.

"Right. And tomorrow things will be fine—for driving and skiing. It's a mess out there right now."

"My truck can handle it." Tucker rubbed his hands together in anticipation. "We can swing by your place for your skis, Kris, and find a good steep hill in no time."

"Steep?" Jillian echoed.

"If it's not steep, what's the point?" Tucker countered.

Jillian grimaced.

"You don't ski." Kris pulled her arm from Jillian. "It must be hard for you to understand."

Jillian glared. "Why not go tomorrow? See what the accumulation turns out to be and how much it adds to the snowpack. Fresh powder and all that stuff."

"Why choose? We can go again tomorrow," Tucker said. "After all, I'm here to ski. I go every day."

"I'm in." Kris had one arm in her jacket.

"We won't go far," Tucker said to Jillian. "I just want us to feel this storm under our feet while it's fresh."

"It could be dangerous," Jillian insisted.

"And you could slip in the shower and crack your skull," Tucker said, "but I bet you still take showers."

"It's not the same," Jillian said. Tucker's charm was wearing off fast.

"Stop it, you two." Kris headed for the door. "Catch you all later."

"Well, there you have it," Nia said.

"Ooh la la." Veronica batted her eyes at the departing pair. "What have we here? Shall I add a name to my party list?"

"I need to go back to work." Jillian stood up. "No snow days for me."

Jillian rarely took her small SUV out of the garage for short jaunts over to the Inn to see Nia or down Main Street for the shops, and a little snow didn't scare her. At the moment, though, she wished she had an extra layer under her perfectly warm jacket. The sky was grayer than an hour ago, and the flakes denser.

The street corner outside was barely visible. What was Kris thinking?

"I'll walk with you to my corner," Nia said. "This is turning out to be quite a storm."

Jillian yanked her knit cap down low, pulled up her hood, fastened it under her chin, and pulled on her gloves as she stepped outside. The temperature had dropped since she left her cozy office.

"So Kris?" Nia said. "Tucker?"

Jillian restrained herself from taking a public position on that question. "Did you know he's planning to ski Hidden Run?"

"He talks about it every morning at breakfast." Nia pushed her hands into her pockets and walked more briskly against the frigid air. "He keeps pumping Leo for information about it, and Leo keeps pulling out ski books I didn't know we had."

"Well, you did name your inn after it."

"We thought it was a bit of local color, some interesting history. We only chose it because it seemed like of all the lost ski runs of Colorado, it was the closest one to Canyon Mines. Neither of us has tried to see the actual location ourselves, which is what Tucker is after with all his maps and books."

"My guess is he knows exactly where it is by now. But he'll have to hike up to it."

"It's been eighty years since it was in commercial use. Surely the trees have grown over."

"One would think."

"Have you ever seen it?"

"Never. My dad has a topographical map where it's labeled. I imagine he could find it if he needed to, but as far as I know he never has."

"It's called hidden for a reason."

"Right. Has Tucker said how long he plans to stay at the Inn?"

Nia shook her head. "He paid in advance—with cash—when he first checked in. Every couple of days, he leaves more cash at the registration desk and a huge tip for Joelle."

"You don't have conflicting reservations for the room?"

"Not so far. He's paying twice as much as the room is worth. I tell him that's not necessary, but he says the money is cleaner in our hands than his."

"What an odd thing to say. What does that mean?"

"No clue. Here's my corner." Nia shivered. "It's too nasty out to stand and chat. Get home safe, my friend."

Jillian slushed the remaining blocks to the blue-gray Victorian with white trim and rusty red accents, let herself in the back door, paused to remove her damp boots, and padded toward her office. Even though she'd just come from the Cage, the frosty walk home had chilled her straight through, and she hit the power button on the coffee machine on her way past. She couldn't work if she didn't warm up. Maybe later she could face a round of shoveling if she layered up.

Her dad's footsteps came down the back stairs that led to the kitchen.

"You okay?"

"Frozen, but sure." She hit the space bar on her computer to wake it up.

"Some black coffee will fix that."

"Dad, can I fix you a delicious double caramel latte?" Jillian could dish it out as fast as he could. In the kitchen, the coffee machine made promising noises.

"I shall put on a pot of homemade potato and leek soup for us to enjoy for lunch a little later," Nolan said. "We can agree on that, can't we?"

"Of course." Jillian never complained when her father cooked. She didn't even mind if he sang arias from Verdi and Puccini in the process. The sounds of her childhood were comforting—though she maintained a strict rule against his uninhibited musical outbursts in public. He had too strong a tendency to go full throttle. "Really glad you didn't drive to Denver today, Dad."

"Me too. I pulled my topographical map out of the frame today." Nolan took his soup pot from the lower cabinet and began amassing ingredients on the counter.

"Did you find Hidden Run?"

"It's marked, topographically speaking."

"What does that mean?"

"The map shows elevations and a few historic landmarks, such as the names of well-known mines and so on. But it doesn't include existing roads."

"Or hiking trails."

"Correct."

"So without a rope to pull up like in the 1930s, how would someone get to Hidden Run?"

"That's something we'd have to research or figure out."

"Like overlaying road maps over the topography."

"That's my girl."

"There's got to be an easier way to find out."

"If there is, my guess is Tucker is on the trail ahead of Team Tucker."

Jillian made her coffee and returned to her office. Nolan got the soup simmering, and the fragrance of potatoes and leek filled the house while they worked, Nolan upstairs and Jillian downstairs. Ninety minutes later, Nolan came down and sliced up some Irish soda bread to go with the soup and called Jillian to the kitchen nook. Outside, inches of white piled up, but inside they were cozy and warm.

Another two hours of snowy productivity passed before Jillian's cell phone rang—with a number she recognized but didn't often receive calls from.

"Carolyn?"

"Where's Kris? I can't get hold of her."

The fright in Carolyn's voice rattled Jillian. "What's wrong?"

"She's not answering her phone. She didn't say anything to me about closing up for the day, but I suppose it's the snow."

"She went skiing," Jillian said.

"In this storm that's getting worse by the moment?"

"I don't think she knew it would get worse when she left. What's the matter, Carolyn?"

"I don't suppose you can come down here? Somebody needs to."

"Carolyn, tell me what happened."

"The building has taken some damage from the storm."

"Oh goodness. Are you all right?"

"Yes. I was working in the back cleaning my equipment. I thought it might be safer to wait out the storm than try to get home right now, but now this."

"My dad's home today. I'll grab him, and we'll get there as soon as we can. Did you call 911?"

"It's not that kind of emergency," Carolyn said. "Besides, I think the power is out up and down the street."

"Stay safe. I'll keep trying to reach Kris." Jillian ended the call and called up the stairs. "Dad!"

Inside two minutes they were in Nolan's truck and creeping along Main Street, which had slicked over.

"This has turned into an ice storm," Nolan said.

"No kidding." It might have been faster to walk through the thickening snow to the building Kris and Carolyn's shops shared. Jillian spent the time hitting Kristina's speed dial number repeatedly, hoping that seeing one incoming call after another would prod her to call Jillian back. In between calls, she sent three text messages and left two voice mails, but she wasn't any more successful than Carolyn had been at eliciting a response.

Main Street was deserted. Nolan had no trouble parking directly in front of Digger's Delight. Inside, Carolyn was moving pails around beneath drips.

Jillian scowled at the ceiling. "There's a second story up there. Where's the water coming from?"

"I haven't been up to investigate," Carolyn said. "Burst pipe? At one point the space up there was living quarters. It's worse over on Kris's side. Water everywhere. I shut off the main valve to both stores, just in case."

"Good thinking," Nolan said. "Why is it so cold in here?"

"The windows in back blew out. I don't have anything to shutter them with. It's literally snowing in the kitchen where I make my candy."

"I'll see what I can find," Nolan said. "Maybe something in the alley. You have lights. I didn't expect that."

"Both the generators kicked in, thank goodness."

"I should take you home."

"And leave all this mess? I'll just worry things are getting worse."

Nolan looked around and pointed at a corner table. "You two stay put right here. I'm going to have a cautious look around upstairs and see if it's safe. The last thing we need is the ceiling falling in." He put a foot on one step up the narrow stairs to the level that had once been the loft of the town's livery and then another, gradually winding his way up.

Jillian exhaled as she sat. "It must have been awful to be here alone."

"Not my smoothest day." Carolyn lowered herself into a chair. "I realize there may not be much we can solve today, but I'm grateful not to be alone."

"We'll solve what we can. As soon as we're sure there's not some obvious danger of somebody getting hurt while we try to clean up."

"I've got mops and buckets." Carolyn laughed and waved a hand toward her display cases. "And plenty of chocolate for fortification."

"At least the true valuables were protected!" Jillian said. "Dad will be relieved to see the chocolate-covered cherries are unharmed."

They heard Nolan creaking overhead. Jillian's phone dinged and she wrestled it from her coat pocket. "It's Kris."

Sorry. Terrible service, the text said. Why all the messages?

Where are you? Jillian thumbed back.

A couple doors down from my store.

Jillian jumped up and went to the shop's door, pushed it open, and craned her neck out. The snow promised reprieve at last. Two lone figures, arms linked, hustled toward Digger's Delight, one wearing purple and the other bright green.

"Jills, what happened?" Kris broke pace from Tucker's arm and crunched ahead. "Why didn't you say something?"

"I didn't know myself until I got here a few minutes ago." Jillian held the door open for them.

"My store?"

"Carolyn said it's bad."

Kris unzipped her jacket and dug in her jeans pocket for keys. "I have to get into my side of the building."

"Carolyn already used her emergency key."

Tucker's hand was on Kris's back. "What can I do to help?"

"My freezers."

Carolyn was right. The water was worse in Ore the Mountain than in Digger's Delight, but the generators were still running on both sides, and the freezers were holding a temperature that would keep the ice cream solid.

"How big is your generator?" Tucker asked. "Running on propane?"

"The tank's big enough for six or eight hours," Kris said.

"After that?"

Kris pulled off her knit cap and ran fingers through her hair. "In the summer I bank on selling out of ice cream by then. But today. . .I may just have to let it melt if the power doesn't come back on. I doubt room temperature will get cold enough even with the power out."

"Or we can eat it," Tucker said.

Kris dropped her head into a palm, but she laughed. "Get serious. What am I going to do?"

"*We* are going to figure this out." Tucker touched her elbow, and she looked at him and nodded.

"That's right," Jillian said. "We're all here to help."

Nolan came down the stairs. "Oh good. Reinforcements. The water's off, but there's some accumulation of water upstairs above the ice cream shop. We'll have to find a way to get the water out before it weighs down the ceiling. Then we can get at the broken pipe."

"Broken pipe!" Kris said.

" 'Fraid so," Nolan said.

"Piece of cake," Tucker said. "We'll bail what we can, or get a wet vac, and then we'll get some guys in here, clear out the mess, make the repairs. The downtime will be minimal."

"You think so?" Kris asked.

"I do."

She scratched a cheek. "Well, it's the slow season for ice cream. I'll just have to officially close if the main problem is on my side of the building. I hope my insurance covers this."

"Don't worry about that," Tucker said. "I have it covered."

Kris gazed at Tucker with acceptance and none of the fiery refusal of the day he wanted to buy her boots. Jillian didn't believe in love at first sight. But what about love in five days?

"Okay," Kris said. "But we should get Carolyn open as soon as we can."

CHAPTER TEN

Maple Turn, Missouri, 1946

Finally, the war was over.

To Matthew's mother's great relief, his father hadn't been drafted. At forty-six when Pearl Harbor exploded, Judd had aged out of the peacetime draft registration. But while the war had not silenced talk of Judd's starting his own business, it did slow the reality. He'd settled on plans for a small manufacturing and retail business for cabinet handles and screws. As soon as the United States entered the war, metal went into short supply for anything other than the war effort.

Judd and Alyce bided their time. The war jump-started the economy, sales picked up even in hospitals, and Judd shot to the top of his region. In addition, he became an adviser for supplying army hospitals without having to leave North America. He traveled even more.

And added to his capital.

Matthew didn't have to listen through the radiator hole as much. When Judd was away from the house, his home office was uncluttered, but when he was home in the evenings, he took out the plans for the new business even though implementation was put on hold. Potential real estate sites that could accommodate a factory and a nearby home. Drawings for a factory and a retail store with room for future expansion. Staffing projections. Financial models. Five-year growth charts. A business plan to present to the bank for a loan application. If Alyce had objections to where the down payment came from, she kept them to herself.

If anything, Judd became more aggressive, arguing among other things that Matthew's college years would be upon them in the blink of an eye once the war was over. They would have to be positioned for positive revenue rapidly. Matthew understood more and more of the business terminology every year. New metals would gradually become more plentiful with the war over. For now, Judd planned to melt scrap so he could create original designs for the cabinetry hardware. He had dozens of sketches. He would start with a few he believed would be the strongest mass sellers and gradually add in a premium line. Already the construction of new housing was taking a rapid upward turn everywhere in the country, and all those new houses needed new cabinets, and all those new cabinets needed hardware. Judd had big plans.

In the year Matthew turned fourteen, the family moved to their new, larger home separated by a grove of wide, mature maples from the gleaming factory and showroom.

Grand opening day arrived.

Judd straightened his tie in the mirror beside the front door. "We're counting on you today, Matthew. It's an important day for your mother."

"Yes, sir."

"You understand what to do?"

"Of course he does." Alyce patted Matthew's cheek, her green eyes lit and dancing, before tugging his shirt collar on both sides. It wasn't crooked, but if it made her feel better, he didn't mind.

"I just want to hear it," Judd said.

"Show people around the factory floor and main offices," Matthew said. "Give basic directions. Answer simple questions. Refer harder questions to you or Mr. Harding, the office manager."

"Good." Judd offered an arm to Alyce with a big smile. "This is our day. We've certainly waited long enough."

She laid her hand in the crook of his arm, and they walked together down the steps of their new home. It certainly made his mother happy. Matthew wondered how large the mortgage was on this house compared to the old one. Judd followed through on every promise to give Alyce what she wanted. Her ivory brocade dress was fancy for daytime wear, but other than her wedding, she'd probably never had such a fancy day to celebrate. Matthew made sure the house was locked—no point in tempting fate when half of Maple Turn would be coming through the new building out of curiosity today just on the other side of the trees—and followed his parents around the maples to the lawn in front of the showroom.

Grandpa Ted and Grandma Bea were waiting and looked as proud as Matthew had ever seen them. Even Uncle Alan seemed impressed, and he didn't often let on that anyone impressed him.

Grandpa Ted kissed his daughter's cheek and offered his son-in-law a firm handshake.

"You've done a fine, fine thing here, Judd," he said. "I've never met a man who could put something together as well as you have here. You could have gone into high finance. I'm sure if your own parents had lived to see this day, they would be incredibly proud. I'm honored to stand in their stead and tell you I couldn't be prouder of your perseverance to bring your dream to life. What you've achieved here will change the future of Maple Turn."

"Thank you, Ted," Judd said. "That's my intention. Make a contribution. Give the town an employer they can count on for decades. As long as I have anything to say about it, Ryder Manufacturing will be here with the jobs Maple Turn needs."

"Well done, Judd. Well done."

"Matthew," Judd said, "find Mr. Harding and ask him to open the building. The tours can begin."

"Yes, sir."

Matthew had been in the factory several times during construction and while machinery was being tested, and of course with others being instructed how to give tours and answer questions. Townspeople now came in droves. Some lingered in the showroom to inspect samples of the wares for sale, or even to make purchases, while others knew this might be their only opportunity, apart from employment, to see the factory itself. Hiring had already proved a competitive process. Judd intended to keep it that way—enough jobs to reassure the community of Ryder Manufacturing's commitment but not enough that anyone would ever think a subpar performance would be acceptable. Excellence would be the standard. There would always be more people who wanted to work at Ryder than could.

"Hey, Mattie."

Matthew spun around. "Jackson, careful!"

"No one's listening."

"Look around. People everywhere."

"Gawking. Not listening."

Jackson was not wrong.

"Okay," Matthew said, "but don't do that again. If Judd hears you, he'll banish you on the spot."

"How about a private tour?"

"You already went through once."

"I mean the other stuff."

"What other stuff? The showroom. The factory. The offices. That's the tour."

Jackson grinned, his double dimples breaking the cheeks beneath his black hair. "There's a door in your father's office. Where does it go?"

"Private storage."

"What does that mean?"

"Private. Storage. A place to store things that are not the business of the public."

"Aren't you curious?"

Matthew shrugged. He was curious about very little concerning Judd. What did it matter what he did with a closet in his office?

"You haven't been back there even when it was empty?" Jackson asked.

"Nope. Off-limits from the start."

"Somebody must know what's in there."

"It's a short hallway that leads to a storage room. Maybe nothing's in there yet."

"Then what's it for?"

"I don't know, Jackson. He designed a lot of the building to accommodate future growth. Maybe that's all it is. Why does it matter?"

"Does it have a keyed lock?"

"Judd locks everything."

"I could get you in there."

"I don't care, Jackson. I have to get back to the front to see if there's another group ready for a tour."

"Fine. Just keep it in mind. My uncle has been teaching me how to pick locks."

"Your uncle? Your dad is the pastor!"

"Not that uncle. My mother's brother."

"Still."

"It's all in good fun, of course. No criminal background, I assure you. But I'm getting pretty good at it."

Matthew waved off Jackson. "Stay away from Judd's office."

Matthew gave one tour after another—strictly the factory floor and the main offices—until it was time for the ceremonial proceedings. Mr. Harding had arranged a small stage and public address system on the lawn. Matthew's parents and grandparents were grouped near the front of the crowd. When Grandpa Ted caught his eye, Matthew waved but hoped he would not be beckoned.

Jackson's father took the stage to offer an opening prayer invoking God's blessing on Ryder Manufacturing.

The president of the Chamber of Commerce gave a speech about how Ryder Manufacturing would put the sleepy town of Maple Turn on the map.

A local real estate agent assured everyone that the boost in employment base would improve property values.

The mayor's wife welcomed Alyce as a founding member of the newly formed Maple Turn Women's League for Town Improvement, which made Alyce flush with pleasure.

The mayor gave Judd an oversized key to the city. Matthew was sure it would be framed and hung in one of his father's offices.

Last, Judd stepped to the podium and pulled notes for his speech from the inside pocket of his black-and-gray pin-striped suit.

Matthew had heard the speech already—many times. Judd rehearsed it. Alyce commented. Judd revised. Alyce remarked further. Judd rehearsed until the performance barely varied by more than a few words. Even the pauses and cadence were predictable. Matthew wasn't sure why Judd bothered with the notes. Perhaps he was more given to nerves than Matthew knew. In any event, Matthew was bored, the speech would take twenty minutes to deliver, and he wanted to sit down for a few minutes of peace and quiet before the mass town picnic began. No doubt Judd would expect his son to help clean up the building and lawn at the close of the day, no matter how many people he was already paying for the task. This could be the only opportunity for respite.

Matthew ducked inside the building, where Mr. Harding nodded at him but did not interfere with his wandering. Theoretically the building should be empty at this point, the tours finished and the showroom unattended except for Mr. Harding's presence to discourage entrance.

Judd's voice droned over the public address system. Matthew shuffled past displays, recognizing the knobs and handles that already decorated the family's new home as part of the initial manufacturing runs to stock the retail bins. He was surprised to find the double doors leading to the offices unlocked, and pushed through them. He had supposed everything would have been battened down once the tours concluded, but he was relieved he had the option to find an empty chair.

First he sat in the reception area. That should have been enough. He was off his feet. It was quiet. He was alone for a few minutes before going back on display during the picnic.

Why was it not enough?

The door to his father's office was wide open. Matthew walked through it and sat in one of the visitors' chairs. He wouldn't sit behind the desk. He couldn't imagine ever doing that.

"Aren't you curious?" Jackson had asked.

Should he be? He'd seen the hallway on the drawings and the room marked Private Storage, but he'd never seen the room, not even during construction. But someone must have.

Matthew eyed the doorway that, if he was mentally matching up the drawings correctly, would lead to the private hallway. It did have a lock. But was it locked? Was there anything so valuable that Judd would really lock it? He got up, crossed the office, and laid his fingers on the handle.

"What the blazes are you doing?"

Matthew's heart pounded under the grip of Judd's hand on his shoulder. He'd come too far into the building to realize he could no longer hear when the speech ended.

"Matthew!" Even his mother's voice scolded him.

"Did you somehow think you were exempt from the instructions that no one is permitted in the area beyond that door?"

Judd's weight on Matthew's shoulders threatened to grind him through the floor, like one of the screws his machines would manufacture, while his brown eyes bore straight through Matthew's thin frame.

"You must not ever disobey your father on this matter," his mother said. "Do you understand?"

"Yes. Yes, I understand. I won't." He might faint from fright and shame if Judd didn't let go of him. Jackson could afford to be flippantly curious. He wasn't the one taking chances. "I promise. I understand."

"Outside," Judd said. "Find your grandparents. Eat some lunch and mind your own business. Don't spoil this day for your mother."

"No, sir." Matthew scrambled out of the building as fast as he could. Jackson was waiting for him out front. "Where have you been?"

"Get away from me."

"What did I do?"

"Got me clobbered, that's what. You and your incessant curiosity." Matthew paced past Jackson.

"The hallway?" Jackson sidestepped to keep up with Matthew's pace while watching his face. "Did you try the door?"

"Stupidest thing I ever let you make me think about doing."

"Did it open?"

"I got caught."

"Whoa." Jackson circled ahead of Matthew, hands up.

"I'm supposed to find my grandparents and eat." Matthew pushed Jackson off. "That's it."

"Nothing says I can't eat with you."

"Not advisable."

"Then let me look for the door from the outside."

"You're crazy." Matthew's steps punched forward. "Besides, there are a bunch of doors. I don't know what they all are. I haven't memorized every detail of the drawings. It's a factory loading dock. Why do I care?"

"It'll be yours someday."

"I'll choose my own career, thank you very much."

"I could get in any one of those doors."

"Pick locks on your own time. And when you get arrested, don't call me."

"You're breaking my heart." Jackson pulled Matthew's elbow. "Okay, today's not the day. Go eat your potato salad with your grandma. But don't forget this. The day will come. And I'll always be here for you."

CHAPTER ELEVEN

Wednesday was no better for sliding down the mountain and into Denver, making Nolan glad he had instituted his winter schedule of working from home three days a week rather than two. Despite an arduous day of pumping water out of the second story above Kris's shop and a long evening of catching up on work, he was up two hours before daylight, grinding through his email inbox from his home office, donned in his gray-and-red plaid flannel bathrobe and slippers. Working during the early hours, when no one in the office in Denver and no clients around the region would be sending new messages or picking up the phone with questions, bolstered productivity. Nolan sorted his messages into folders: those on which he was copied for courtesy, those he could direct to a paralegal for next steps, and those he would add to his own list of tasks to ponder more deeply.

Mediation questions most made him twist his mouth in puzzlement. In a family law practice, mediation meant something had gone wrong at a fundamental level in a relationship that once had at least held the promise of beauty if not beauty itself. Where had it gone wrong? What was the plot twist that brought sad and angry parties armed with lawyers to glare at each other in a legal conference room? Nolan could sort out what was fair from a legal standpoint, but he always hoped also to figure out something that might bring some degree of healing even when the relationship was beyond restoring to what it had been.

Patrick.

Sigh.

The mediator needed a mediator.

Nolan printed a document that had arrived attached to an email and slid it into a folder to read and mark up later when his brain moved into an in-depth groove. He had a yellow legal pad with a list of tasks jotted for this day, and he starred the essentials to accomplish what he could in the hours while Canyon Mines was waking up and perhaps come back to in the evening when it returned to rest. But this sweet town that had been his home for twenty-six years had taken a hit in yesterday's storm, and Nolan couldn't stay warm and dry in his home office all day knowing that people he cared about were trying to restore their property.

By the end of Tuesday, it was clear that several blocks of downtown had lost electricity. The building Kris and Carolyn shared had the worst damage because of the burst pipe, but other structures had assorted issues. The Heritage Society volunteer director, Marilyn, discovered a window well filled with snow, and the aged window leaked moisture into a stack of recently donated boxes up against the cement wall. Marilyn panicked about the potential damage before she'd even had a chance to inspect the boxes. Homes were without heat. A roof that should have been replaced last summer was collapsed from the weight of the snow. The hardware store was doing its best to get more propane in stock. Half a dozen families had significant vehicle damage. No doubt more stories would emerge.

Nolan raised his eyes to the view outside his office window. The home, situated toward the western end of Main Street, where structures petered out into wider spaces, boasted mountain vistas through the seasons. Today pink glare returned Nolan's glance, snow canopied across towering evergreens draping into valleys as sunlight inched upward. Before long it would be a blinding dazzle of white, and the residents of Canyon Mines and the other towns along I-70 would shovel themselves out.

At the sound of Jillian's bedroom door opening, Nolan cocked his head to listen to her shuffling steps.

"You're up early." She rubbed one eye with the heel of her hand, just as she had since she was a toddler.

"Wanted to get some work done." Nolan stacked a couple of folders. "I'm sure it will be all hands on deck on Main Street today."

"No doubt. I'll get the coffee going before I jump in the shower."

"Eggs and bacon? We should have a good breakfast before we head over to help."

"Maybe I'll shovel before I shower."

"Let me do that."

"I can pull my weight around here, Dad. I get free rent, after all. And you were already sore before everything you did yesterday."

"Tucker did most of the heavy work yesterday. I'm fine."

"You're bluffing."

"I guess we're going to have to flip for it." Nolan reached for a nickel in the coin dish on his desk, their strategy for resolving rare impasses about household chores. "Winner gets to shovel. You call."

"Heads."

Nolan tossed the coin, caught it, and flipped it on his wrist. "Tails. I win. I'll shovel."

"I was going to say tails."

"But you didn't."

"Then I'll make breakfast." Jillian padded out of the room.

Nolan hit SEND on three emails, his mental to-do list already shifting to supplies he should be sure to load into his truck before they left the house.

Both showered and dressed forty minutes later, they sat at the breakfast bar, their favorite place to eat.

"I heard from Kris while you were pushing snow around," Jillian said. "Tucker arranged for some company to come out and assess. She says they can fix the pipe, restore the damage to the flooring upstairs, get everything properly dry, the whole business. Tucker claims they can keep downtime to a minimum for both businesses."

Nolan swallowed a bite of eggs. "Do you suppose he thought to tell them it's a historic building?" They couldn't just haul in some PVC and slap down linoleum.

"Valid question. I guess they'll see that when they come. But Kris says we shouldn't worry about that building today."

"I don't suppose there is any point in cautioning her about accepting this massive level of generosity from a man she barely knows."

Jillian pushed her shoulders up toward her ears. "She seems to have gotten over that. In any event, if we want to help, there are plenty of other places."

"Marilyn is in a tizzy about those boxes at the museum. They're related to a family that has been in Canyon Mines forever, apparently."

"I feel bad. She wanted me to help sort them, and I just haven't had a day to give her. I had promised her I would next week."

Nolan picked up his coffee mug. "My gut says she's not going to get a lot of sympathy about old papers when there are broken windows around town and leaky roofs and the power is still sketchy in places."

"I know." Jillian crunched bacon between her teeth. "I guess if Kris doesn't want me, I'll check in with Marilyn. Everybody around town will be rearranging things today."

"I can make sure that window well is shoveled out and get a proper cover for it from the hardware store so this doesn't happen again. The leaky window will need to be replaced, but that is a task for a warmer day."

"I'll let Kris know where we are in case she changes her mind." Jillian reached for her phone.

"I'll warm up the truck." Nolan reached for his keys.

Marilyn was overjoyed to see them. "Finally, someone who understands the potential importance of these papers."

"Where are the boxes now?" Nolan asked.

"Still downstairs." Marilyn led the way. "The best I could do last night when I discovered the catastrophe was pull them away from the wall and try to sop up the water with towels. Whoever packed them put too much in them. The bottoms are falling out, so we have to be careful. I cleared tables in the group education room and plan to work in there."

"Let me get the boxes," Nolan said. "You and Jillian can see what to do with the papers, and I'll work on making sure there's not a repeat performance with the window."

"The Heritage Society would be so grateful."

Nolan moved the boxes, grimacing at the reality that the bottoms and sides of several were indeed soggy and the contents at risk. He did his best to deliver them to the group education room before the cardboard gave way entirely, left Marilyn and Jillian to devise a strategy for sorting and salvaging, and went around to the back of the building to attack the window well with a snow shovel. At first its width made it fairly easy to shovel, but soon he realized it was deeper than was first apparent, making the task awkward enough to assure Nolan's sore back muscles would need an extra day to recover.

"There you are."

Nolan straightened up and pushed his hat off his eyes. "Tucker."

"You're a hard man to track down, my friend."

"Have you come to help?" Nolan was beginning to think this was a job for a younger man.

"To rescue you! Wouldn't you rather go skiing?"

"Skiing?"

"Inches more snowpack, fresh powder. I thought it was great yesterday when I took Kris out, but this will be fabulous today. Perfect for remedial recreational refreshment."

Nolan stuck his shovel in the mound of snow he'd been transferring out of the window well and leaned on it. For the sake of conversation with Tucker, the invitation was tempting.

But no.

"I'm afraid not," Nolan said. "There's a lot to do around town. When I get this window well sorted out, I'll see if I can help inside. If not, I'll go on down the street and find another project."

"I essentially got the same answer from Kristina. I tried to lighten her load, and she just plunged into someone else's project."

"I'm sure she appreciated the arrangements you made. Canyon Mines pulls together on a day like today."

"Okay then," Tucker said. "Another time."

"Right. Another time."

Tucker tramped off through the alley, and Nolan turned back to his shoveling. His back creaked as he bent over again and protested with every load of the wet snow, but at least the job was done. At the hardware store, he found the last of the window well covers and returned to install it before going inside the museum to warm up.

"I'm happy to report that window well will see no more snow," he said.

"Thank you!" Marilyn said. "I'll mention to the maintenance committee that the window replacement is rising in urgency."

The front door opened, and a man came in. "Hello!"

"I'm sorry, we're closed today," Marilyn called across the education room.

The man came closer.

"It's Tucker," Jillian said.

"Who's Tucker?" Marilyn asked.

Nolan made introductions and said, "I thought you were going skiing."

"I changed my mind." Tucker shirked off his green jacket and dropped it on a chair with his backpack. "I thought maybe I could help. Now, what's the system here?"

"It's pretty basic at this stage." Jillian stood up to point at various tables. "We're just getting everything out of the boxes to start. Dry documents go on that table there. Damp ones can be spread out on the other side of the room. Dry photos on this table here, and damp ones over there. Try to make sure nothing is sticking to anything else. And then we'll just see what we have and go from there."

"I can handle that." Tucker opened a box with a damp splotch on one side. "Looks like mostly photos here."

"Watch out for any notations on the back," Marilyn said. "If they're wet, please try not to smear them."

"Got it." Tucker positioned a chair and began extracting photos from the box. "These look really old. Do you mind if I ask if we know who we're looking at?"

"We know the general family," Marilyn said. "We hope to learn more about specific individuals by going through all of this in an organized manner at some point."

Tucker glanced at Jillian. "Genealogy heaven?"

"Might be," she said. "Hard to say yet. Any names or dates?"

Tucker flipped a photo. "Howard Blankenship, 1932."

"Mmm," Marilyn said, "that's not the surname of the family who donated the boxes."

"Could be another branch of the family tree," Jillian said, "or just an old family friend. Anyone really."

"That's the year my grandfather was born," Tucker said. "This dude could be about the age of my great-grandfather, I guess." Nolan caught Jillian's eye.

"Do you have any photos of your great-grandfather?"

"Not that I'm aware of," Tucker said. "Doesn't matter anyway."

"Why not?"

"Just doesn't." Tucker set the photo aside and picked up another.

"In my line of work," Jillian said, "we like to think it all matters."

"Believe me, it doesn't." Tucker flipped another photo. "Someone labeled this one in pencil. And really bad handwriting. I doubt anyone will ever read that again."

"We'll at least try," Jillian said. "We may get clues from other context. You might notice a similar photo that has a better notation, for instance, or a date stamp, or a studio marker if it's a professional portrait."

"My mom has so many photos of my Grandpa Matt," Tucker said. "I keep telling her she has to let me digitize them, but she refuses to let me take them out of her albums."

"I feel the same way about pictures of Jillian when she was little," Nolan said. "Digital photos are just too hard to press against your heart in a sentimental moment the way you can hold an entire album against your bosom."

Tucker laughed.

"Dad, stop," Jillian said. But she was laughing as well. "Somewhere we have a photo of me with my great-grandfather. Pop Paddy. I was just a baby. He passed not long after that."

"That one's in your baby album," Nolan said.

"Well, I'm keeping my photos right where they are," Tucker said. "In the cloud, safe and dry and uncontaminated by chemicals."

"We're in the process of digitizing everything," Marilyn said, "but it's a slow process. We have to depend on volunteer extra-credit hours from high school students and the limited hours when the machine is free at the library."

"You don't have your own machine?" Tucker seemed surprised.

"Look around," Marilyn said. "The city leases us the building for a dollar a year, but everything else is donated services or we have to fund-raise for what we need."

"You need a machine," Tucker said. "And not a low-grade library scanner, but one worthy of a museum handling delicate documents. Maybe I can make a donation."

"That kind of machine is expensive. I may be a small-town archivist, but I read museum publications."

"I'll see what I can do. In fact, make me a list of what else you could use that might be hard to fund-raise for."

Marilyn's eyes widened.

Jillian and Nolan exchanged glances. Was Tucker's first impulse always to buy something for strangers?

Tucker looked around the room, nodding. "My grandfather would have liked this place. He always enjoyed giving to a good cause."

CHAPTER TWELVE

"Dinner guests, Dad? Tonight?" Jillian trudged into the kitchen behind her father. "It's been a long day. A long two days."

"I know." Nolan dropped his keys into the copper bowl on the counter. "But the streets are plowed, the power is back on, and we were major help to Marilyn even if papers are still in piles. It's worth it to end the day with a bit of normalcy, don't you think?"

"I guess so."

"We have to eat," he said. "Cooking for four is no more trouble than cooking for two, and maybe we'll get somewhere with Team Tucker."

Jillian unzipped her jacket and let it fall off her shoulders onto a chair. "For someone who runs a company, he sure doesn't like to talk about it very much."

"See? You notice that too. He'll stay with it for a couple of sentences and then change the subject."

"Or minimize what he does."

"Exactly." Nolan waved a hand in a grand gesture. "I shall prepare a royal feast and ply him with my culinary skills."

"Um, Dad, your culinary skills are vast. Truly. Kingly. But Kris and Tucker will be here in less than an hour. You didn't give yourself much time to prepare a royal feast."

"Well then, how about Irish bacon and cabbage stew? It's hearty fare on a wintry night."

"Perfect. Bacon twice in one day. You won't hear me complaining."

"Ah, but I saved the good chunky stuff for a special occasion. There's time for some quick buttermilk biscuits too."

"I'll set the table," Jillian said. "To celebrate that the power came on and everything didn't melt into a giant puddle, Kris is bringing three kinds of ice cream and some of Carolyn's fudge for dessert, so don't get ideas in that department."

"Cobbler? Pie? A three-layer cake perhaps?"

Jillian rolled her eyes. "Give me your jacket. I'll hang it up."

Nolan exchanged his winter jacket for the white chef's apron he claimed made him feel inspired and began humming as he set to work.

"Why are you humming 'Take Me Out to the Ball Game'?"

"I'm not."

"Yes, you are."

Nolan sang, "Take me out for some ice cream; take me out to the store. Buy me a triple-scoop jumbo cone. I won't share it. I'll eat it alone!"

Jillian laughed. "Ice cream on the brain."

She went into the dining room to select dishes and settled on the eclectic pieces her mother had collected over the years, colorful rich-hued plates beneath contrasting deep bowls to hold generous portions. Nolan's stew, with its dark green cabbage and red bits of tomatoes, would add to the festive palette. With just four at the table, she laid the place settings two on each side rather than having anyone on the ends. It seemed cozier for soup and bread on a cold night.

Her duties discharged, Jillian had time to run upstairs, splash water on her face, pull a clean sweater over her head, brush her unruly dark hair and tie it up in the back, and be back downstairs well ahead of the expected arrival time of Kris and Tucker. She descended the back stairs into the kitchen.

"Need any help, Dad?"

"I believe I have everything under control," Nolan said.

To Jillian, it looked very much as if he didn't have anything under control, but she reminded herself—again—that this was his cooking style. She was more likely to clean up as she went along and always have a clear spot for the next food she needed to chop or mix. Nolan described himself as a visionary chef who couldn't be bothered with such mundane details, so the kitchen was likely to look like a tornado had blown through. But his end result was far superior to hers, and he wouldn't go to bed before the kitchen was spotless, so she had nothing to complain about. He did have a simmering pot on the stove, and ingredients for biscuits were open on the breakfast bar.

"Go put your feet up in the living room, Jilly," Nolan said. "Keep an eye out for them."

"I could roll out the biscuit dough."

"No need. Go relax."

Jillian took a paper napkin and wiped flour off his cheek and then kissed it before going into the living room to turn on the porch light. She sat for a few minutes in the comfortable purple chair with the companion ottoman, her favorite place to relax, and flipped pages of a magazine. A few minutes later the sound of an approaching vehicle and then closing car doors called her to look out the front window. Tucker offered an open hand to Kris, who laid her own in his. Fingers entwined, they swung their arms while they progressed up the walk. Tucker's backpack dangled casually off one shoulder, as it always did when he wasn't wearing it.

Kris, who was so often all business and whose shop had suffered significant damage in the last twenty-four hours, was laughing. Jillian didn't imagine she would be doing the same under similar circumstances. Then again, she didn't have someone in her life who made her relax and laugh the way Tucker apparently did for Kris.

Jillian was pretty sure she and Kris could never make fun of a Hallmark movie together again.

"Dad, they're here," Jillian called.

"Good, good, good," came his response.

She pulled open the heavy main door on one side of the house. "Come on in."

"It smells amazing in here," Kris said.

"Is it true Nolan does most of the cooking?" Tucker asked.

"Lucky for me, yes." Jillian put out her arms. "Let me have your coats."

Nolan came out of the kitchen. "Welcome to the Parisi-Duffy home, where a delectable menu awaits your taste buds in just moments."

Jillian hung the coats in a closet, and Kris handed a sack of goodies to Nolan.

"Dessert!" His eyes lit up.

"He's going to sing, isn't he?" Kris said.

"I think so," Jillian said.

"On top of my sundae, all covered with sauce, I lost my poor cherry, it really got lost." Nolan's tenor filled the room.

"How did you know he was going to do that?" Tucker asked.

"Sometimes he just can't help himself," Jillian said.

"It rolled off the table, and onto the floor, and then my poor cherry, it rolled out the door."

"Dad, the ice cream." Jillian pointed to the package in his hands.

"I shall endeavor not to let it melt," he said.

"You'd better not," Kris said, "after what I've been through to keep it solid up until now."

"It rolled to the garden and under a bush, and then my poor cherry, it turned into mush. If you. . .if you. . ." Nolan faltered. "Can't quite remember the last bit."

"I do," Tucker said. "Old camp song."

"Oh no," Jillian said.

Tucker sang in a baritone octave. "If you like your sundae all covered with sauce, hold on to your cherry, or it will be lost."

"By golly, that's it. You're a fine man." Nolan wagged one eyebrow and disappeared back into the kitchen.

Tucker laughed. "This looks like a fantastic house."

"We think so," Jillian said. "I work from home all the time, and Dad's here two or three days a week. The layout gives us both the space we need."

"You never think about getting your own place?" Tucker asked.

"Nah. I'd have to cook and pay my own internet bill."

He laughed.

It wasn't that Jillian never imagined living away from Nolan. Maybe someday she'd find somebody and the time would be right. But for now, this was where she belonged.

Tucker had his hand on the small of Kris's back as they moved into the living room, and when they sat on the navy sofa, they didn't leave more than six inches between them. Kris did live on her own, and maybe she was ready to change that circumstance.

"Canyon Mines is a great place," Tucker said. "I see a lot of old houses that remind me of the small town I'm from—not as small as Canyon Mines, but the same kind of charm."

"And where's that?" Jillian asked. Maple Turn, Missouri. She knew the answer. She just wondered whether he would say.

"Near St. Louis."

"East? West?"

"Sort of south. It's like so many towns in the Midwest. It's been there a long time. Maybe once upon a time it had a chance to be bigger than it is, but time passed it by."

Nice dodge.

"I suppose that's true of Canyon Mines," Jillian said. "In the mining heyday everyone had great expectations. But here we are, a sleepy little mountain town with mining history and not much else."

"Great access to ski slopes," Tucker said. "You have that in your favor."

"I suppose. Why do you live in—where is it?"

"South of St. Louis."

"Right." He wasn't going to give anything away. Had he even told Kris the name of the town? "Do you stay for your work?"

"It's a family business, so I have to."

"Do you like it?"

"It was Grandpa Matt's business, and I loved him."

Jillian nodded, though it wasn't really an answer.

"If you could live somewhere else," she said, "where would it be?"

Tucker glanced at Kris. "Probably ski country. But realistically, I'll have to settle for vacations."

Nolan emerged from the kitchen with a soup tureen and set it in the middle of the dining room table. "Dinner is served. I'll just grab a few things, and we can say the blessing."

Kris didn't wait for instructions about the seating arrangement. She automatically chose a place beside Tucker. While Nolan ferried the biscuits and butter and a pitcher of ice water, Tucker leaned back and stretched an arm across the back of Kris's chair.

How can they possibly become an old couple from Friday to Wednesday? But they had. Kris was relaxed, comfortable, as if her place had been beside Tucker Kintzler for years, not days.

"I think that's everything." Nolan pulled out his own chair. "If I may, I'll share a family blessing. May you always find nourishment for your body at the table. May sustenance for your spirit rise and fill you with each dawn. And may life always feed you with the light of joy along the way."

"That's an Irish blessing if ever there was one," Tucker said.

"Straight from one of my Irish grandmothers." Nolan passed the biscuit basket. "So Tucker, you left the museum to go meet someone you hired to look at Kris's building. What's the report?"

"They'll be at it first thing in the morning," Tucker said. "The first step is to fix the pipe, which surprisingly they believe they can accomplish in one day, along with drying up the floors downstairs."

"They see no reason why the shops can't open again on Friday," Kris said. "We already have power back, and once we have water, we'll be ready for a grand reopening!"

Nolan chuckled.

"Then they can work on the damage upstairs without interfering with anything," Tucker said. "Carolyn and Kris can choose a day to close in order to have the floors downstairs refinished, but that can be at their convenience."

"Carolyn's convenience, really," Kris said, "since it's her shop that loses more business at this time of year than I do."

"Dad, Tucker was telling us a bit about his business before you announced dinner."

Tucker ladled stew into his bowl. "Not much to tell. It's been around a long time, so it's well established and seems to weather the bad times and come out on top. I've only been at the helm a little while and haven't rushed to fix something that isn't broken as far as I can tell. Just building on the assets we have and keeping people employed."

"Seems like a sound strategy," Nolan said.

"Are you staying in fairly close touch with the office while you're out here?" Jillian asked.

"I'm on vacation," Tucker said. "What's on my mind is skiing."

Tucker's next comment had to do with how knowledgeable he found Leif Mueller on ski equipment and how satisfying it was to come to Colorado for some challenging skiing. The curtain closed on talking about his life in Missouri. But it hadn't opened on discouraging him from skiing Hidden Run. Jillian stirred her stew gently, watching steam rise, and sized up the pair across the table, unsure whether her starry-eyed friend was still committed to persuading Tucker not to ski the dangerous run.

They ate stew, warm biscuits, fudge, and ice cream. They swapped what information they had about recovery efforts around town. They yawned and debated the virtues and vices of caffeinated coffee in the evening.

"The crew's coming early," Kris said at last, "so I'd better have an early evening."

Once Tucker and Kris were gone, Jillian helped Nolan clear the table and clean up the kitchen. Then, after he'd dragged up the back stairs saying he still had work to do before he could sleep and had to drive to Denver in the morning, she went into her office and powered up her computer. She had to find out more about Tucker. She wouldn't use any secret portals of the internet not available to anyone—say, Kristina, if she was curious. But the local and regional newspapers that ran obituaries of Matthew Ryder were full of links to archived articles about the family and the business, and it was time to do more than scan the highlights. The articles only went back to a certain date. Before that, articles were available on microfiche at St. Louis regional libraries. She could make requests for copies, which might take a couple of days or a few weeks to fulfill. In the meantime, Jillian settled in to read what she could and, as was her habit, used a yellow legal pad to keep handwritten notes of the bits of information that caught her interest.

Just in case.

In case of what?

In case she needed to tell Kris.

For what purpose?

She wasn't sure.

Just in case.

The whole point of "just in case" is you don't know what the circumstances might be.

Tucker spoke of the business being his grandfather's, but Jillian was fairly sure it went back at least one generation before that. Surely Tucker knew that. Jillian smelled a story.

Accounts of the organization's history praised "bold investments of capital in the early days" for paying off rapidly in profits that were reinvested in the company and formed the core of its financial strength for decades to follow.

Ryder Manufacturing had been a steady and growing employer in Maple Turn that brought economic stability to the town along with a tradition of philanthropy around children's causes. It was true that Tucker's grandfather got the credit for the philanthropy.

An old newspaper photo celebrating the fiftieth anniversary of Matthew Ryder's marriage indicated that his best man, Jackson, had been a childhood friend. Jackson had still been alive on the date of the Ryders' fiftieth anniversary ten years earlier. The two men had their photo taken together at the more recent occasion.

A quick search of death and obituary records suggested Jackson was still alive.

CHAPTER THIRTEEN

Nolan stood in front of Ore the Mountain two days later and laughed out loud.

Kris opened the door and stuck her head out. "Like it?"

"Where did you get that thing?"

"Tucker. Not sure where he pulls his magic from, but it's eye-catching."

"That it is." Nolan stepped back to the edge of the sidewalk for the full effect of the giant red lettering of the GRAND REOPENING sign strung across the front of the building. "Not a bit much for only being closed two days?"

"Three, if you count the day of the storm."

"Three then." Nolan stepped inside.

"Fun, don't you think?"

"Absolutely." Nolan looked around. The wood floor showed water damage, of course, but between the mopping he and the others did on Tuesday, the fans they left running on Wednesday, and the work the professional crew did on Thursday, it was dry and could be sanded and refinished at a convenient time. The worst-case scenario was that some planks might have to be replaced. Otherwise, the shop looked the way it always did. "Looks like things are coming along well."

"The cleanup was so fast! Tucker thought the sign might drum up some winter business," Kris said. "I guess he's heard me whine enough times in the last week about how slow this time of year is for selling ice cream."

"Let's hope it works."

"I'll keep it up for the weekend traffic and make extra hot chocolate."

"Good idea." The sign was visible halfway across town. "And the weather warmed up, so that's in your favor."

"It's perfect timing. Carolyn's daughter had her baby last night, so she's gone down to Golden for a month to help. I can't depend on traffic from the candy shop spilling over into my store for a while."

"Then this will be just the boost you need." Nolan rubbed his hands together. "Now, what have you got on offer today?"

Kris narrowed her eyes. "I'm thinking you want pralines and cream."

"But of course." Considering that he rarely varied from his three favorite flavors, she had a one in three chance of being right. "Jillian's coming down soon. Any excuse to eat ice cream in the middle of the morning, you know."

"I do know." Kris had a dish in her hand and filled it with two scoops, just the way Nolan liked it. "I feel like I should give you a prize for being the first customer at the grand reopening."

"Balloons dropping over my head, perhaps?"

"Something like that." Kris handed him the bowl.

"All the ice cream I can eat for the rest of my life?"

"I'll make you up a certificate."

"In the meantime, take my green certificate." Nolan left cash on the counter and moved to a small table near the window. "Who's that out there?"

"Who?"

Nolan chuckled. "A dancing ice cream cone."

"What?" Kris came around the counter and hustled toward the window. "I didn't know anything about this."

"A little more of Tucker's magic."

"He never said a word."

"The ice cream cone's hands are cherries. Nice costuming touch."

"An ice cream cone has hands?"

"How else can he wave the customers in?"

Kris's thumbs were busy texting when the door opened.

"Have you got hot chocolate?" A young man with an infant in his arms, two children behind him, and a woman bringing up the rear made the inquiry.

"Absolutely." Kris shoved her phone back in her pocket. "I can add extra milk to cool it down for the little ones."

"That would be great. We'll have four, two with extra milk. I'm glad you're open again. We were afraid the damage would close you down permanently."

"No way."

Nolan flashed a smile of encouragement at Kris and dug into his pralines and cream.

Tucker arrived next. "Hey, great! Customers!"

"Your little old-school promotion scheme seems to be working," Nolan said. "How in the world did you do all this so quickly?"

"I know people who know people. There are benefits to being in business."

"Apparently."

"Do you plan to stay awhile?"

"Awhile. Jillian is coming down."

"Perfect. Keep sitting near the window. It's better if people walking by see people inside."

"Will do."

"Do me a favor and keep an eye on this." Tucker pushed his backpack into a corner between the window and Nolan's table. "I'm going to go out and do some street duty. You can't let it out of your sight."

Nolan laughed. "Go for it."

Tucker waved at Kris and went back outside. While the door was open, Luke O'Reilly came in.

"Just the man I wanted to see," Nolan said. "Now, about the theme of your winter party."

"Forget it," Luke said. "Need-to-know basis, and you don't need to know, my friend."

"I'm sure I could advise you on the legality of something or other. Quid pro quo."

"Your fancy lawyer words don't work with me."

"Fine. That's how you are." Nolan heaped his spoon with ice cream and raised it to his mouth. Luke joined the line.

Jillian came in—with three other people who went directly to the counter.

"We all want an ice cream cone, ice cream cone, ice cream cone!" Nolan sang to the tune of "Mary Had a Little Lamb." He held nothing back on the volume. Three little girls giggled.

"Dad, we came to an agreement about public singing when I was in high school."

"I wish to renegotiate the terms."

She narrowed her eyes. "Perhaps you'd like to join the dancing ice cream cone."

"It's been quite an entertaining morning so far." Nolan eased another luscious spoonful of ice cream down his throat. "Much better than reviewing the final mediation agreements on my desk."

Jillian dropped into a chair beside Nolan. "Is that Tucker's backpack?"

"I have been authorized to supervise it."

Jillian drew back. "He's more protective of that thing than most women are of their purses. He didn't even give it to me with his coat when he came to dinner the other night."

"What can I say? People trust my face."

Outside, the joint antics of the dancing ice cream cone and Tucker Kintzler gathered a modest number of onlookers, some actually stopping to shift their glances toward the door of Ore the Mountain. Hoods were down and jackets unzipped on the warmest day Canyon Mines had seen in a week. The door opened twice as people made the decision to follow the ice cream cone's advice and come in.

"I came across something, Dad," Jillian said. "About Tucker."

"What's that?"

"I've been reading archived articles about his family. There's a name, his grandfather's best friend, Jackson. He's still alive. Has Tucker mentioned him?"

"No, he hasn't."

"They were childhood friends, and he was best man in Matthew Ryder's wedding. They had their picture taken together at his fiftieth anniversary."

"That is a long friendship."

"I'm making some inquiries to try to find him."

"What do you think he could tell us?"

"I'm not sure. But people tell their secrets to somebody, don't they?"

"I suppose a friend that old is a good candidate."

"I guess if I want ice cream, I'd better get in line," Jillian said.

"I'll hold the fort here." Nolan ran his spoon around the inside of his bowl, scraping up the last of his treat.

"No singing."

"You're no fun."

Jillian was only a few steps away when her phone rang and she answered. "Uncle Patrick?"

Nolan's head pivoted.

But Jillian didn't turn back toward him, and she kept moving forward with the line as she talked.

If it weren't for that silly backpack in the corner left in his charge, Nolan might have caught his daughter's eye, waved, and left to go back to work. But in the moments he was watching Jillian, Tucker had dropped out of sight, so Nolan couldn't simply return the backpack and leave. Nolan jiggled one leg under the table and awaited the inevitable.

Jillian returned with her waffle cone and two napkins. "Dad, Uncle Patrick says you never called him back. It's been a week."

"He shouldn't have called you."

"But he did. He says he's been leaving you messages."

Nolan sighed. "That's right."

"This is not like you, Dad."

"It's a complex dynamic, Jillian."

"He's your brother, Dad. I always thought Patrick was some sort of black sheep of the family, but I don't know why."

"No, it's not that."

"Then what? I've heard Nana say he had a temper when he was younger, but the few times I've met him, I never saw anything more than someone who looked like he needed a break. Sulking at best. The Duffys are loud when they get together, you know."

"I do know."

"How is it that I come from a large Irish family and I have this uncle I don't know? He's your brother. He's reaching out, and you're not taking his calls."

"You don't have to tell me the obvious, Jillian." Instantly, Nolan regretted his tone. "I'm sorry. I shouldn't have snapped at you."

"Dad."

Her green eyes, the ones she got from him, pleaded with him.

She put a hand on his closed fist. "He wants to talk to you. What don't I know?"

Tucker burst through the door and spread his arms to put one hand on Nolan's shoulder and the other on Jillian's.

Nolan flashed him a grin. "You are doing a fabulous job directing traffic this direction. Have you set up a roadblock or something?"

Tucker's forefinger shot up. "I wonder if I could do that! Maybe not in the street—there's probably a city ordinance about that—but a few orange cones on the sidewalk gently guiding the path."

"They sell them at the hardware store," Nolan said. "Buy six and they'll give you a deal."

"Dad!" Jillian said.

"What? Just trying to do right by Kristina. It is the grand reopening, after all."

The door opened again and another customer joined the line.

"Whatever you're paying that guy in the costume," Nolan said, "it's not enough."

"Who is that, anyway?" Jillian asked.

"My secret." Tucker pointed to the corner. "I need to grab that backpack. If Kris gets a break, tell her I'll be back."

Nolan stood up. "You'll have to assign that duty to Jillian. I'm afraid I need to get back to my desk."

"Jillian it is then," Tucker said. "Your cone is dripping."

Jillian lifted the cone and ran her tongue around it to contain the leaks from the hard shell chocolate dip.

"Nolan, how about we ski tomorrow?" Tucker said.

"I can do that. Let's make a day of it."

"Good. Walk with me and we'll make a plan."

"Dad?" Jillian said, dabbing the corner of her mouth.

"Yes?"

"What we were talking about—we'll talk again?"

"When we have a chance." He didn't meet her eye. He was only digging a deeper hole.

CHAPTER FOURTEEN

This time Tucker was driving his gray rented pickup, and Nolan was the passenger as they headed deeper into the mountains toward a ski resort.

"I haven't been there in forever," Nolan said when Tucker announced the destination. "Exactly how many different places have you skied since you came to Colorado?"

"Half a dozen." Tucker adjusted his dark sunglasses. "That doesn't count the informal hills around town. Canyon Mines makes a nice home base. There are places close enough to run out to for the afternoon, but others farther out that are still very doable as a day trip."

"You are not wrong," Nolan said. Bella had loved the location for the same reason. Even venturing to one of the more distant locations, she could put supper in the slow cooker, take Jillian to school, arrange for Nia to babysit after school, ski several runs, and be home in time to put the meal on the table before Nolan was home from Denver.

"This one has a great ski shop," Tucker said. "We could see about getting you some new skis. What do you say?"

Nolan shook his head. "That might be premature for my remedial phase."

"If you had better skis, you could move out of the remedial phase more quickly."

"You have an answer to everything."

"I try to."

"I'm afraid I'm sentimentally attached to the skis I have." Bella had given Nolan those skis. Jillian was eight at the time and already had declared she didn't want to ski, no matter how much Bella cajoled. Even with new skis Nolan wouldn't be able to keep up with Bella, but it gave her such pleasure to help him pick them out, and at the time they were considered a good set for someone of moderate ability. But twenty years?

Even Leif, who agreed that technically the skis were safe, raised an eyebrow about why anyone would still want to use them.

"Fair point," Tucker said. "I have skis I'm sentimental about. I'll probably never get rid of them, but I don't use them either. How about we rent something for you today?"

"Rent?"

"Sure. As your ski instructor, I think you're ready to experience what kind of skier you could be on more modern equipment."

"You mean like, faster?"

"Exactly."

"Tighter turns?"

"Precisely."

"Better stops?"

"All of that."

"More likely to break a bone?"

"Wait a minute." Tucker laughed. "You set me up. I won't let you do something that's not safe."

Nolan nodded, tucking away that promise. "Okay, but we start with the bunny hill again until I get the feel of them, and this time you do not use me for demonstration purposes with a group of children."

"I'll have to settle for that deal, because I already reserved the equipment."

"What?"

"I couldn't take a chance there wouldn't be anything available."

The thing about Tucker Kintzler was that he was fully and entirely likable. Nolan reminded himself of the specter of Hidden Run and the reason he'd taken up skiing with Tucker in the first place. Allegedly Kris had the same motivation, though it seemed her reasons were deepening into a more personal investment. Nolan might be alone on the Stop Hidden Run Crusade. He just hoped he didn't have to stop two skiers rather than one.

They did rent the equipment.

"Where's the other half?" Nolan asked when he had everything on at the top of the bunny hill.

"What do you mean?" Tucker straightened Nolan's helmet.

"They feel like they weigh nothing!"

"This is what I've been trying to tell you. You're going to love it."

A couple of kids lined up next to Nolan and positioned their poles with some coaching from their parents. Tucker smiled at them. "Great day for skiing, isn't it?"

"Don't even think about it," Nolan muttered.

"I'm not allowed to be friendly with the other skiers?" Tucker made no effort to keep his voice low. "My friend here needs some encouragement on his new skis."

The kids giggled.

Nolan sighed. "Well, then, children, shall we do this?"

They all pushed off at more or less the same time. Every promise Tucker made about the updated skis proved true. They were light and slick and smooth, and Nolan was at the bottom of the long bunny hill ahead of the kids with Tucker right behind him.

"See?" Tucker flipped up his goggles. "You survived. You did great, in fact. Let's try the blue."

"If I remember right," Nolan said, "blue at this resort is a little steep." Bella had skied circles around him here, fearless of the pitch and terrain even when many of her friends found it out of their comfort zone.

"You don't want to stay on the bunny hill all day with your new cool skis."

"Well, I suppose I don't."

"Then we're doing blue."

"Maybe I should have stayed on my slower skis," Nolan said.

"Where's your spirit of adventure? You're here to *ski*. You've got the right mechanics. I'm confident of that. All we're doing now is speeding things up slightly."

"More than slightly."

"I'm just trying to encourage you, my friend. But if you don't want to try. . ."

"I'll do it." Nolan turned toward the lifts. "I'm not old yet."

"Not by a long shot."

Tucker took the blue hill at Nolan's speed, eyeing the skiers passing them on both sides but offering patient encouragement for adjusting to the feel of the lighter, faster skis. The second time down, Nolan felt comfortable to push off hard and go faster all the way down. About halfway,

Tucker took off at full speed. Nolan opted to sit out the third run and instead watch from the bottom as Tucker took the entire hill at lightning speed.

"Next up, black!" Tucker said.

"I'll find a ringside seat for that one," Nolan said.

"I think you're ready," Tucker said.

Nolan shook his head. "That's out of my league, and I'm pretty sure it always will be."

"Don't talk like that. You've seen the difference the right skis can make. We'll get you a pair of your own that you can really get used to. I'll have you on double blacks before you know it."

"I don't think so, Tucker. For that you need Kris."

"She is a terrific skier. I should bring her here. We could do the double black together."

"She'd probably like that. But today you have me for a cheerleader for anything more than blue."

"All right," Tucker said. "Let's go see how crowded the black is, and maybe we'll come back so you can do the blue again before we have to turn in your skis."

Tucker's bright green jacket made him easy to track even from the bottom of the slope as he got off the lift, pushed off, and made tight turns around bumps in the steep terrain of the black diamond run. Even though there were other skiers on the hill, Tucker was the most eager and aggressive to gain speed, take the turns at the last possible moment, and find the points of lift that would send him airborne for a few seconds before whooshing him into powder swirling up as his skis cut back into the snow. Nolan couldn't begin to estimate his speed. Breathtakingly fast. Bella would have been impressed. No wonder Kris was smitten and willing to close her shop in the middle of the day for the chance to ski with Tucker.

Finally, Tucker glided to a stop at the base of the run, and Nolan pushed over on his skis to join him.

"Wow." Nolan planted his poles in front of Tucker. "That's all I have to say."

"What the teacher can do, the student can learn," Tucker said.

"Not one this remedial, I'm afraid. If you want to take another pass here instead of going back to blue, I'm happy to watch again."

"What about double black?"

"If all I'm doing is watching, sure. I can call 911 from anywhere."

"Put your phone away. You won't need it."

Spotting Tucker atop the double-black diamond hill was easy. Only four skiers were there. Even from the bottom, Nolan could see the run was more rugged, with more places to find lift. Knees bent, leaning slightly forward, poles behind him, Tucker found every spot. Another skier came down wrong and didn't land on her feet. Fortunately, her binder did just what it was supposed to do and released her ski. Tucker whizzed past her as she was setting up to continue down. He took every maneuver flawlessly, aimed for Nolan, turned his skis, and slid to a perfect stop.

"You are amazing," Nolan said.

"I wish you could know the feeling I get on a run like that," Tucker said. "You could do it. I know you could."

Nolan shook his head. "Time to turn in these skis."

They headed back to the rental shop, had a hot beverage and a snack in the lodge, and returned to the truck for the drive back to Canyon Mines.

"Do you compete somewhere that you've failed to mention?" Nolan asked once they were on the highway.

Tucker shook his head. "I'm in it for pure joy, and doing the thing that challenges me next."

"Where is the most challenging place you've ever skied?"

"United States or Europe?"

"Fair question. Let's stick with Stateside."

"Jackson Hole, Wyoming, is a pretty good adrenaline rush. Thirty-foot-drop through the chute and some amazing cliffs."

"So it's about the thrill?"

"Partly."

"And Canyon Mines?"

Tucker glanced over at Nolan. "I needed a vacation. Everyone knows skiing in Colorado is great."

Nolan nodded. Jackson Hole. He couldn't ask for a better opening for Jillian's line of inquiry. "I knew someone named Jackson once. A client. It seems like it's a name making a comeback for little boys, don't you think?"

"Maybe. The only Jackson I know is old."

"Does he ski?"

"Doubtful. I'm not sure he's ever been out of Missouri—except maybe over the river into Illinois."

"Really?"

"He was a friend of my grandfather's. A locksmith by trade. He's a curious soul about how things work but largely content to stay close to home."

"There's something to be said for a life of contentment," Nolan said. "Not everybody needs big thrills—like, say, skiing Hidden Run."

"You heard about that."

"Yep."

"Why shouldn't I? You've seen what I can do."

"You are pretty amazing." Nolan trod carefully. "But no one has skied Hidden Run in decades. It's dangerous."

"But it's still there, right?"

"The land is, sure," Nolan said. "The run is another question. It was never fully cleared in the first place, and enough time has passed for it to be overgrown again. We're not above the timberline."

"I know I can't just take a ski lift up there. That's why I had Leif order some backcountry skies. They'll be in any day now."

"Tucker, you're an amazing skier," Nolan said, "probably the best I've ever seen. But Hidden Run wasn't safe even when it was operating commercially."

"Now you sound like your daughter. I didn't expect that from somebody who skis."

"Jillian has a good head on her shoulders," Nolan said. "There were several catastrophic accidents at Hidden Run in the few years it operated, and dozens of lesser ones."

"I know. I've been reading everything I can scrounge up about it. But my guess is those were not experienced skiers. I'm different."

"That may be true, but it doesn't remove the danger. What does Kris think?"

Tucker shrugged behind the wheel. "She was trying to persuade me off, but I think she might actually come with me."

"Well, she is a fine skier too." Nolan sobered. "Does anyone else in your family ski? Was your grandfather a skier?"

"Grandpa Matt? No. Between the business and all his children's charity work, he didn't have a lot of hobbies."

"But you were close."

"We spent a lot of time together. He was always interested in what was going on in my life. We talked every day, right up until the end. About everything. Well, not everything, it turned out. But I didn't know that."

Nolan felt a pang for all the days he'd avoided talking to Paddy. Because of Patrick.

"What do you mean?" Nolan asked.

"It got complicated."

"I'm an attorney. I understand complicated things."

Tucker stared at the highway. "He got sick, and it was like there was something he wanted to say and never did. Couldn't, somehow. The last thing he said to me should have been how much he loved me. That's what I wanted to say to him. Instead, he wanted to talk about some hideous secret and leave me in a quandary about what I'm supposed to do."

"Anything I can help you with?"

Tucker gripped the wheel more tightly. "I doubt it. It's massive stuff."

"I'd like to help if I can."

Tucker shook his head. "Thanks, but I don't think so."

"So you've come to Colorado to think."

"I just knew I couldn't stay there right now."

"Have you talked to Kris?"

"Not really."

"She's a good listener."

"I just want to ski, and doing it with Kris is a lot of fun."

"Do you talk to Jackson?"

"Not about this."

They rode in silence for a few miles. Paddy was seventy-nine when everything blew up. He and Nolan talked again after that, but not about Patrick. Things were never the same.

"Tucker," Nolan said, "families come undone. That doesn't mean they can't be put back together." The words of Patrick's messages burned in his mind.

"Sometimes the fabric may be too unraveled." Tucker thumped the steering wheel several times with a thumb.

"From everything you've said over the last week, I believe your grandfather loved you and you loved him."

"That's true. But things go wrong that you don't even know about. Things people never told you. And you can't fix that. Not when they leave you."

"Your grandfather's last words?"

Tucker didn't answer.

"We can do what we think is right—as well as we are able at different points in time. That's a starting point." Nolan watched Tucker's face, which had grown steely.

How could he advise Tucker without knowing what Tucker faced—and knowing he was dodging the task of repairing the unraveled fabric with his own brother? He couldn't go back and change what he thought was right at a different point in time. But he could choose differently now.

Tomorrow. Starting with Jillian, and then Patrick.

CHAPTER FIFTEEN

Maple Turn, Missouri, 1947

Even the ceiling fans his mother insisted on installing in every room in the new house couldn't battle the midsummer heat and humidity. Matthew wrestled out of the damp sheet, swung his feet to the floor, and settled his eyes on the shape of his bedroom window in the shadows. It was open as wide as it would go, but even the night air brought insufficient relief. It didn't move through the screen perceptibly.

Or maybe it was his tangled thoughts that tortured him and stole his sleep yet again.

His parents didn't know he ever left the house in the middle of the night when slumber eluded him, much less how frequent the habit had become recently regardless of the outdoor temperature. The new house's design, with a main staircase in front and a smaller one in the rear, left little challenge for a teenage boy to slip out of bed, down the steps, through the kitchen, and out the back door without disturbing his parents, whose bedroom hung over the front porch. Matthew had mastered the small movements of soundlessly clicking locks open and doors closed behind him. At least outside he didn't feel the walls closing in, distorting every wish and thought.

He loved his mother, but his days in Maple Turn were numbered. He was fifteen now. If he went to college, it was only three years off, and he would go farther than St. Louis. Even if he didn't go to college, three years from now he'd have his high school diploma in his hands. Maybe he wouldn't finish high school. Judd hired people without high school diplomas, and there were other factories all over the country that would hire a hard worker. Or he could join the army. The war was over. There wouldn't ever be another one like that, not after two world wars. He'd be safe, and his mother wouldn't have to worry. Judd wouldn't care whether he was gone. Matthew had been working in the showroom the last few weeks, earning a little money. He'd barely spent a penny. He'd keep working after school in the fall and save everything he earned. When he was seventeen, he'd have something to leave with. By then he would pass for eighteen, or even twenty.

In the backyard, he paused at the stone bench in the flower garden that gave his mother such pleasure. In the old house, she'd only had a couple of small beds to putter in. Now she had a real garden, and this was the first summer they had fresh flowers in the main rooms of the house every day all summer. Primrose and coneflower and red columbine and foxglove and lobelia and cardinal and iris and day lilies.

Matthew would figure out a way to make it right with his mother. He still had a couple of years to sort that out. But he couldn't stay. Surely she could see that. Or she would by then.

Looping around the side of the house, he crossed the front lawn. It didn't slope like Grandpa Ted's, but he was too old to roll down a hill anyway. His mother was the one who insisted on leaving the grove of maples standing between the house property and the business, rather than leveling everything when the equipment was there to work on the grading and dig the foundations. It was healthy for the family, she said, to have boundaries between home and business. They should be able to look out their windows at home and see natural beauty, not reminders of work to be done. It was convenient to live next to the business, but Judd needed a place of retreat.

The speech was nice. She had practiced it—Matthew could tell. *"What do you think this character might be feeling?"* Miss Lampier's question had hung over his childhood in ways she had never known. His mother was proud Judd made something of himself and gave something to the town. But it had come at a cost, and she didn't want to see the cost when she gazed out her windows or sat on the front porch. That's why the maples still stood, why she hadn't let the landscapers even thin them.

She hadn't ever been inside the showroom or offices of Ryder Manufacturing after opening day. Not once.

Matthew rounded the maples and considered the sleeping building. Already Judd had expanded the parking lot. He knew how to sell into the hardware stores in the area as well as manage retail sales and fill orders outside the region. The shipping dock was always busy. Matthew knew which doors were which now. Two led into where supplies were delivered. Two led out when shipments were ready to leave. Two served for employees to come and go, and two more for the fire and emergency exits. By process of elimination, the remaining door must be the external entrance to the private storage area in the private hallway behind his father's office. But he had never seen that door open, not from the outside nor from the inside. Not a single time in more than a year of being in business.

Most days he thought nothing of it. He went to school, helped his mother around the house and yard, went to church as expected—at least Jackson was there—played some baseball with Jackson and other friends when he had time, and stayed out of his father's way. Only this summer had he begun working in the showroom for the first time because Judd announced that he would, and complying was easier than causing his mother distress. Judd still traveled occasionally, but not with the same regularity as when he had sold supplies to hospitals in the region. He had a business to run, and he had a sales staff of his own now. Matthew just kept his head down and counted the days.

He circled to the rear of the building, following the wide route he always took on his nocturnal excursions. If he wasn't sleepy, he would take another lap. If he could, he'd go farther, but it wouldn't do to be two miles away if he was ever discovered missing. His mother would panic, and Judd would nail him to the wall for causing her panic. This way, if the lights suddenly came on at home and voices shouted his name, he could call back and claim he had only needed some air. Especially at this time of year it was understandable.

Mr. Harding had been pleading with Judd to install a security light at the back of the building, but Judd perpetually dismissed the notion as a waste. Matthew stepped carefully through the darkness.

A door opened, and a quick shaft of light illumined a figure with a sack.

The door.

Matthew ducked under the loading dock.

The sack looked like a rumpled bag of laundry. The door shut, and the figure—a woman—moved toward a dark sedan. The factory did have some minimal laundry needs, but why would it be picked up at this hour? This was far later than the normal janitorial hours. And there was no laundry service truck, just the sedan. When the car door opened, a cry came.

He thought it was a cry. It was too brief to be sure. A child? That made less sense than the laundry.

Matthew stumbled over something soft and lumpy, and a cat gave an angry snarl before shooting out from behind his legs.

He exhaled heavily. No child. Just a stupid, grungy, stray cat. The sedan's engine started, and it pulled away.

The cat didn't explain laundry from the storage door. Sometime, in the daylight when Judd was not around, Matthew would have a look. He was not as good as Jackson at jimmying a lock, but he could try.

Matthew's heart raced. This walk hadn't been calming at all.

At breakfast in the morning, Matthew's mother, who still preferred to cook for her small family even though Judd urged her to hire help, had eggs and bacon on the stove. Judd was already eating.

"You're late," Judd said. "We had to say grace without you."

"I'm sorry," Matthew said. "I had trouble sleeping."

"It was awfully warm last night." His mother filled a plate and set it in front of him. "Papa was just saying that he plans to be out of town for a while."

"Oh? Where are you going?"

"Various places," Judd said. "I'll be coming and going quite a bit for the next few weeks. We invested a great deal of money in equipment. If we want it to pay off, we need far more sales of our original designs at mass-produced scales. I'm going to need to travel to increase sales and secure additional financing for the necessary expansion. We can't stay a small shop for long."

"Will you take someone from the sales team with you?"

"No. I will handle these matters personally. They are delicate, and our future depends on them. Your future, Matthew, since this company will be yours someday."

Matthew swallowed some eggs. It was surely his mother's idea that the company should be his someday.

"When will you leave?" She refilled Judd's coffee cup.

"Today, I think. For the first meeting."

Matthew crunched bacon between his teeth and guzzled his glass of milk. "I should get to work."

"No need for that," Judd said.

"Sir?"

"These next few weeks will be intense for me," Judd said. "I imagine I will be coming and going at unpredictable hours, meeting with people at their locations as well as here—whatever can be arranged on short notice. I suggest you and your mother go to your grandparents' for a few weeks until school starts up again."

Matthew set down his milk glass. He wasn't dull-witted, and he had a better memory of peculiar events of his childhood than his parents gave him credit for. And he'd heard far more conversations than they knew. This had something to do with his mother getting what she wanted all those years ago—and perhaps the house they were sitting in right now—because of the way Judd did business. Maybe it had something to do with what just happened a few hours ago in the middle of the night.

"Mama can go," he said. "I can take the bus out on the weekends. But I'd like to stay and work in the showroom. I enjoy being around the business." How easily the falsehood passed his lips.

"You'd be on your own too much," Judd said.

"I could stay with Jackson's family. I'm sure they'd let me." What objection could there be to leaving him in the care of the pastor?

"I'm afraid that won't do."

"I'm old enough."

"Matthew," his mother said, "you need to be with me. Out of the way."

Out of the way? Out of the way of what?

"I'm fifteen," he said. "I don't need looking after."

"The decision is made." Judd picked up his newspaper. "Stop arguing. I'll let Mr. Harding know not to expect you any longer and drive you out to St. Charles after lunch."

"Can I at least go tell Jackson goodbye? We had plans." And the door. Maybe it was time to let Jackson jimmy the door after all—as long as he was sure Judd was out of town.

"There's no time for goodbyes." His mother's voice held firm. She might not like what Judd was up to, but she didn't want Matthew anywhere near it. He was certain of that. "You can send Jackson a postcard from Grandpa Ted's store. The two of you will survive until school starts in the fall. Get your things together."

"Fine." Matthew pushed back his chair, made no effort to tuck it back under the table or put his dishes in the sink, and walked out of the room.

Forget the job. Forget Jackson. Forget the door. Forget Maple Turn. He *would* figure a way out. If his mother kept choosing to close her eyes to whatever Judd was doing, eventually she'd be closing her eyes to Matthew too.

CHAPTER SIXTEEN

Coffee wasn't the only enticement Nolan's nostrils detected on Sunday morning.

Jillian was cooking.

He slid his feet into shoes, straightened his tie, and descended the back stairs.

"Breakfast!" Nolan said. "And here I thought I'd barely have time for toast before church."

"You have time for oatmeal and fruit with a side of family history honesty." Jillian topped a bowl with blueberries and set it on the breakfast bar in front of the stool where Nolan usually sat.

"Patrick," he said.

"Patrick." Jillian filled her own bowl at the stove and came around the bar.

Coffee. Spoons. Napkins. Cream. It was all there. Nolan had no excuse to get up and procrastinate. The best he could do was splash some cream over his oatmeal and buy four seconds to collect his thoughts.

"The first thing I want to say is that if I could change one moment in my life, it would be that moment with Patrick." Nolan stirred the milky liquid into his breakfast.

"Dad, what happened?" Jillian turned sideways in her stool, her eyes pulling for his.

He looked at her square on. "Patrick and Pop Paddy argued, and Patrick left. It broke Pop Paddy's heart. Patrick was the apple of his eye. He found out I was there when Patrick left, and he blamed me for not stopping him." This was the sparse version, but it was essentially accurate.

"Could you have? Should you have?"

"At the time, I didn't think so." Nolan took a bite.

"And now?" Jillian said.

"I don't know. I'll never know, because I didn't try, and I was the only one who had the opportunity to try. He didn't come back. Pop Paddy died a few years later without ever seeing Patrick again, or even talking on the phone, and he never really forgave me. Things were never the same between us."

"Oh Dad."

Nolan ate more oatmeal and sipped black coffee. Patrick hadn't been interested in what Nolan had to say, but Nolan hadn't tried very hard to say anything either. He deserved whatever fury Patrick had unleashed on their grandfather. He hadn't seen that this time Patrick wouldn't come back in a few weeks and act like nothing had happened. And then it was too late. But this was not the time to tell only one side to Jillian when there had been so many sides during the events.

"What are you going to do to fix this, Dad?" Jillian put a hand on his knee. "You can't keep doing nothing. Not when Patrick keeps calling you—and now me."

"You're right. I'll do something. Soon."

All those years ago, every moment was laden with choices that might have told another story. Picking up an item. Admiring it. Coveting it. Not putting it down when doing so would have changed everything. Savoring a glimpse of favoritism. Feeling the power of being the youngest. Knowing what it meant to Patrick and wanting it anyway. Accepting that piece of Pop Paddy. Not stopping Patrick. Not saying anything. Not being sorry.

So many unchosen simpler fixes so long ago now snowballed into the avalanche of dodging his brother's calls in shame.

"If I can help," Jillian said, "just ask."

"Thanks, Jilly. Pray that I will be wise."

"You are wise. And you're a wonderful family mediator."

"I will have to rely on the Holy Spirit to mediate between Patrick and me."

"Patrick is reaching out, Dad. Find out what he wants. That's the starting point, isn't it?"

Nolan nodded.

"Eat," Jillian said. "Your oatmeal is getting cold."

Not everyone knew their grandparents. Nolan had been lucky to know all four of his. To love and be loved. If it spoiled at the end with Pop Paddy, it was his own doing. A lifetime—Jillian's lifetime—did not change that.

"Something happened with Tucker's grandfather, you know." Nolan spooned food into his mouth. "That's why he's here."

"Not just to ski like a maniac?"

"He is a phenomenal skier, no question. But the maniac leanings have something to do with his grandfather. I'm sure of it."

"He seems like an upstanding guy so far," Jillian said.

"Tucker takes a liking to kids. I suppose he got that from his grandfather. But there must be a reason why his grandfather would choose children's causes to give to."

"I didn't come across a personal connection, but I can keep looking." Jillian scraped her bowl clean. "The one thing I thought was interesting is that his grandfather was a very young man when he took over the company."

"There could be any number of reasons for that."

"Of course. I just found it curious. In any event, he died a few months ago, as you know. The local newspaper was full of glowing coverage of a beloved citizen. That's about it, on the surface of things."

"Then we have to find something below the surface for you to go on," Nolan said. "My gut tells me we have to get to the bottom of what happened with Tucker's grandfather if we're going to stop him from skiing Hidden Run."

"Maybe he's always been a risk-taker. We don't really know him."

Nolan shook his head. "I don't think he's a chancer. There's a difference between excitement and foolhardiness, even for a person of his skill."

"You think he's knotted up about something and that's why he's so bent on Hidden Run?"

"It's a reasonable working theory."

" 'The truth shall make you free,' " Jillian said.

"Jesus was on to something, don't you think? Nothing on Jackson?"

"Not yet."

"Who knows, an old friend might have a piece of the truth a grandson doesn't."

Jillian slipped off her stool and picked up the empty oatmeal bowls. "Time for church. I'll be right back down."

She put the bowls in the sink and went up the back stairs. Nolan took his phone out of his pocket. The weather had cleared, and his afternoon was uncommitted. Patrick's latest message said he was still in Denver. Maybe they could meet today. Nolan scrolled through his contact list and found the number he almost never used. The last time he'd called it was when his father was hospitalized for unexpected bypass surgery and Nolan was appointed to let Patrick know, even if no one in the family thought he would come from Seattle. He hadn't, but he did call their mother during the long hours of waiting while Big Seamus was in surgery.

Patrick didn't answer. After four rings, his curt voice mail greeting came on, and Nolan spoke into the cyber void of wherever phone messages went.

"Patrick, it's Nolan. If you're free today—Sunday—I could drive over to Denver to meet. I'm headed to church now, but let me know. Anytime in the afternoon or evening will work."

Nolan ended the message and exhaled. He might have missed his chance. Patrick had called Jillian two days ago. Maybe he'd gone back to Seattle. He could be on a plane right now. If he didn't call back, Nolan might feel the same repugnant soup of culpability and reprieve as that day Patrick's car squealed away and Nolan didn't stop him. That's what Paddy had not forgiven Nolan for in the end.

Not just failing to stop Patrick.

But not *wanting* to stop him.

Being glad the volatile brother was gone.

And Paddy had been right. That's what Nolan couldn't forgive himself for.

CHAPTER SEVENTEEN

Near St. Louis, Missouri, 1948

The tinge of antiseptic tickled Matthew's nose, but he had no free hand to assuage the itch and had to settle for scrunching his nostrils.

"Don't do that," Judd said. "You are not four years old. I'm conducting business here."

"Yes, sir."

Matthew hefted the box of cabinet door samples. Though not full-size, they were heavy nevertheless. Judd insisted on quality. If expanding from producing hardware that went on the cabinets to also selling the cabinets themselves was going to succeed, Ryder Manufacturing would take no shortcuts. In only two years, Judd's pace of expansion had been unrelenting. One capital crusade followed another, and while Matthew knew nothing of the details, the evidence of success was clear. Ryder didn't yet manufacture its own cabinets, but Judd had his eye on that prize as well—and the promise of increased jobs and prosperity it would bring to Maple Turn.

"We've been here before, haven't we?" Matthew asked.

Judd eyed him peripherally. Matthew had his answer. He was small, not in school yet the last time his nose twitched this way. Antiseptic, yes, but also a faint scent that reminded him of the English lavender his mother worked hard to grow in a sheltered corner of her garden, as if in this particular medical establishment someone made an effort to blunt the harsh chemical odors wafting in the halls. When his mother brought lavender into the house, Matthew had sneezing fits.

They weren't all that far from home, or from St. Charles and Grandpa Ted's general store and rolling property and fishing holes. Matthew was sixteen now and mentally marshaling arguments for why his father should allow him to drive the Buick. So far he hadn't asked. He wanted a failsafe approach before he raised the question, including his mother's support, but ultimately, driving was an essential skill for his exit plan. Wherever he landed, he wanted to be able to say he knew how to drive and held a valid license.

"I'm dressed for the meeting, aren't I?" Matthew would be sure to straighten his tie once he set down the load in his arms.

"I won't require your assistance today beyond setting up."

Matthew stifled a sigh. Judd's response was not unexpected. Matthew's read of his father was rarely wrong. Judd always required that Matthew dress in nice slacks and a shirt and tie when he traveled with him on sales calls, but Judd's mood in the car would signal whether Matthew would be at his side learning the business, as Judd would explain to customers, or sitting outside a closed door in a rickety wooden chair or, if he was lucky, a more modern aluminum one styled after chairs designed to withstand use on naval vessels.

This clinic was recently updated and not quite finished, so it wasn't too late for Judd to pitch his cabinets and hardware. Operating in the wing of a hospital fairly separate from the main services, it occupied space that formerly belonged to administrative offices. Judd pointed with an elbow, and Matthew turned a corner into a waiting area. At least the new clinic already had new chairs. His gaze took in the side tables. The magazines, stacked neatly in overlapping rows, weren't even out of date yet. He could pass the time comfortably. In truth he didn't care about learning the business. He was only there to placate his mother and because Judd had him on the clock after school. He'd get paid whether he was in the meeting or not. His seventeenth birthday was within sight, bringing options with it. If only his shoulders would fill out to match his height, it would be easier to pass for eighteen when necessary. Maybe he would finish high school, or maybe he wouldn't. He refused to tie himself down on that point. He just needed to learn to drive. Already he had a list of notes he would write to his mother on postcards from wherever he went. A visit home would only come when enough time had passed for her to accept the permanence of his move away from home.

Judd spoke softly to a young woman at the reception desk. The name plate said Miss Couchman. She waved them through a gray door and pointed to where they could set up their wares.

"We don't have a conference room," she said. "Dr. Kemmons suggested using the hallway so he could get an idea what the cabinets might look like out here. Then you can talk in his office about the details."

"Good thinking," Judd said. "This will work fine."

"He's got a couple of patients, but he should be free soon."

Matthew set his box on the floor and began unloading it, following Judd's lead to set door samples on the narrow table and lean them against the wall. Then they began sorting an array of hardware options that would complement the samples.

"I want to see my baby!" A woman shrieked behind them and pushed past the patient being escorted through the gray door.

"Mrs. Liston, you can't be back here without an appointment." Miss Couchman's stern steps followed the distraught woman.

"Don't tell me where I can't go." Mrs. Liston shirked off the receptionist's touch. "They said my baby died."

"I was very sorry to hear that."

"I don't want your pity. I want to talk to somebody."

Matthew released a half dozen pewter knobs in his hand from an unplanned height, and they clattered to the tabletop.

"Matthew!" Judd's hushed rebuke was instant.

"It's very sad when a mother loses a baby during birth," Miss Couchman said, "but it's a matter to discuss with someone at the hospital, not the clinic."

"No one at the hospital will talk to me. I've been to every office they have. Do you know I never even saw my baby?"

"Again, I'm very sorry, but I'll have to ask you to leave."

Judd nudged Matthew and whispered, "Mind your own business."

Matthew picked up another box of handles, this one polished black with gray rims, and set them out, but his head was cocked toward the commotion. Miss Couchman maintained an astringent demeanor for someone as young as he judged her to be—surely not yet thirty.

"If my baby died, why didn't I see him?" Mrs. Liston wanted to know.

"I'm afraid I can't answer that question," Miss Couchman said.

"Or why don't I have a death certificate? It's been a month. Is my poor little baby in a cold refrigerator somewhere in the bowels of this place?"

Mrs. Liston's pitch was so shrill Matthew's spine shivered in reaction.

"Matthew, this has nothing to do with you." His father's voice was low and firm. "Turn away."

"She's pretty upset," Matthew said.

"But you are not the one who upset her. You are here to work, not to get involved with patients you know nothing about."

"Yes, sir."

Matthew opened another box. Judd turned his back to the upheaval and pulled a notebook and catalog from his briefcase to study.

"They just say they'll take care of things, but they tell me nothing. Nothing!" Mrs. Liston jabbed the air toward the receptionist. "Since I can't get anywhere with the hospital, I decided to see the doctor who was looking after me before the baby came, and that's Dr. Kemmons."

"I'd be happy to schedule an appointment if you'll just step into the lobby."

"You don't understand," Mrs. Liston growled. "My appointment is *now*. I'm not leaving without answers. I can take care of my own baby. I want to see him, and I want a death certificate. Then I will bury him myself."

"Mrs. Liston," the receptionist said, "it's not really my place, but I did work for the hospital from the time I left school until we opened the clinic a few months ago. In cases like this, the baby is cremated and a grave is provided. It's for the best."

Mrs. Liston screamed. Matthew faltered backward into his father, who was still flipping pages in his catalog.

"Matthew, watch where you're going."

"Pop," Matthew said, "something's going on here."

"And it's being taken care of. Maybe you should just go to the waiting room right now."

Matthew shook his head.

A nurse exited one of the exam rooms, and Mrs. Liston rushed toward her. The nurse caught her wrists as her arms flew up.

"Tell me where my baby is!"

"Stillbirth. I've tried to explain," Miss Couchman said. "She'll be notified in due time where the grave is."

The nurse released Mrs. Liston's arms but gripped her around the shoulders. "I'm sure that's the case. Perhaps we can help shake loose the paperwork."

"Yes, of course," Miss Couchman said. "Do we have your phone number in our records, Mrs. Liston? I'll look into it and call you."

"I haven't got a phone." Mrs. Liston glared, her face streaked with angry tears. "Somebody knows something about what happened to my baby, and I want to know what it is. My baby was not stillborn. I heard him cry. I want to know what happened to him. There should be a death certificate. There should be a cause of death. What sort of hospital would cremate a baby and not tell the mother?"

"A kind hospital," Miss Couchman said, "full of people who want to spare you any more pain and expense than you have already endured."

The nurse patted Mrs. Liston's back.

"Let go of me." She jerked out of reach of anyone and set her feet in a defiant dare. "Where's the doctor? I want to talk to him right now."

The nurse glanced at Miss Couchman and nodded. "Fine. I will let him know you are here."

Matthew glued his back to the wall. Judd flipped another catalog page.

When the nurse returned, a second nurse followed along with the doctor.

"Hello, Judd," Dr. Kemmons said. "I'll just be a few minutes."

Judd nodded without looking up.

"You must know something," Mrs. Liston bellowed. "There must be something in my records. You were my doctor when I was expecting. You were supposed to be there when my time came."

"Yes, I'm sorry that at the last minute I couldn't be there, but I assure you the man I sent to attend you was a fine doctor."

"He wasn't *my* doctor. He was a stranger who came at the last minute, patted my hand, and took my baby. Now they're telling me I didn't hear him cry. But I did!"

"Mrs. Liston, please. You're not doing yourself any good getting all worked up."

"Don't insult me. Wouldn't the hospital give you information about what happened when my baby was born?"

"I would have to look and see."

"Fine. Do it."

"Mrs. Liston, I have a full schedule today. Patients in the exam rooms, more in the waiting room, a meeting with these gentlemen."

"My baby died! My *baby* died!" Every word rising through her throat twisted into a sob.

"Perhaps we should see about admitting you to the hospital," Dr. Kemmons said.

She recoiled. "You mean the mental ward again."

"If you calm down and become reasonable, it might be for your own good. You can get some rest, and people there can help you through your grief about the baby you lost. It's been a month, and you still seem to be in crisis."

"I'm sorry I'm not grieving on your convenient schedule." Mrs. Liston's eyes flashed toward Judd. "You! You were there! I saw you. Tell me what happened."

Matthew's breath drew sharp.

"Look at me when I'm speaking to you." She lunged toward Judd and yanked on his elbow, sending his catalog and notebook flying and forcing him off balance before pummeling his chest.

Matthew might not have the broad shoulders he wished for, but he towered over the woman, and his reflexes kicked in. In two long strides he had hold of her and pulled her off Judd. No one should get hurt, not even dispassionate Judd. That wasn't how his mother or Grandpa Ted raised him.

"Can someone call security?" Matthew wrapped his long arms around Mrs. Liston's thrashing.

"Already did," a voice responded from the reception area.

Judd couldn't help looking at Mrs. Liston now.

"You know something about this," she said, digging her fingernails into Matthew's hands. "I don't forget faces. I know you were there, right outside the door as it opened when I heard him cry when they took him away."

Two hospital guards arrived and escorted the flailing Mrs. Liston out.

Dr. Kemmons followed. "I'm going to admit her," he said to a nurse. "Try to reach her husband. I'll be back as soon as I can, but this could take awhile." He glanced at Judd. "Sorry about your boy."

"I'll get something for your scratches," the second nurse said to Matthew.

He shook his head. "I'm all right."

"Some disinfectant would be wise."

"Do it, Matthew," Judd said. "You don't know anything about that woman."

"I'll be right back." The nurse scurried off.

Other clinic staff scattered in their efforts to restore order to the patient flow.

"You all right, Pop?" Matthew said.

Judd picked up his catalog and notebook and smoothed them. "Yes, thank you."

"You don't know her from anywhere, do you?"

"Of course not. Look at her state of mind. It's complete nonsense. Why would I know anything about a woman's deceased baby in a town I only visit occasionally for sales calls?"

"I thought she might be confused about where she recognized you from."

"I've never met her, Matthew."

"What will happen to her?"

"That's not our concern. But under the circumstances, I suggest you get your scratches disinfected and we pack up. We can reschedule this call for another day."

CHAPTER EIGHTEEN

Jillian hit Send.

The unidentified body in the morgue in Denver had a likely name and two candidates for next of kin that detectives could look for. Jillian had done her work based on the personal papers found among the man's possessions. Three old letters, long out-of-date documents from across the country showing three different names and assorted addresses, a couple of photos with first names written on the backs, a twenty-year-old church bulletin, three spiral notebooks of smeared ink. After the coroner determined the man had died of natural causes and there was no foul play to investigate, the Denver police kept the originals of everything except the mostly illegible spirals and sent those, along with copies of everything else, to Jillian to decipher. In cases like this, she had to remember the parameters of what she was being paid to do and a reasonable time frame for results. Otherwise she'd be tempted to try to reconstruct the narrative that would bring this man to such a dismal end.

But they weren't writing a movie script. All they wanted was an identity they could verify and a next of kin to notify, and Jillian was confident she'd accomplished that, so today she closed the file and sent her invoice.

She glanced at the time. A pile of work still awaited, but her back was stiff. Her dad would say she spent too much time hunched at the computer, and she would be hard-pressed to argue.

Get up and move, Nolan would say. *Talk a walk. And go farther than the coffeepot.*

Uncle Patrick hadn't called back. Nolan had fidgeted around the house all day yesterday waiting. By supper he was berating himself for goldbricking. For more than a week he had avoided Patrick's calls. If his brother never wanted to speak to him again, he would deserve it, he said.

Jillian hoped that would not be the case—for both brothers' sakes. And for hers. Her dad hadn't revealed the full story. Maybe she didn't need to know it, but he needed the weight of a long-ago moment off his shoulders, if it was possible—and he had to talk to Patrick before she could press him for more details.

Jillian shuffled folders around on her desk, bringing to the top of the stack the unofficial one that bore no label. It held a couple of sheets torn from a yellow legal pad where she had written notes about Matthew, Tucker, and Ryder Manufacturing, along with a handful of articles she'd thought worth printing from newspaper archives around the region. One she'd come back to again and again, looking between the lines for a glimpse of the true Matthew Ryder. It was one of those quick Q&A formats, with fairly simple questions intended to elicit brief answers to run in a format that took up the same amount of printed space every week. This one had appeared in a local business journal nearly thirty years ago. Jillian had highlighted three questions.

Q. Tell us why family is at the heart of your business.

A. We all make choices that reflect the connections that we ourselves seek. Family is where some of the greatest conundrums can happen, and we rise to face the greatest challenges.

Q. Your family is well known for religious activity as well as business contributions. Do you have a favorite Bible verse?

A. John 8:32. "And ye shall know the truth, and the truth shall make you free."

Q. What gives you the greatest satisfaction in your work?

A. Sometimes in our work, we must step up to a call we never pursued, and the greatest surprise is finding that somehow we were able.

Matthew Ryder hadn't wanted to answer these questions. Jillian would bet her professional expertise on it. Both family members and his public relations team must have been scratching their heads when they saw his answers in print. When asked a question about family, he said nothing about his own heritage, nothing especially warm and fuzzy. When asked about his faith, he responded with a verse that left room for great struggle. And it was questionable whether his work gave him any satisfaction at all.

"I own shoes," Jillian said aloud. Nia thought she should get a cat. She couldn't be trusted to take care of a dog, in Nia's opinion, but a cat was lower maintenance and would give her somebody to talk to instead of just herself.

The problem with being friends with your former babysitter was that she knew your old habits, like talking aloud to yourself when you thought no one was listening. But she'd learned the habit from her father and thus felt no shame.

Jillian decided she would walk farther than the coffee machine. It wasn't a pot, as she was always telling her father. He had to accept that the days of having an ordinary coffeepot in their kitchen were long gone. In the small space off the kitchen, she pulled on her fur-lined ankle boots and her perfectly warm jacket before double-checking her pockets for keys and phone, and locking the door behind her. She wanted to talk to Kristina, and not by text. The walk would be good for her back and good for her curiosity.

Downtown, the red-lettered GRAND REOPENING sign was visible from down the street, though the dancing cone was gone. Inside Ore the Mountain, Kris was wiping tables while Lindy worked the counter serving a couple of customers.

"Wow." Jillian stamped the remains of gray snow off her boots. "You had Lindy come in?"

"I had to on Saturday." Kris straightened a chair under a table. "Granted, we sold more hot chocolate than we did ice cream, but all that snow last week made for a big ski weekend. And that silly human cone on the sidewalk was surprisingly effective."

"He was back on Saturday?"

"Yep. I didn't know until I got here."

"Missed you at church yesterday."

"Tucker and I went skiing. He wanted to get an early start."

"I imagine it was beautiful. The weather was so clear."

"Spectacular!" Kris started another table. "Do you want some ice cream? Hot chocolate?"

"I'm pretty sure I still owe you for the last two indulgences."

"Your credit is good with me."

"Good to know." Jillian chose a chair. "Hot chocolate if you have time to sit with me."

Kris glanced toward the counter. "I don't see why not. Be right back."

"Don't forget—"

"I know. Extra whipped cream."

"Lots."

Kris returned with two large cups. Jillian inspected hers.

"How am I supposed to drink this without getting whipped cream on my nose?"

"Make up your mind."

"Fine." Jillian licked some whipped cream as if it were ice cream. "So how's Tucker?"

"Seems great. At least as long as he's skiing."

"Still planning on Hidden Run?" Jillian might as well get a Team Tucker report in between the nuances of a Kris and Tucker report.

"I stayed away from that yesterday. Just didn't seem like the day for it."

"You're entitled to some fun." *Or, you might be losing focus.*

Kris chuckled. "I'm tempted to have some fun by buying Tucker a new man purse."

"That backpack is pretty sad." Jillian licked more whipped cream and started to wonder if Kris had filled the whole cup with topping and no chocolate.

"He always has to know where it is, like a woman and her purse. Worse, actually. Do you know he wears it under his jacket while he skis?"

Jillian ran her tongue over her top lip to clear whipped cream. "Can't he just leave it at the B&B or in the truck? He doesn't keep his wallet in it, does he?"

"He carries around so much cash that he probably should," Kris said, "but no. As far as I've noticed, the only thing in it is a padded envelope."

"Sealed or unsealed?"

"Sealed. Definitely sealed."

"Strange."

"That's what I think. But it's the one thing I've ever seen make him anxious—when he thought he'd left it at the restaurant in Genesee last week. He almost turned around and went back when we were halfway home, and then I found it stuffed between the seats."

"That's when you got a look at what's in it?"

"More of a solid feel," Kris said. "Tucker took possession, and we didn't talk about it again."

"So what do you think is in it? Ski maps? Research on Hidden Run?"

"Why would that be sealed?"

"Legal documents for work?" Jillian was beginning to be hopeful there was hot chocolate under the whipped cream after all. She could smell a hint of it.

"Maybe. Something important he just doesn't want to do?"

"Perhaps the family business doesn't run itself as smoothly as he would have us believe."

"That's possible, I guess," Kris said. "We haven't talked all that much about the business."

"What do you talk about?"

"You know. Stuff."

"Kristina. We've been friends a long time."

"We ski, okay? We go to dinner. He's easy to relax with. And he's been incredible with fixing up this place after the storm last week. It's been nice to have someone to lean on."

"You deserve to have someone, Kris."

"Thanks, Jills. I promise I haven't forgotten about Team Tucker. I know I'm supposed to be trying to talk some sense into him. If anything, I have even more reason not to want him to get hurt."

"Has he ever talked about a family friend named Jackson?"

"Sorry, no."

"What about his great-grandfather, Judd?"

"Definitely not. I don't think his Grandpa Matt liked his father much."

"That's what my dad says. No family scrapbook?"

"Hardly something he'd bring on a ski trip."

Jillian shrugged. "Could be in the backpack."

Kris's phone pinged with a text, and she took it from a pocket. "It's Tucker. The backcountry skis are in at Leif's."

"That makes Hidden Run closer."

Kris nodded. "He wants me to meet him at Catch Air right now."

"Are you going?"

Kris looked around. "Lindy can handle things here. It's only a couple of blocks away. Come with me."

"I might want to clock him for considering this."

"Me too. But if we go, we can make sure Leif knows Tucker has in mind to ski Hidden Run on these skis."

"True. But will he be for or against it?"

"At least he'll make sure Tucker's prepared." Kris stood. "Give up on that cup of whipped cream."

"Did you put any hot chocolate in this at all?"

"Two full ounces."

It was a twelve-ounce cup. "You are a rotten friend."

"I do my best."

They traipsed over to Catch Air and found Tucker stroking the new skis on the long counter—two sets.

"Here you go," Tucker said. "Mine were actually here a few days ago. I waited for yours."

"Mine?" Kris said.

"Well, I don't have four legs," Tucker said.

"I never said I wanted backcountry skis."

Kris's words were out of sync with her movements. She walked to the counter and lifted a ski. She wasn't as tall as Tucker, and the second set of skis was proportionally shorter.

"They're so light." Kris was enchanted. "Such narrow waists."

Tucker leaned over and ran a finger over the notches at one end. "I got the skins too, so you'll be all set for climbing in the backcountry."

Like on Hidden Run.

"I've never done any backcountry skiing, Tucker." Kris laid one ski across both hands to feel its weight.

"You'll love it."

"How much have you done?"

"We'll learn together."

Kris tilted her head upward at Tucker. "So you're not actually a backcountry skier?"

"It's just the next progression. We're ready."

"It could be dangerous."

Say you won't do it. Say you can't accept the expensive skis. Jillian moved closer to the counter, hoping her presence might bring Kris nearer to reality.

"It's such a generous gift, Tucker," Kris said, "after you've done so much for me already."

"I didn't pick out the bindings," he said. "I thought you should do that."

"Definitely."

"Kris," Jillian said.

"Yes?" Kris reluctantly shifted her gaze toward Jillian.

Jillian smiled vaguely and scratched her head.

Kris put the ski down on the counter. "This is too much, Tucker. I can't accept it, and I don't think I'm ready for a rugged backcountry environment."

"Of course you are. Tell her, Leif."

"You could learn," Leif said. "There are places that aren't so scary."

"No, no, no." Tucker wagged a finger. "We're going for the good stuff. Hidden Run."

There it was.

"I'm definitely not ready for that," Kris said. "It's a legend—a *lost* legend. I've never even seen it."

Thank goodness.

"What do you think, Leif?" Tucker said. "Kris is one of the best. She could do it, couldn't she?"

"I wouldn't," Leif said.

Thank you, Leif.

"But that's just me."

What?

"Exactly," Tucker said.

"But if someone is bound and determined," Leif said, "these would be the right skis. And of course you want to be up on your mountaineering and avalanche awareness skills for safety."

"But you wouldn't do it," Jillian said, "and you're an excellent skier. The best, right?"

Tucker scowled at Jillian.

"Nah, personally I wouldn't," Leif said. "Too many trees to get good speed. But it's an individual choice."

"And individually I'm choosing to do it," Tucker said. "With good speed, I assure you. And I'd like Kris to come with me. Please fit her for the best bindings you recommend that she feels comfortable with."

"Tucker," Kris said, "that's incredibly generous—you're incredibly generous. But Hidden Run? We could both get hurt."

"I wouldn't let that happen to you."

"And I don't want it to happen to you."

"Just take the skis, and we'll go from there a step at a time."

"She already said she doesn't want to do it," Jillian said.

"That's not exactly what she said." Tucker glowered. "You don't even ski, so you're hardly qualified to have an opinion on the question of Hidden Run."

Heat rose through Jillian's face. Confusion flashed across Kris's eyes.

Leif picked up the shorter set of skis. "Shall I just hold on to this pair while you think about it? I can always send them back for full credit as long as we don't put bindings on."

"No," Tucker said, "we're not returning them. We waited a long time for them to come. The skis are a gift from me to Kris, and they're useless without bindings that fit her."

Kris looked from Leif to Tucker. "I guess it wouldn't hurt to put bindings on them."

Jillian couldn't believe what she heard. Kris couldn't seriously be considering skiing Hidden Run.

"You don't have to rush to a decision," Jillian said. "The skis will be here."

"It's my gift to Kris, and she can decide." Tucker glared at Jillian. "Might as well get them ready and take them home, because they're not going back."

"Leif," Jillian said, "what exactly is involved in avalanche awareness skills? Do you offer a class?"

"Let it go, Jillian." Tucker pulled cash out of his wallet to pay for the bindings. "There must be YouTube videos. It's probably not that much of a risk around here anyway. Hidden Run is not even that far out of town, and a lot of the ski resorts are higher elevation."

Kris was not kidding when she'd said he was doing his homework.

"Let's get down to business on the bindings," Tucker said.

Jillian slipped out of the shop. Kris didn't need her, Tucker didn't want her, and she had homework of her own to finish up. On her way back to the house, she found in her phone the number for a contact where she'd sent an email and called it. Maybe she could speed up the process of a response.

"Yes," said the St. Louis librarian on the other end. "I found the old microfiche for the article you requested and was just about to send you a scan. On the other matter, I think it will be more fruitful to refer your question to a local source I think can be more helpful. But it might take persuading."

CHAPTER NINETEEN

Nolan adjusted the shades on his home office windows. As much as he hated to do it, he had to shut out some of the glare. A sunny day mixed with last week's snow still freshly adorning the mountainside equaled distracting brilliance streaming through the windows and bouncing off his laptop screen and reading glasses. He settled into a comfortable chair with a mediation file to try to find the heart of the story. What had alienated this family to the degree that a disagreement became legal strife? If he could find that answer, he could bring tempers down and the needful emotions forward to find a solution during next week's face-to-face meeting.

His cell phone jangled.

"Hey, Tucker."

"Beautiful day to ski!"

"Sorry, nose to the grindstone for me."

"All day?"

" 'Fraid so."

"I might run out for a quick ski," Tucker said, "but I was hoping you could meet me later at the Heritage Society."

"Oh?"

"Marilyn still needs help, right?"

"I'm sure." Nolan tapped his pen against his yellow legal pad. "If I hustle for a while, I could probably meet you there midafternoon."

"Good. I don't think she thought I was serious when I said I wanted a list of what she needs. She'll believe you if you vouch for me."

"Perhaps."

"Three o'clock?"

"I'll be there."

Nolan wasn't the only one having a nose-to-the-grindstone day. He hardly heard movement from Jillian's office below his all day. Occasionally the back stairwell, just outside her office off the kitchen, carried the clatter of her printer as it spat out a page or her indistinct voice on the phone for a couple of minutes. More often he heard the spatter and hiss of her coffee contraptions. At lunchtime he offered to make her something to eat, but she said she wasn't hungry. Coffee yes, but not food. She was like her mother in that way. He made her a sandwich anyway and set it on her desk.

At a quarter to three, Nolan marked where he would want to pick up in his own work when he returned and popped into Jillian's office. He was glad to see she'd eaten the sandwich and picked up the plate.

"Thanks, Dad. I'll bring you an apple or something tomorrow."

"I'll hold you to it," he said. "I'm leaving now."

"Where?" She glanced at him and then back at her monitor.

"Meeting Tucker at the Heritage Society."

Now she turned around. "Well, that's interesting."

"We did leave things rather a mess the other day, and I doubt Marilyn has much help."

"True."

"He also wants to make a donation."

"Also interesting. Try to bring me back some information."

"I'll do my best."

"And I'm glad you're doing something where I don't have to worry that Tucker is going to break my father."

Nolan laughed.

"Don't laugh, Dad. I don't want him to break Kris either—her body or her heart. He bought her those ridiculous skis."

"Kris has a good head on her shoulders."

"I always thought so. But Tucker does something to her. Now they both have the right skis for Hidden Run."

"Do you want to come along?"

Jillian sank back in her desk chair. "After bungling things yesterday, I'm sure I'm a *persona non grata* at the moment. Biscuits to a bear. Isn't that one of your expressions? Waste of time."

"I can recommend a mediator, if it comes to that."

"Ha ha."

"What about Matthew's friend Jackson?"

"Still trying to track him down. I'll keep at it though."

When Nolan reached the Heritage Society, Tucker was waiting outside.

"Does Marilyn know we're coming?" Nolan asked.

"I left a message on the museum line." Tucker held the door open.

Marilyn stood up from behind a small desk. "It's kind of you both to come back."

"Glad to help," Nolan said.

"I've made some progress since last week," Marilyn said, "but with the usual schedule, it's hard to undertake the project with full steam. I've shifted the children's educational activities to another room in order to leave that space undisturbed."

"Children's activities?" Tucker perked up.

Marilyn nodded. "School groups, mostly. Class field trips. We try to make history as interesting as we can by making local connections, but children these days expect more technology than we can afford."

"Perhaps a donation to technology would help," Tucker said. "I was serious when I asked for a list of what you need."

"He's very serious," Nolan said. "I'm supposed to vouch for him."

"Subtle," Tucker muttered.

"Yes," Marilyn said, "and thank you. I promise I will make a list. How long do you plan to be in town?"

"That's open-ended at the moment," Tucker said. "I have one or two more things I want to do before I leave."

"Long enough for the winter party? I hear Veronica and Luke have something fantastic planned."

"I'm not sure."

"I will make the list a priority." Marilyn started walking toward the community room. "Now about all those documents."

She updated Nolan and Tucker on the organization of the documents and photos and gave them a quick set of instructions on how to create labels, prepare boxes where the documents would be properly stored, and, if they had time or interest, begin reading documents for significant information on the history of the family who donated the boxes that might help further identify the contents. Then she left them to work while she greeted visitors to the museum and prepared for a school visit the following day.

Tucker tossed his jacket and backpack on a nearby chair. Nolan slung his coat over the back of another.

"The good news," Tucker said, "is laying things out to dry seems to have helped."

"A little curly around the edges in a few cases," Nolan said, "but major casualties seem to be minimal."

Marilyn had separated a box of documents and photos that sustained the most damage from the water. They were dry now but stained or blurred, and she would have to determine whether they retained enough value to keep. Everything else was ready to be organized more specifically and stored appropriately in sturdy, lined, acid-free museum boxes Marilyn had supplied.

"Why didn't I see these before?" Tucker—wearing the gloves Marilyn had also supplied—picked up a set of photos.

Nolan moved closer to see. "Old ski resorts."

"Look at those skis! I can't imagine skiing with what they must have weighed."

"Those photos must be at least fifty years old." Nolan examined the one Tucker held now. "We were there last week. That's the blue hill. I recognize the view of the mountains behind it."

"You're right." Tucker moved the photo to reveal another. "I bet these are all area ski locations that have been in business a long time. Or some of them could be gone—lost ski runs. Marilyn could make an exhibit of them."

"That's a good suggestion."

"Or postcards. She could sell them, and the Victorium Emporium could sell them. Leif too. People in his shop would pay good money for a nice collection."

"I like the way you think. A good fund-raiser for the museum."

Tucker moved through the photos. "I don't know who the man is who keeps showing up in the photos, but the places tell a story through the decades."

"Indeed." Nolan was drawn in.

Tucker paused on one photo. "Is this what I think it is?"

Nolan leaned in. "Hidden Run?"

"From 1934." Tucker gave a low whistle. "I've seen a few other old photos in its heyday."

"Look at all the trees. Even then it was a difficult course. I'm sure it doesn't look anything like that now, Tucker. It must be very overgrown."

"Not this again. I thought you were the fun Duffy."

Nolan swallowed his reply.

"Let's just have a nice afternoon, Nolan." Tucker carefully set down the photos. "Not everyone should go down Hidden Run, but I know what I'm doing, and Kris is equally qualified. I've taken her skiing enough times to be sure of that, and I made certain we both have the right skis."

"It's still dangerous, Tucker."

"Drop it. Arguing about Hidden Run is not on the list of things Marilyn gave us to do." Tucker picked up a box. "Where's that instruction sheet about making box labels?"

Nolan found the sheet, handed it to Tucker, and pulled a chair up to a table full of documents. He read documents all day every day at work. Perhaps that would help his brain find information to highlight about the family history preserved in front of him here that might be helpful to Jillian's genealogy work later.

"Maybe these papers will reveal who the skier is in the photos," Nolan said.

"A name to go with the face would be cool," Tucker said. "Obviously he loved skiing. He started as a young man and skied a long time."

"He could be a grandfather or great-grandfather or even great-great-grandfather of someone here in Canyon Mines."

"If that's the case, why would people just give boxes of unsorted papers to the Heritage Society?"

"Maybe they didn't know what was in them," Nolan said. "They could have been sitting in somebody's basement for years. An elderly relative dies, and the family needs to clear out the house to sell it. Nobody really wants to go through everything. The boxes could just as easily have ended up in an estate sale or a dumpster."

"I guess. I got a few things like that from my grandfather."

"Did you go through them?" Nolan asked.

"Not yet. I just transferred them from his basement to mine because we put the house on the market. No one in the family needs it. It's just too big, and the money will help take care of my grandmother."

"Maybe you'd find some interesting things about your genealogy," Nolan said. "Great-grandparents and that sort of thing."

"Bits of me, I guess," Tucker said. "Grandpa Matt was adopted. That rather scrambles the family line when it comes to genetics."

Adoption. Jillian would need this information as soon as possible. This could explain the disconcerting feelings between Matthew and his father.

"I suppose so," Nolan said. "Did he have any information about his birth family?"

"Not that I knew of. And my father left when I was two. I grew up with a last name I know nothing about. I've never even met a single Kintzler in my life, and the Ryder name is an adopted name, so I don't have much of a family tree, do I?"

"The Ryders are still your family. They were your mother's family, and your grandfather's family, no matter how he came to them."

"He loved Great-grandma Alyce. I know that. Judd, not so much."

"Is that what he said?"

"Some things don't have to be said for you to know they're true. He never would even use his middle initial because it stood for Judd's name. He never kept a single picture of Judd around the house. Even my mother gave me a photo of the father who abandoned us. She thought I had a right to it."

"She sounds wise."

"She is. But Grandpa Matt never liked the man who raised him, and I only found out why after he died."

"About the adoption?"

"Among other things."

"Jillian could try to help with the family tree."

Tucker finished his label and raised his eyes at Nolan. "Maybe we should just leave things be with Jillian as well."

"She's very good at her work, Tucker. Yours wouldn't be the first family with an adoption she helped."

"I believe you."

"Why not give her a chance to find some answers about your grandfather? You cared about him a great deal."

"I did." Tucker got up and selected another stack of photos to examine. "All my life. But he spoiled it right at the end."

Nolan lurched a few inches. "What do you mean?"

"Never mind." Tucker spread photos of strangers on the table.

"Tucker?"

"You've been in town a long time." Tucker flipped a photo, looking for a notation. "Maybe you recognize some of these older people."

"Tucker, you can talk to me."

Tucker's hands stilled. He stared down at the old photo. "Why did he have to do that?"

Nolan waited.

"He was in his right mind. He knew what he was doing. He shouldn't have put that burden on me. Not like that."

"How?"

"On his deathbed! We both knew it was our last conversation. I was barely holding it together. I just wanted to tell him I loved him. And he told me to find a letter and that I had to do the right thing when he hadn't, no matter how much he wished he had."

"That sounds rough."

"It was gruesome. The worst thing is he did it on purpose—made it too late for me to ask questions or have his help or understand what any of it means. A letter that made no sense and a sealed packet that I can't bring myself to open." Tucker glanced toward his backpack. "It's like every good thing we shared was undone, and I'm supposed to fix it all on my own. And now that's what I have to remember. It's not fair."

"No, it's not."

"I'm tempted to shove his mystery envelope into one of his boxes in the basement for someone else to deal with. Or maybe I'll take them all straight to the dumpster." Tucker waved a hand over the table. "What's the point of any of this, anyway? Somebody just didn't have the courage to choose the dumpster."

"I'd like to think there's more to it."

"I'm not so sure. Maybe it's better just to put things in boxes and tape down the lids. What we do now is what matters. Just live."

"In the moment."

"That's right."

"Life can change in a moment."

"Exactly."

Nolan's life had changed in a moment. In a way, he'd been handed a sealed envelope and had chosen not to open it all these years. It was easier to stuff the loose ends banging around his family into a metaphoric envelope. He never should have let Paddy give him something he *knew* Paddy had promised to Patrick. He played the little brother card. He was so good at being indulged in those days.

He had to try again with Patrick.

"I've changed my mind about today." Tucker straightened his stack of photos. "I meant to do more. Please give my apologies to Marilyn."

"I will," Nolan said. "I'll stay for a while and see what I can do on my own."

"Do me a favor and try to forget everything I said." Tucker fiddled with his backpack and jacket.

"Do me a favor and believe that you can trust me," Nolan said.

Then Tucker was gone. Nolan pulled out his phone to call Jillian.

"This changes a lot," she said.

"Can you crack adoption records?"

"I'll certainly try. I have a friend who has more experience with adoption histories than I do. It's easier if a family member cooperates. If the records are sealed, which is likely for records of that era, not just anyone can request they be opened."

"Try, Jilly. I have a feeling this is where it all turns."

"It takes time, Dad. It's a bureaucratic process."

"Well, see if your friend knows any shortcuts."

Nolan ended the call and scanned the tables. He and Tucker had managed to bring more disorder than anything else in the few minutes they'd worked. He made some progress on the piles over the next hour or so, choosing to start with the simpler tasks and clear them from the tables and into labeled boxes so that what remained would be more evident. Before he left, he reviewed with Marilyn what he'd done so she could easily undo anything she wasn't happy with. When he stepped outside to the relative privacy of the sidewalk, he scrolled his contact list for Patrick's number and selected it.

"It's about time," was Patrick's greeting.

"Hi, Patrick." Nolan resisted the urge to point out that he'd left Patrick a voice message two days earlier. "Are you still in Denver?"

"I am."

"How are you?"

"Well enough."

"Have you seen Ma and Dad?"

"Quite a bit."

"Good."

"It's a good thing you called, or you were going to have them on your tail soon."

Nolan doubted that. His parents had stayed carefully neutral between their sons for decades, grateful for every small attention Patrick paid them while Nolan saw them often.

"I can come into town tomorrow," Nolan said. "I'd love to buy you lunch."

"I'd love to let you."

They set up a time and place and clicked off. Nolan knew no more than before the call about what was on Patrick's mind, but he had taken the needed step on his end. He knew what he would say if given the chance.

The museum door opened.

"Nolan!" Marilyn called.

He was standing right there beside the door. "What is it?"

She showed him a fist gripping a stack of hundred dollar bills. "I found it on a chair in the community room. It's three thousand dollars with a sticky note that says: 'Not lost. A gift for the children.' "

Tucker.

"What should I do?" Marilyn asked.

"Receive the gift."

CHAPTER TWENTY

Maple Turn, Missouri, 1948

Don't forget the file your father asked you to get from his office." Matthew's mother looked up at him over her knitting needles. "He specifically said he'll want it when he gets home from his meeting at the church."

"I'll go now," Matthew said.

"The keys are there on the table by the door. When you get back, I want to measure your arms. My guess is I need to make these sleeves two inches longer than the last sweater I made you. I can't keep up with the rate you grow."

Matthew nodded. Grandpa Ted would give him any sweater he wanted from his store, but his mother was an expert knitter. His friends couldn't tell the difference between the ones she made and the ones he got from a store or the Sears catalog, and at least her sleeves would cover his lanky wrists.

He scooped up the keys from the table and loped across the property, around the stand of maple trees, and in the front door of Ryder Manufacturing. These were his mother's keys, which she never used. "For an emergency," Judd said when he gave them to her. She hadn't wanted them, insisted that she had no need for them, no intention of going in the building. And she hadn't so far in the more than two years the business had been operating. But on occasions like this one, Matthew used them for brief errands.

Judd was not one to leave a cluttered desk at work or at home. Loose papers were sorted into appropriate folders, and folders were put away in locked drawers or cabinets or given over to the care of his secretary to do the same. Folders he intended to take home with him went to the corner of his desk, which otherwise was clear and polished cherrywood except for his telephone, green banker's lamp, and a brass rack that held three fountain pens. On this day, Judd had made the rare oversight of leaving his office without the single manila file he intended to take home before having his supper and driving to the church for an evening meeting of the deacon board. The length of Matthew's errand to fetch it and return home to his sleeve measurements and homework should not exceed ten minutes. In the building, through the showroom, down the hall to the offices, into his father's office. The key ring gave Matthew access to Judd's tidy domain. He turned on as few lights as necessary to navigate the path. With the file in one hand—he wasn't even interested enough to read the typed label—he pivoted to leave.

His hand was on the doorknob, checking to be sure it would lock behind him, when the phone rang. Twice. And stopped.

It was neither the phone on his father's desk nor the one on his secretary's small desk outside the office. There were other offices in the hallway—the accountant, the sales team, the production manager—but Matthew was certain the ringing had come from within Judd's office and was heavily muffled. He turned around and scanned the possibilities. Judd's office held little interest for him normally. Now he moved into the room again, standing beside the desk as he examined the trio of bookshelves on the wall behind the desk, peering into the openings between books and gaps behind vases and photos and a clock and assorted items of decor people typically didn't notice. Matthew wouldn't have been able to name most of them in a memory game. He wasn't in any of the photos, but his mother's face smiled from several of them.

But there was no second telephone.

It rang again. Twice.

It was in the desk. Matthew threw himself into Judd's black leather chair and tugged at a lower drawer.

Locked.

A lifelong friendship with Jackson had taught Matthew a few skills. He'd never had any luck with that outside back door, once he'd identified it, though he'd tried a couple of times in the middle of the night before deciding it wasn't worth the bother. It wasn't an ordinary lock and would take more practice than he had opportunity for without prying eyes. But he'd learned from Jackson on simpler challenges, and they practiced for fun to see how fast they could get in. A locked desk drawer would be little obstacle.

Matthew reached into his pocket and extracted the tool he needed. Half his face turned up in pleasure at how speedily he heard the click he sought. The drawer opened, and there it was.

A phone.

His heart pounded.

Why would an upstanding businessman, or a deacon, keep a phone locked in his desk? Matthew waited for it to ring again, trying to reason through what he would do if it did. Answer? Impersonate his father? Just pick it up and listen for a voice?

He took the phone into his lap and waited. Five minutes. Eight minutes. His mother, with her clicking knitting needles, would start to wonder about him. But she wouldn't come looking.

It didn't ring again.

Two sets of rings, about three minutes apart, twice each time. It could be a code. Perhaps his father was supposed to have been there to hear it and do something. Call a number? Take some other action without speaking to anyone—just know what to do?

Ten minutes. Eleven minutes. It wasn't going to ring again. It wasn't like Judd to forget something like this. Perhaps it was the caller who was off schedule, calling on the off chance that Judd would be there to take the call anyway.

Matthew lifted the phone from his lap to put it away. Turning it over for a few seconds to move the cord out of the way revealed the keys taped to the bottom.

Matthew knew instantly what they were for. And he took them and moved through the darkness, letting his eyes adjust to the shadowed scene as he went.

The first opened the door from Judd's office into the private hall.

The second opened the door labeled Private Storage.

Matthew stood in the doorframe, his heart pulsating against his rib cage so fast it strangled his breath. He forced an exhale to ground himself and assessed to be sure he would not be locking himself in without a way out. For good measure, he moved a trash can in front of the door to prevent it from closing fully as he fumbled for a light switch. This part of the building had no windows. A light now would not give away his presence.

The trash can had fresh additions, papers towels not yet crusted dry and hair trimmings. The room itself—larger than he'd ever imagined—was furnished with three sets of bunk beds and three cribs, all with folded blankets and bedding. At one end was a bathroom and sink. At the other was an open rack of children's clothing. Some looked used and washed while other garments appeared brand-new. Going closer, Matthew saw the range of styles was narrow, the same clothing in various sizes and a small variety of colors, like a shopper might buy from the Sears catalog. Even the shoes were arranged that way beneath. A bag of laundry—soiled by the smell of it—was drawn tight, as if ready for pickup.

Matthew didn't have to wonder if the walls were soundproof. Of course they were. No light. No sound. A secret room furnished for children.

A four-drawer wooden file cabinet stood sentry beside the door—locked, of course. He could pick it, but he was running out of time. His mother would get anxious.

Matthew backed out of the room, retraced his steps down the hall, taped the keys back to the bottom of the phone. At the last minute, he remembered to grab his father's folder again before returning to the house.

His mother looked up. "I was beginning to wonder."

"Sorry."

"Come here and put your arms out."

"Do you have to measure both? Won't they be the same?"

"Just to be sure." She took a measuring tape out of her knitting basket and stood up.

"Mama," Matthew said.

"Yes?"

Matthew swallowed hard, digging for words.

"What is it, Matthew?" She snapped back the measuring tape, satisfied with the numbers, and sat down again to pick up her needles.

Matthew dropped to the ottoman where he could see her face clearly.

"I found the keys in Pop's office and I used them."

"I don't know what you're talking about."

"There's a phone in a locked drawer, Mama. Normal people don't do that. And a room full of beds and children's clothing."

"What on earth are you talking about?"

Her words spoke denial, but her face paled.

"Mama, what does Pop do in that room?"

For the first time in Matthew's life, his mother reached forward and slapped him.

"What are you suggesting, Matthew?"

"I'm not suggesting anything, Mama." Matthew snatched his mother's flailing hand as it readied for another assault. "I'm asking questions. I'm old enough."

"Not for this, you're not."

"Then there *is* something."

Perspiration poured out of her tidy hairline, and she wrestled her hand from Matthew's grasp. "You should mind your own business. You were told to mind your own business."

"I'm not four years old."

"This is your father's business."

"And yours?"

With both hands, she picked up her knitting basket and pitched it across the room. The contents scattered in every direction. "Not mine! Not mine!"

"Mama, tell me."

She shrieked like the woman in the clinic a few weeks ago who couldn't find anyone to tell her what happened to her baby. A quilt Grandma Bea made by hand was draped across the back of the davenport, and now his mother grabbed it and drew her knees up to her chin to huddle under it.

"Mama." Matthew tried to pull the quilt away from her head, but she resisted, only sobbing louder.

What have I done? He had forgotten to take care of her temperament in the urgency of his own mood.

"I'm sorry, Mama. We don't have to talk about it. Can I make you some tea?"

"I only wanted a baby. Judd wasn't supposed to snatch things."

"Mama?" Matthew was dizzy with questions that would have to wait. His mother was disappearing before his eyes. Form folding. Size shrinking. Countenance contracting.

All those years ago. *"It's the same way you got what you wanted."*

Matthew saw dots. The lines were not quite connecting. He grasped for meaning.

"Mama, please come out of there. Let's have tea. I'll put extra honey in yours."

"I don't want to know. I can't know!"

"Know what, Mama?"

Without coming out from under the quilt, she toppled sideways on the davenport.

The front door opened. Matthew lurched up.

Judd dropped his Bible on the table beside the front door. "What in the world?"

"I'm sorry."

"Matthew, what did you do?" Judd rushed into the room.

"I might ask what did you do?"

"Don't get insolent with me. Explain what happened to your mother." Judd went to the davenport and wrapped his arms around the frightened bundle that was his wife.

"I found the keys, and I used them to find the room," Matthew whispered.

Judd clutched Alyce to him, clawing at the quilt to free her head and glaring at Matthew at the same time.

"You destroyed your mother's life because you broke the one rule I told you never to break only two years ago. You see that, don't you? Was it worth it? Are you satisfied?"

"I had questions." *Have questions.*

"Which you wouldn't have had if you had obeyed."

Matthew bit back his response. He'd always had questions.

Judd had Alyce's face free now and kissed her forehead. "I'm here, Alyce. I'm here. You'll be all right."

"We should call the doctor," Matthew said.

"No." Judd's reply would tolerate no argument. "Here. If you think you can manage a moment of kindness rather than self-indulgence, hold your mother."

Matthew took Judd's place on the davenport. Judd left the room for a moment, returning from his office with a syringe.

"What are you giving her?"

"Your questions have done enough harm for one night."

"You're drugging her? Have you done this before?"

"Matthew."

Of course he had.

"She has spells," Judd said. "We've protected you all your life, but she depends on me to take care of her at times like this. The medicine helps her through."

Judd freed Alyce's arm from the bundling and administered the injection before straightening her out on the davenport and covering her with the quilt.

Neither father nor son spoke as they listened for her breathing to find a pattern that told them she was settled and no longer hearing.

"She said she only wanted a baby and you weren't supposed to snatch things," Matthew said softly but with undiminished determination. "What did she mean?"

Judd held one of Alyce's hands between both of his, taking his time in answering. Finally, he said, "I have assisted with a few adoptions because of connections from my hospital sales days. I make children comfortable during the transition before they are united with the loving families that are waiting for them."

"The room?"

Judd nodded.

Alyce's breathing deepened.

"Judd," Matthew said. "I'm adopted. That's what she meant. That's why she. . .broke."

Judd's dark eyes turned their fury on Matthew. "You are a lucky child. You have a loving home with a mother who adores you. You have never wanted for anything. And all you have in return is ingratitude."

Matthew pointed at the sleeping form. "I love her. But something tells me she is not the only mother broken at the thought of losing me."

"Stop it, Matthew. If you care about your mother at all, you will never speak of this again. Look what it did to her to even come close to the question. She would give her life for you, and I would give mine for her. Your mother takes very seriously what Jesus said about there being no greater love than being willing to give your life for another."

Matthew's throat thickened.

"And stay out of my office, Matthew. Stay out of my desk. I won't warn you again."

Alyce was unconscious. Judd kissed her cheek before lifting her in his arms and carrying her up the stairs with befuddling tenderness.

Matthew left the house.

CHAPTER TWENTY-ONE

Sorry, it will have to wait until tomorrow." Nolan checked his pocket for keys and phone and fastened the latches on his soft-sided briefcase.

"I didn't realize you would be in the office today," the associate said. "I need a senior-level opinion on this document. If you could just give it a quick read."

Nolan shook his head and reached for his gray overcoat hanging behind his office door. "I wasn't planning to be here either. I have an appointment I can't be late for, and I'm not sure if I'll be back. If it can't wait until tomorrow, you can email me the file and I'll try to read it tonight, or you'll have to find someone else to consult."

"It's only two pages," the associate said.

"Sorry." Nolan gestured that the younger man should leave his office and pulled the door closed behind them. He wasn't taking any chances being late and having Patrick think he wasn't coming, and he had cleared the afternoon so he could be ready for whatever turn events might take.

Two red lights and a fender bender snarling traffic in a third intersection meant Nolan arrived at the restaurant four minutes late despite his precautions to be early. He satisfied himself that Patrick was not already waiting in one of the booths and let the hostess seat him where he could watch the entrance.

Another five minutes passed. Surely Patrick's grace period had not expired in those first four minutes.

Nolan sent a text. I'M HERE.

Nothing pinged back, but Patrick was probably driving or negotiating insufficient parking.

Or. . . Or what?

Outside, snow had begun, and for a flash Nolan wished he were home in the mountains, looking at the view out his office window. Even for January, the season was bringing more snowy days than usual, piling inches of powder on the slopes. Tucker could not have known his ski vacation would be this productive. Nolan fiddled with his phone, tempted to call and reassure himself that Tucker wasn't on Hidden Run at that very moment.

One thing at a time. He put his phone away. Patrick was the thing right now.

At twenty minutes past the original meeting time, Nolan ordered a cup of coffee as an earnest payment on tying up a booth during the busy lunch shift. At the thirty-minute mark, he ordered an appetizer, the Irish cheddar and mushroom potato bites Patrick had always liked when they were kids. Nolan didn't know what he liked now. At forty minutes, he was calculating how much money he would leave on the table if Patrick never turned up and he didn't order a full meal. When the potato bites arrived, Nolan faced the reality of how gelatinous and clammy they would be cold and regretted the choice.

But they were still steaming when Patrick slid into the booth three minutes later. Nolan had never seen his brother with a full red beard before. It looked good, showing none of the gray streaking the hair on his head. He tried to think of the last time he'd seen Patrick. Five years ago? Or seven?

"Hey," Patrick said, "you remembered."

The potatoes were the right choice after all.

"For old times' sake." Nolan nudged the plate toward Patrick, who reached for it with gusto. Patrick offered no explanation or apology for being forty-five minutes late, and the reason didn't matter enough to Nolan to risk inflaming the atmosphere with an inquiry. He said simply, "Thanks for coming."

"I thought maybe you were trying to wait me out and hope I was going away," Patrick said.

"I was wrong not to take your calls."

"Did Seamus talk to you?"

"Seamus? No, should he?" Nolan hadn't spoken to his oldest brother since Christmas.

"I thought maybe he wrangled you into calling me. He threatened to drive out to Canyon Mines and choke some sense into you."

"Well, he didn't," Nolan said. "You can thank Jillian for the sense-choking. But I should have come to it on my own."

"You could have taken my calls or answered my texts."

"You're right."

"Didn't you even wonder about the sheer number of times I tried to contact you?"

"I'm sorry. I really have no excuse."

"Okay then. We got that out of the way."

Nolan nodded. He deserved the scolding and much more.

"I had some extended business in Denver, so I've been staying with Seamus and commuting back and forth," Patrick said. "And of course visiting Ma and Big Seamus."

"I'm sure they've been glad to see you."

Patrick fidgeted with his fork. "Big Seamus wants peace between his sons, Nolan. It's time. He's not a young man. We can't do to him what we did to Paddy."

"No." Their father had already had the near–heart attack that awakened them all to his mortality. No one had argued with Big Seamus, as Patrick had with Paddy, but the silence of unresolved tension screamed just as loudly through the decades.

The waitress showed up, having patiently invested nearly an hour into whether she was going to make any money off having this booth tied up when it ought to have flipped by now.

"They have St. Paddy's Irish sandwiches," Nolan said.

"Corned beef brisket, cabbage, sourdough. Pop Paddy's favorites."

"The spicier the mustard, the better. And always dripping on his shirt."

They laughed softly together at the memory.

"More than thirty years, Nolan," Patrick said softly. "Longer than. . ."

"I know. It's been there longer than it wasn't."

"I've grown up. I want you to know that. It's taken awhile. Too long. I might have put a therapist's kid through college. Or bought a boat. But between Seamus and Big Seamus and Grace sticking by me all these years when I didn't deserve her, well, I'm here. And I wasn't going to leave until you agreed to see me even if I had to take off work."

"Patrick." Nolan worked to swallow past the knot in his neck. "Pop Paddy promised it to you. I knew that. I had no business admiring it the way I did. I knew what I was doing that day, the things I said, the way I phrased them. I knew it would make Pop Paddy give me what I wanted even though he'd always promised it would be yours. That's where it all started."

"Yeah, well, we all knew you were a spoiled brat in those days," Patrick said. "But you were also a grown man, and so was I. I shouldn't have argued with Pop Paddy. I should have taken it up with you."

"You probably would have punched my eyeballs out if you had."

"Probably."

"I would have deserved it."

"No. It was a thing. You were still my little brother."

"Not a very good one," Nolan said. "I was very good at thinking about myself though."

"Seamus says you grew up too."

"I like to think so."

The food arrived.

"The family blessing?" Nolan said.

Patrick nodded, and they spoke it together. "May you always find nourishment for your body at the table. May sustenance for your spirit rise and fill you with each dawn. And may life always feed you with the light of joy along the way."

Patrick exhaled, and his green eyes gripped Nolan's. "I've always had that—a true inheritance there was never any reason to squabble over."

Nolan picked up his fork and separated his fries from the edge of his sandwich for no particular reason. "I shouldn't have let you leave."

"I'm not sure you could have stopped me."

"I could have tried," Nolan said. "I was there. No one else was. I should have thought about what it would do to Paddy, to Big Seamus and Ma—to the whole family—if you stayed away. Even to my own child someday, who I didn't know would be born but who has grown up without you in her life. She feels the hole, all because in that moment I just wanted the peace and quiet of having you gone." He'd watched as Patrick threw a couple of hastily packed bags into the silver Grand Am he was so proud to be driving and peeled away. Not one word left Nolan's mouth. No urging to stay. No plea to cool off. No apology. No reasoning about what Patrick's departure—which was not the first one—would do to their mother. Just unadulterated relief.

"I was the one who stayed away except for those few visits when Ma practically begged. My own parents weren't even at my wedding. Pictures of Brinlee are not the same as a flesh-and-blood granddaughter."

"Because you didn't want to see me. Everyone paid a huge price because of my selfish stupidity."

"Ma and Dad say you're really good at your job," Patrick said. "They didn't mention you're really good at beating yourself up."

"That's because I haven't apologized to them for blowing a hole in our family. But I will."

"You had some help, Nolan."

"Maybe I can also have help putting things back together."

"More your area of expertise than mine, but it's why I've been hanging around waiting for you to stop ignoring my phone calls, even if I did feel like punching your eyeballs for how long it was taking."

"Sorry about that." Sorry about so much more. "How much longer does your business keep you in Denver?"

"A few days. I promised Ma another weekend, and I have a meeting on Monday. I've seen you now, so I can fly home after that."

"Come to Canyon Mines before you go," Nolan said. "Have a proper visit with us—with Jillian. She would love it."

Patrick scratched under his beard. "I'm unencumbered tomorrow."

"Perfect." Nolan would push a couple of meetings into next week. When Jillian found out the reason, she would free up her time as well. "Come spend the day."

"Does Jillian know any of this?" Patrick asked.

"Just the bare bones," Nolan said. "But she's plenty old enough now to know that parents are people who make mistakes."

"By the way," Patrick said. "I am sorry for being so late today. No more games."

CHAPTER TWENTY-TWO

Maple Turn, Missouri, 1952

The Oldsmobile churned up dust as Matthew spun into Maple Turn on a Friday afternoon toward the end of his sophomore year of college. He would only make the drive, at least in this direction, a few more times before his parents expected him to work full-time at Ryder Manufacturing for the summer. Last summer had been in the showroom. This intolerable season would be learning to operate the machines that made hardware. He couldn't talk his father out of it. No argument about his lack of aptitude around machinery was persuasive. In fact, Matthew's pleas only persuaded Judd all the more of the importance of Matthew's starting at the bottom to fully understand the business. How could he ever solve engineering and productivity issues if he didn't understand what a machine could do and how? So he would spend his summer wearing a leather apron under the tutelage of a series of machinists who probably wouldn't trust Matthew to tie their shoes much less operate the expensive machinery Judd relied on for the business's profits. Judd had already laid out a schedule for Matthew to cram in learning the basics of cabinetry carpentry during school breaks next year.

Meanwhile Jane would be three hours in the opposite direction in central Illinois. He'd be lucky if he could finagle a couple of long day trips to see her on Sundays. And all he could tell her was that he had to work, not that he had to stay home on Saturdays to look after his mother because his reckless running at the mouth had destroyed her mental health four years ago and she'd never recovered. And likely never would. As if to cement Matthew's ties to Alyce and Maple Turn, Judd had bought the brand-new Oldsmobile for Matthew's seventeenth birthday—but kept the title in his own name. Matthew read between the lines clearly. *You did this. You're not going anywhere. You're going to use this car to pay the price.*

The honking horn from the car riding his rear bumper made Matthew laugh, something he didn't often do anymore in Maple Turn. He eased to the shoulder and let the car pull up beside him.

"Jackson, you old dog."

"Mattie! Did your old man tell you he took me on?" Jackson's dimpled grin was as devilish as ever.

"How did you swing that?"

"I'm not entirely sure his new manager knows the boss considers me a bad influence, even if I am the preacher's kid."

"Well, my mama always thought you were cute."

"I still am."

"What are you going to be doing?"

"Machinist in training."

Matthew threw his head back and laughed again. "You and me both, buddy. Come summer."

"I'll be machining circles around you by the time summer rolls in."

"Maybe they'll make you my tutor."

"That would really give the old man a stroke."

"Maybe I should drop by and talk to the preacher." What would Jackson's father think if he knew the truth about one of his deacons?

"About what? Got some repenting to do?"

Matthew ran his index finger around the top curve of the steering wheel. "Just haven't really talked to him in a long time. I always liked him."

"You see him in church, don't you?"

Matthew did. Twice a month. And every time his conscience stabbed him. The last time he preached on "The truth shall make you free." Matthew knew the truth—at least some of it—and he didn't feel free. He'd wanted to know the truth and destroyed his mother. He knew the truth, and he let his best friend's father—a man of God—think Judd was a fine, upstanding Christian. That all the Ryders were. The longer Matthew kept the silence, the more he was no better than Judd. Would more truth truly free him or bind him more tightly?

But Mama.

"Let's go fishing this summer," Matthew said.

"Maybe pick a few locks."

Matthew smiled and nodded.

"You ever going to let me pick that lock on the back of the factory?" Jackson winked.

"Probably not. I rarely even think of it." If only Jackson knew the locks he'd gotten past four years ago. At least then he'd appreciate why Matthew was even still in Maple Turn.

"Then there's no harm in trying, is there?" Jackson said.

"Only if you want to keep your new job."

"There is that."

"I have to go, Jackson. Mama will be waiting."

"She looks good these days, Mattie. She really does."

"Good to hear."

Matthew turned into the long driveway and waved out the driver's window. His mother returned the gesture from the porch, where she was waiting as he was sure she would be. She always wanted him to telephone when he was leaving his dorm in St. Louis, and she knew how long it took to make the drive home. During the winter months, he might be able to persuade her to wait for him inside the house, but she'd be watching nevertheless and checking her watch.

The cost of stumbling on his own adoption, and whatever Judd meant by helping with adoptions, was his mother's mental breakdown. She'd never been herself after that night. He was bound to her afresh in her raw need. He missed so many classes after that to look after her that it was a wonder he graduated high school at all. Getting into a decent college in St. Louis under those circumstances probably had more to do with his father's influence than Matthew's achievement. Judd paid more attention to him, but everything had a price.

First came the car when he was seventeen—so he could drive his mother around and so he could easily travel back and forth from college on weekends.

Then college of course. Judd insisted he attend and study business, because Alyce had always wanted it. How could Matthew decline? One look at his mother made him agree to anything. She was too frail to risk seeing what would happen if he did not do as she wished.

And Judd knew it.

So Matthew finished high school, enrolled in the college Judd selected, and came home on the weekends twice a month, bringing his studies with him, even though there would be a slate of obligations awaiting him at the big house.

He got out of the car, removed his briefcase and overnight bag, and climbed the porch steps. His mother offered her cheek, and he kissed it.

"So lovely to have you home for a bit."

She said this every time, as if he came home once a semester rather than every other weekend.

"Always good to come home." Matthew stuck to the script.

"Have you met a nice girl yet?" This line in the script put hope in her eyes.

"Not yet, Mama." Matthew couldn't let her hopes rise. She would love Jane. But he wasn't sure he could let his own hopes rise, so it was unfair to let his mother start planning a wedding in her mind. Maybe the best thing was to stay away from Jane all summer and let the spark fizzle out. They weren't much of anything yet. A few dates. Running with the same crowd. She was only a freshman, barely finished being a schoolgirl, while he was a businessman in training with a jaded view of life he wouldn't wish on anyone.

"Well, soon, maybe," Alyce said. "You'll be a catch when the right girl comes along."

They went inside, where Gertrude's dinner preparations filled the house with tantalizing aromas. Somehow they'd gotten through Matthew's high school years by eating charred dinners or Judd or Matthew going out for food and bringing it home. Matthew had taken on keeping the house in order, but he was never much good at cooking. Alyce always intended to make a meal or straighten a room, as she always had even after they moved into the big house, but more and more Matthew and Judd would find her staring vacantly. Even her garden was half the masterpiece it once had been, and she'd never knitted another stitch after that night she'd measured Matthew's arms before throwing her basket across the room.

Judd kept her busy. That was the best he knew to do, and Matthew had no better ideas—at least none Judd would accept. Once Matthew's departure for college was imminent, Judd persuaded her that a woman of her position in the community ought to have hired help, and Gertrude joined the household. She understood from the start that her duties involved being a companion to Alyce as much as housekeeper and cook. The ladies' auxiliary at church had regular activities, and Judd made sure Alyce got there. The Maple Turn Women's League for Town Improvement honored her presence even though she no longer had creative suggestions. Garden society events, civic committee meetings, lunches—she did fairly well at these occasions if she had someone at her side to keep her attention focused so she didn't fall into staring.

"I want to cut some lavender," Alyce said. "We should have fresh flowers in the house."

"Isn't it early for lavender, Mama?"

"There must be something in the garden. I'll go look."

Matthew watched her move through the house and caught Gertrude's eye.

"I'll get your garden scissors, Mrs. Ryder," Gertrude said, trailing after her.

Judd came out of his study.

"Matthew."

"Judd."

At least his mother spoke to him in sentences.

"She needs more than this," Matthew said.

"She's doing well," Judd said. "She gets out nearly as much as she used to, and most people don't notice anything off."

"How can you say that? They don't even know what happened, but after four years, they've just gotten used to this is how Alyce is. But maybe she could get well again with the right help. Doesn't she deserve that chance?"

"You know why we can't do that, Matthew. We can't have her talking to people, answering probing questions. We can't risk it."

"You mean *you* can't risk it."

"You did this, Matthew. You made a choice that brought on this change."

"As if your choices have nothing to do with it."

"Don't get smart with me."

"What about the pastor? Wouldn't he understand? Couldn't he be some help somehow?"

"Matthew, we're not having this discussion."

Matthew clamped his mouth shut. This was how it always went. They orbited around each other in the same house, caring only about Alyce. But they didn't talk about the room. Ever.

On Saturday Matthew took his mother to lunch in town. She loved it when they did this. He hated it. She always chose a prominent restaurant and a table smack in the path of everyone coming and going. Her friends would see them and stop by the table to say hello and grill him about how college was going. Alyce's face would flush with the pleasure of showing him off and hearing how tall and handsome he was and how much he favored Judd—even though that was impossible. Inevitably someone would make a comment about how before he knew it, he would be going into the family business or that soon enough the whole business would be in his hands when Judd retired.

Today was no different. Matthew had learned long ago to order food that was palatable at room temperature when he was out with his mother. His plate would always grow cold before he got to eat his lunch. Mrs. Babcock from church. Miss Bizwell from the library. Mrs. Caldwell and Mrs. Booker from the garden society. They all paraded past the table, and each time Matthew put down his fork and stood politely to shake hands and answer questions.

Going to college wasn't the worst thing in the world, but going into Judd's business? Knowing that room was there? Wondering what was happening in it? Not being allowed to ask questions because of what it might do to his mother and having Judd hold that over his head? For how long?

He never got an explanation four years ago about the circumstances of his own adoption, but he'd lain awake enough nights to be persuaded that Alyce was tormented by the knowledge that he'd been stolen.

And if he did sleep, he faced his own torments—visions of Mrs. Liston demanding to know what happened to the baby she'd heard cry and insisting Judd had been outside the delivery room.

Wondering if another woman had heard him cry.

Alyce must have known where Matthew came from. Maybe not at first. Maybe she found out after she'd fully and wholly become his mother in her heart, when it was too late to think of giving him up. Giving him *back*. She might even be implicated in some way. He was a grown man now, but what would happen to her frail state if legal action descended on her because Matthew exposed Judd?

What a weak man he was that he could not see right from wrong and choose the moral path. Instead, he went to college to get a degree in business and met a nice girl named Jane who captured his heart. He pretended they could have a future when he would be dragging her into a big, ugly secret.

Jane didn't deserve that.

He didn't deserve Jane.

But he loved her already.

He would have to break her heart—and his—for her own good.

CHAPTER TWENTY-THREE

Sweats and a bathrobe might not be a professional wardrobe in most businesses, but Jillian was in charge of her own articles of incorporation, and on mornings when she woke early and reconciled to the truth that sleep was over for the next sixteen hours or more, it wasn't unusual for her to start her day in garb aimed more at warmth than fashion. Chic was never foremost in her mind, but she'd eventually progress to jeans and a long-sleeve tee and a more publicly presentable second layer of insulation against January weather than the tattered favorite fleece robe.

She inspected the taupe coffee cup, already filled and emptied twice on an empty stomach. The milk and sugar in her morning concoctions should count for something toward food groups—practically the same as a bowl of cereal.

Her dad's steps descending the back steps made her mutter. "Shoot."

"Did you say something?" Nolan stuck his head in.

"Nothing," Jillian said.

"Pretty sure it was something."

"Nothing important." She'd missed her chance for a third cup of coffee without his lifting one eyebrow—how did he do that?—to question how many she'd already had.

"I'm making breakfast," Nolan said. "Why don't you get dressed?"

"Am I twelve and late for school? People all across America eat breakfast in their bathrobes."

He cocked his head. "But not today. Something tidy. Green, perhaps, to go with your eyes?"

"Dad!" Jillian wasn't budging out of her chair. "What are you talking about?"

"Just breakfast." He clapped his hands twice. "Hop to. By the way, what do we have for breakfast options?"

"Are you sure you don't want me to fix breakfast?"

"I wish I'd had time to go to the store. But I shoveled our walks and the neighbors' when I got home yesterday. No time now."

"The bigger problem is you're a terrible grocery shopper, but why the urgency?"

"We have eggs?"

"Yes, I just bought two dozen."

"Cheese?"

"Cheddar and swiss."

"Sausage?"

"Italian."

"The usual assorted vegetables?"

"Dad."

"Go on, scoot," Nolan said. "You get dressed. I'll throw together a breakfast casserole and squeeze some fresh oranges."

Jillian laughed. "When have you ever squeezed fresh oranges?"

"There's always a first time. Do we have oranges?"

"Sadly, no." She would like to have seen him squeeze them.

"I will make do." Nolan tugged at the back of Jillian's chair. "Go on."

"Dad! What is this about?"

"Can't a father make breakfast for his daughter?"

"Well, sure, but you're being especially demanding about it today."

"Do as I say, Jillian. You'll be glad you did." Nolan rolled her chair toward the door, nearly dumping her out of it.

"I see I have no choice."

"Now you're getting the hang of things."

Upstairs, Jillian jumped in the shower. If Nolan had time to bake a casserole, she had time to clean up from start to finish. She found the green sweater he'd given her for Christmas a couple of weeks ago, a perfect match for both their eyes, and scrounged up a clip to tame her hair on top of her head and let the dark waves hang loose around the sides of her face. The aroma filling the house suggested Nolan had found more than enough to work with and had a promising meal in the oven. Now he was banging around making cleaning-up sounds.

The doorbell rang, and Nolan called up, "Can you get that?"

"Sure." Jillian scrunched her eyebrows. It was still early for someone to drop by.

Except Nolan had been acting strangely all morning. Crossing the wide living room, she saw he'd even managed to set the dining room table.

Three places.

"Who are you expecting?" she called toward the kitchen.

"Just get the door, please."

In thick wool socks, Jillian finished the path to the door on the side of the house that served as the main entrance, turned the bolts, and opened the door.

"Uncle Patrick!"

"In the flesh." Patrick stepped over the threshold.

Jillian glanced toward the kitchen. "You and Dad?"

"He finally called me back." Patrick opened his arms for an embrace.

Jillian hugged her uncle. She'd been in college the last time she saw him, and before that—she'd have to think. Their visits had been so few. She'd tracked the progress of Patrick, Grace, and their daughter more through the photos that turned up at Nana and Big Seamus's house than personal contact.

"This is amazing," she said.

"He didn't tell you I was coming?"

"No. The goofball. Come on in."

Nolan leaned against the banister, watching the reunion and grinning.

"How was the drive?"

"Snowy, more this morning on top of last night's," Patrick said. "Was it this wintry when I lived here?"

"We've had quite a January," Nolan said.

"The house looks awesome." Patrick's eyes swept the downstairs layout before lifting to the crown molding.

"Full tour after breakfast," Nolan promised. "Who's hungry?"

In the dining room, the sausage and egg casserole sat in the center of the table, with a bowl of fried potatoes on one side and cut-up fruit on the other.

"What a feast," Patrick said.

"Jillian can whip up any coffee invention your mind can imagine."

"Yes!" Jillian stood at the back of her chair. "Espresso. Cappuccino. Latte. Whatever you like."

"Just black, please," Patrick said.

The brothers howled.

Jillian glared at Nolan. "That better be the last family secret you keep from me."

They sat down, recited the family blessing, filled their plates, and dug into catching up on news of Patrick's family.

A first.

Never before had Jillian seen her father and Patrick making an effort to be at ease with each other, rather than sitting at opposite ends of a holiday family table or rotating out of the room so they didn't have to spend too much time avoiding eye contact in the same space while three generations of Duffys gathered and cousins scampered through the rooms and aunts compared notes on jobs and family life.

Perhaps the next "first" would be a visit that included Grace and Brinlee coming for a visit to Canyon Mines.

"I hear a phone," Patrick said, tilting his head.

"Must be mine." Jillian scooted her chair back. "I left it in my office."

The phone rang incessantly. Whoever was calling wasn't content simply to leave a message but rather dialed again and again. By the time Jillian answered, Nia's tone was curt.

"What took you so long?"

"Excuse me?" Jillian said.

"Sorry," Nia muttered. "Bit of a crisis over here."

"What's wrong?"

"We have a new unplanned guest."

"Don't you have space?" Usually Nia just sent overflow inquiries to one of the chain motels at the edge of town.

"You're going to have to break the news to Kris. Right away."

Jillian dropped into her office chair. "What are you talking about?"

"I think you'd better just come over here, Jillian. Just for a minute. Then you have to find Kris immediately."

"We have a guest of our own this morning, Nia."

"I bet it's not the fiancée of the man your best friend is falling hard for."

"What?"

"Just get over here. Please." Nia clicked off.

Jillian returned to the dining room.

"Everything all right?" Nolan asked. "Client?"

Jillian shook her head. "Nia. We need to go over to the Inn."

"Patrick is here, Jillian. He came to spend the day with us."

"The timing's terrible. I'm sorry. Did you know Tucker is engaged?"

Her father's eyes flickered with alarm.

"To a woman who just turned up at the Inn," Jillian said, "while Tucker is somewhere with Kris."

"Sounds like trouble," Patrick said.

"Someone we care about could get hurt." Nolan turned to Patrick. "The Inn at Hidden Run. It's just down the street."

"I could use another cup of coffee," Patrick said, "while I go over notes for my next presentation."

"There's plenty of casserole left too." Nolan stood. "Back as soon as I can."

"Sorry, Dad," Jillian said as they hustled down the street to the Inn, crunching over fresh snow. "Tucker never even hinted to you?"

"Not once."

Nia was in the parlor with a tray of scones. She'd probably made them that morning to serve her own guests and now offered a choice of strawberry and lemon cranberry to a tall, dark woman in designer jeans and a leather jacket.

"Come on in," Nia said. "This is Laurie Beth. She came to surprise Tucker."

Laurie Beth rose to shake hands with Jillian and Nolan. "Nia is being polite. It's true Tucker will be surprised, but I was also starting to worry when he didn't come home after a couple of days and I didn't even know where he was."

"The skiing has been exceptionally good," Jillian said. "At least that's what I hear. I don't ski."

"But I do," Nolan said, "and it's true. A great season. Do you ski?"

Laurie Beth shrugged. "Some. I'm not in Tucker's league though. When he said he wanted to ski for a few days, I didn't think much of it."

"He's done it before?" Jillian said.

"Sure. Just two or three days at a time. I know it's more fun if he can ski the hills he likes without worrying about me. But this time he didn't even tell me where he was going, and I haven't heard from him at all."

"How did you find him?"

"His assistant finally cracked. She's the only one Tucker has contacted a couple of times." Laurie Beth's blue eyes folded under her dark bangs in puzzlement. "It was all very strange though. I think the only reason she told me where Tucker was is because someone has been fishing around about our friend Jackson. Her sister-in-law works at the newspaper, and they had a call from a library. She said the original call came from Canyon Mines. Tucker's assistant found that very curious."

Jillian startled. "That was me."

"What do you want with Jackson?"

"It's a long story. But I never actually spoke to him."

"He doesn't really talk to people anymore. The death of Tucker's grandfather hit him hard, and he's not in the greatest health himself."

"Does Tucker normally talk to Jackson?" Jillian asked.

"It's been weird lately," Laurie Beth said. "When I suggest checking on how Jackson's doing, Tucker seems to want to avoid him. I don't get it."

If nothing else came from hunting for Jackson, it brought someone to town who knew Tucker better than anyone—though clearly Tucker hadn't been telling Laurie Beth everything, or she wouldn't be here now. Jillian swallowed and moistened her lips. If only Kris weren't the one who was going to be stomped on as a result.

"Well, you're here now," Nolan said. "I'm sure you're eager to see Tucker."

Laurie Beth smiled at her hostess. "Nia tells me you might have some ideas where Tucker might be. Can you help me find him?"

"Tucker has been friendly with some people around town," Nolan said. "Nice man."

Laurie Beth smiled. "I think so." She raised her left hand to tuck her hair behind her ear, and the ring on her third finger flashed.

"I'll tell you what," Jillian said, "why don't you enjoy your scones, and I'll ask around. Maybe someone knows what his plans were today."

"That makes sense." Nolan sat down. "A better plan than driving all over the county looking for him."

Nia walked Jillian out. Nolan already had Laurie Beth chatting about her trip out from Missouri and picking up a second scone.

"Did Tucker tell you anything about where he was going when he left this morning?" Jillian whispered.

"Only that he was planning to try to persuade Kris to take the morning off. Skiing, I presume, after last night's snow."

"She probably would do it," Jillian said.

If Kris had any inkling of Laurie Beth's existence, she never would've given Tucker the time of day. Now what?

"She didn't answer her phone. They sometimes come back here together," Nia said. "You have to stop that from happening."

"Obviously." Jillian exhaled. "Even my dad can't keep Laurie Beth chatting forever."

The first step was to verify that Kris was not at the shop. She could have simply not opened that morning, or she might have called Lindy in for a few hours. Lindy might know her plans for returning. Even if Jillian didn't find Kris now, there could be time to head her off before she and Tucker turned up at the Inn.

Waking up early and working in her bathrobe seemed like half a day ago. Uncle Patrick in the dining room seemed like a dream. It was barely time for most of the shops on Main Street to be opening for the day. Jillian bustled up the two blocks of Double Jack, back to Main Street, and over to Ore the Mountain. The inside lights were on, and the door was unlocked.

Jillian tugged the door open. "Kris?"

She crossed the empty shop, moving toward the counter and called again. "Kris?"

This time the door from the kitchen swung open. "I'm here."

Kris looked a wreck. Blanched. Tear-streaked. Sniffly.

"What happened?"

"Not a great morning." Kris shuffled into the table area.

"Tucker?"

"We had our first fight. I don't know what got into me, Jillian. What universe have I been living in?"

"Where's Tucker now?"

"I don't know. And I don't know if I'm supposed to care."

CHAPTER TWENTY-FOUR

Jillian put both hands up to her cheeks. "There's no right or wrong about what you're supposed to feel. Do you want to tell me what happened?"

Kris gestured toward a table before grabbing a stack of paper napkins. Jillian wished she had something gentler to offer her friend's nose.

"Hidden Run. That's what happened." Kris wiped her nose and sat in a straight-backed chair. "I failed at the mission."

"You don't mean he wanted to take you to ski Hidden Run today."

Kris shrugged. "I think that's what he was getting at asking. He came by early when he knew I would be mixing ice cream. Once he started dropping hints, I tried to head it off by once again saying how dangerous it is up there even for the best skiers."

"And you argued about that?"

"He was insulted that I doubted his ability." Kris blew out breath. "Then he was insulted on my behalf that I doubted my own ability. Then he accused me of not believing that he'd done his homework, that he knew exactly what he was doing, and whatever the risks were, they were worth it."

"What does that mean?"

"The reward of the thrill. You only live once, and you can't be afraid to live life to the fullest. You have to make the most of the opportunity in front of you. It was one cliché after another. The worst was when he said he was disappointed I was satisfied to live a small life in a small place when I could be so much bigger."

"Oh Kris." That was just mean. What got into Tucker? "Do you think he went anyway?"

"Who knows? If not today, he'll do it soon. I couldn't talk him out of it, but I wouldn't go with him either. But he might have just gone back to the Inn to sulk."

Jillian drew a long breath. "Kris, I have to tell you something."

Kris leaned forward. "What is it?"

"Tucker is not at the Inn. But his fiancée is."

"Tucker is engaged?" Kris threw a wadded napkin on the table. "Well. What do you know?"

"I'm sorry, Krissy."

"It's not your fault, Jills. You're not the one who withheld a rather significant fact. Not that I ever asked that specific question."

"It doesn't seem like he gave you any reason to think you should."

Kris shook her head, her face reddening.

"Are you all right?" Jillian asked. "Should I get you some water or something?"

"It's not my finest moment, but I'll be all right." Kris blew her nose into a fresh napkin. "I've been thinking ever since we quarreled, and I realize I was just someone Tucker was having fun being reckless with, and he almost caused me to be reckless. The night skiing. Closing the shop when I don't usually do that. Even looking down my nose at you because you don't ski—I'm sorry about that."

"It's all right." It wasn't when it happened, but it was now.

"All those gifts. Giving into the moment. Not asking enough questions—or the right questions. What was I thinking?"

"None of that justifies being madcap with your feelings by not telling you about Laurie Beth."

Kris peered at Jillian. "You know her name?"

Jillian swallowed hard. "I met her at the Inn. Nia says you sometimes drop in with Tucker."

"And she didn't want me to just show up without a clue."

"No."

"Well, you can all rest easy on that matter." Kris took another napkin from her stack and rubbed the table with it. "What's she like?"

"Don't do this to yourself, Kris."

Kris raised both hands, palms out. "You're right."

"My dad's with Laurie Beth now," Jillian said. "Tucker was shutting her out too. She didn't even know he was here. She tracked him down by being stubborn with his assistant, who seems to be the only person he's been in contact with."

"I'm not used to arguing with people, Jills."

"I know." Banter was one thing. A true quarrel was another. "Tucker has a life in Missouri and someone who cares for him enough to come looking for him. So why is he being so rash with his own life and people who care about him?"

"Laurie Beth showing up won't change any of that," Kris said. "I may not know Tucker as well as I thought I did, but I do know that."

"Maybe she will. Maybe there's a side of him you don't know, and a side of him she doesn't know."

"I don't follow."

"She doesn't ski, at least not at the level he does, like you do. They seem to have an understanding that he doesn't have to go through the motions of taking her along on his trips because she would only drag him down. But you get the skiing."

"And she gets everything else? Is that what you think?"

"I don't know what she gets," Jillian said. "I just met her for a few minutes. I shook her hand. I didn't even sit down. But she's here now and could fill in some gaps. The two of you know Tucker better than anyone else."

"You want me to meet the woman Tucker is engaged to?"

"Are you ready to let him break his neck on Hidden Run?"

They locked eyes.

The jangle of Jillian's phone startled them both.

"It's a Missouri area code," Jillian said.

"St. Louis?"

"Or close by." Jillian accepted the call and put it on speaker for Kris to hear as well. "This is Jillian."

"This is Jackson." The old man's voice wobbled. "I understand you're looking for me."

"Yes, that's right. Thank you for calling."

"The message said it had something to do with Tucker. That's the magic word."

"Is it?"

"Anything for Mattie's grandson."

"I'm glad to hear that." Jillian's eyes still gripped Kris's. "I only met Tucker recently, but everyone here likes him."

"Mattie was always so proud of him."

"I understand you and Matthew were lifelong friends."

"To the very end—though he was one lock I could never quite pick."

"How so?"

"What does it matter now? A couple of old men with a long-ago quarrel about a locked door and a brick wall."

"It might matter to Tucker."

"Then he should ask me about it, I suppose."

Jillian's stomach sank.

"This will sound odd," Jillian said, "but do you mind my asking what Matthew's parents were like?"

Jackson scoffed. "Judd was a cold fish to anyone but Alyce. Nowadays someone like her would have a lifetime of therapy, but Judd wouldn't allow that kind of help. When we were young, I had the idea Mattie would leave Maple Turn, but after his mother got that way, well, he was the only child, you see."

"I do see. I'm an only child. Did something happen to make her. . . get that way?"

"Must have. It's the only thing that would have kept Mattie in town. But Mattie kept that locked away too. Bricked it off just like he did that back wall. Wouldn't tell me about either one."

"I see."

"I don't know what Tucker is doing out in Colorado. Tell him to come see me when he gets home."

"Yes, sir, I will."

Jackson hung up.

CHAPTER TWENTY-FIVE

Maple Turn, Missouri, 1957

I t's still early." Jane's eyebrows lifted and her lips twisted.

Matthew raised an arm to move her silky brown hair off her shoulder. At the library all day she wore it tied back with a ribbon, but she let it hang loose for him in the evenings. The porch light outside her small apartment behind a garage cast a beatific yellow glow across her face. He said nothing.

"I know," Jane said. "Your mother."

"I'm sorry." He spent too much time apologizing to Jane.

"It's all right. I understand. Really I do."

"If I can come back, I will."

She shook her head. "Your father is out tonight, remember. She might be anxious if you're not around."

"I could call Gertrude to come back."

"She was there all day. It's your turn. She needs her family."

Matthew sighed. "You're too perfect."

"No, I'm not. I just remember what it was like when my mom was sick."

That was a lonely stretch for both of them. Jane left college for three semesters when her mother fell ill and ultimately lost her life. By the time her father had his wits again, Jane had to work so hard to make up lost ground that Matthew hardly saw her for another year after that. Her graduation was delayed, and she had to go home for a period of time before she could make her own plans. But finally, after so much lost time, she was here, in Maple Turn with a job and an apartment. They saw each other every day.

And every day Matthew thanked God.

And every day guilt shot through him for letting her come, for continuing to let her believe they could be planning a future, that any day now he might put a ring on her finger.

"Keep trusting, Matthew," Jane said. "I would have been lost without my faith when my life was in such upheaval and I didn't know what the future held. Don't lose yours."

He leaned in and kissed the lips he did not deserve. Her faith would have to be enough for both of them.

"Go." Jane put all ten fingertips on Matthew's chest and pushed him away. "I'll try to get a long lunch break tomorrow and come by Ryder."

"What do you see in this place?" he said.

"It's an adorable town. I fell in love with it the first time you brought me here to meet your parents."

"That was a mistake." In a moment of weakness, he'd admitted to his mother he'd finally met a nice girl. There was no backing out after that. Maybe he'd done it so he couldn't back out. "Are you sure you love me, or is it just Maple Turn?"

"You, silly. But it doesn't hurt that you come from just the sort of town I've always imagined raising a family in. I can't believe they needed a second librarian when I needed a job!"

He kissed her forehead. "Okay. I'm going."

Grinning, she leaned against the wall and watched him walk backward until he bumped into his Oldsmobile.

Matthew waved and pulled away from the curb. Jane thought he had good prospects and said she didn't much care where he worked, but she was increasingly attached to Maple Turn. It was just as well. Realistically, his options were limited. He couldn't leave his mother, not when he was the reason she was the way she was.

And Alyce loved Jane. Everybody loved Jane. Matthew certainly did.

He banged the steering wheel. It wasn't fair. He wanted a life with Jane. She deserved that ring on her finger. But didn't she also deserve the truth?

Driving out to the big house took only a few minutes. As he expected, Gertrude was gone, and Alyce was in the kitchen fixing tea, signaling the beginning of her protracted bedtime routine. For years Judd, Gertrude, and Matthew—who was twenty-five now—surrounded Alyce with structure and routines. It was part of keeping her busy and her mind occupied so she didn't slip into vacancy. There was always the next thing to do, even if it was just time to make a cup of tea and sweeten it with precisely two teaspoons of clover honey.

"Hi, Mama."

"Mattie, there's my good boy."

His little-boy nickname had crept back into Alyce's vocabulary recently. Judd glanced at Matthew the first few times she used it but made no vocal objection.

"You're having your tea," he said. "I'll fix your snack."

"You're so sweet." Alyce carried her tea to the kitchen table, sat in her chair, and reached for the honey.

Matthew took a small plate from the cabinet, laid out eight square crackers, layered tabs of yellow cheese on four of them and spread cream cheese on the others. It was the same every evening. Tea and honey, cheese and crackers.

"Now where is my *Ladies' Home Journal?*" Alyce glanced around the kitchen and started to scoot her chair back.

"I'll get it." Matthew found the latest issue on top of the stack at the end of the counter where Gertrude always made sure to leave it, and laid it on the table. He sat in the spot where he'd been eating breakfast since he was fourteen except when he was away at school.

"And how is Jane?"

Matthew smiled. "Jane is well. Thank you for asking."

"You know, I was beginning to think you were too picky," Alyce said. "All the times I asked if you had met a nice girl and all the times you said no. Then you brought Jane home, and I realized you were just holding out for the very best."

"She really is the very best, isn't she?"

"I've become quite fond of her. I think your grandparents have as well."

"I'm glad to hear that, Mama."

"You should marry her."

"You think so?"

"She's no fool, Mattie. Don't dawdle so long that you cause her to have doubts."

Matthew let the advice settle in. His mother spoke truth. The rest of the Ryder family truth is what concerned him. He would love to rush back over to Jane's apartment, propose, take her in his arms, smother her with kisses, plan a wedding for as soon as possible, and never let her go. But she was entitled to know what life she was signing up for—and why.

Telling her would give her every reason to walk away.

Not telling her would force her to be an unwitting player in a lie.

Someday Matthew wanted to know what lie Judd told Alyce in order to give her what she wanted. When did she learn the truth, whatever it was? Alyce had been fragile ever since the night he asked her about the room. He'd never been back in it or discussed it again. He wouldn't talk to her. The risk that she'd break even more dramatically was one he wasn't willing to take. That didn't mean it wasn't a festering wound weeping for disinfectant and debridement or that he didn't pick at it from time to time.

"Where's Pop tonight?"

"A late meeting over in St. Charles. He said not to wait up."

Matthew tried to think if Ryder Manufacturing had current business in St. Charles that required an evening meeting but shook away the query fairly quickly. He didn't pretend to track Judd's schedule, and it was probably better that way. He had his own portfolio of responsibilities now, overseeing machinery and productivity to make sure there was no shortage of supplies to meet the demand the sales team created. As long as he had time this evening, that's all he wanted to know.

Tonight. For Jane.

Matthew pushed his chair back. "I think I'll go for a walk. You'll be all right?"

"I have my tea, my snack, and my magazine."

From here the routine was about forty minutes of grazing the cheese and crackers and flipping pages. He had time.

Outside Matthew strode around the trees to Ryder Manufacturing. As a grown man and a junior executive, he had easy access to the building with his own set of keys to every part of the building except Judd's office, but he could easily pick that lock and the desk with one hand. He'd done it before.

Judd had moved the keys from the bottom of the phone. Matthew had looked twice before in the last few years. As he'd gotten older, and spent more time around the business, he was better at getting into Judd's head. Judd could carry keys on his person, chained to his vest or trouser pocket, but he would never take the chance that he might be caught in an automobile accident or other medical emergency that could result in the loss of *these* keys. No. They were in the office, locked somewhere.

This time Matthew didn't waste time picking the lock to the desk. Instead, he stood before the trio of built-in bookcases behind the desk constructed from matching cherrywood. He scanned the gaps between sets of books and business binders, looked behind vases and photos and heavy brass bookends, examined suspicious bindings of books that didn't sit quite square on the shelves, sliding doors, and drawers. Picking a couple of locks on the sliding doors and drawers was so simple that Matthew chuckled, but nothing of value was behind them. A paperweight drew his eye. It held no papers in place on the shelf where it sat, and it wasn't particularly attractive for decorative purposes, though it was heavy.

Matthew turned it upside down and flipped it from front to back.

And there it was. A felt backing not quite sealed at the edges. He picked at it and found a tiny lock that required a specially made key.

Or a moderately good lock pick. He was better than moderately good.

Inside a miniature cavity were three keys, more than he'd hoped for. He was prepared to jimmy everything if necessary, including the file cabinet, but keys were so much cleaner.

The room was much as he remembered from almost ten years earlier with some improvements. The overhead lights had been updated, and the bathroom now had two sinks rather than one. Both looked like they'd been used recently for haircuts and not quite wiped clean. Dark strands mixed with red and blond in the corners. Some of the bunks had rumpled bedding, as if someone was supposed to come in and tidy up. A diaper pail smelled like it needed emptying.

A key got him into the wooden file cabinet he hadn't tried to pick the last time, and a rapid rifling ran a list of names. Baker. Delancy. Edgar. Ferris. Garrett. Harrell. Jerrett. Karroll. Mulligan. Newman. Orman. Polis. Dozens of others. Matthew pulled out several at random and looked at dates and notes before shoving them back in and pulling out more. Aimless methods fell into a pattern, and Matthew became progressively unpersuaded that Judd's involvement was simply an occasional way station.

Matthew seethed.

Along with the names were numbers. Some could easily be dates without the benefit of separation between days, months, and years, but the others? More likely amounts. Dollars. Matthew had seen enough of the Ryder company books to recognize that at least some of the dates and amounts, when taken together, corresponded to significant infusions of Judd's capital into the company during expansion schemes.

He yanked open another drawer, and then another. In the bottom drawer, there they were, nestled beneath a set of folded cloths and children's pillows. Actual ledgers. Doctored books. On top of whatever was happening to children in this room, Judd was laundering money. The odds that the two activities were separate were zero, in Matthew's eyes.

He slammed the drawers closed, shut off the lights, locked all the doors behind him, kept the keys and ledgers, and went home.

Alyce looked up from the sink, where she was rinsing her dishes.

"Heading up to bed?" Matthew said.

"I think so," she said. "How about you?"

"Just popped back to check on you." He kissed her cheek. "I realized I have some work to do over at the office. Will you be all right here?"

She waved him off. "Certainly. Go on."

"I'm going to leave Pop a note on his desk in case he needs me."

"That's my good Mattie. You're so thoughtful."

Matthew walked his mother to the bottom of the stairs and watched her reach the top before going to his father's study and composing a stern note and leaving it square in the middle of the cleared desktop. Judd always stopped in his office when he came in the house. There could be no question of his finding it.

Then he locked up the house and went back to the factory, where he sat in Judd's chair behind Judd's desk, with only the small green banker's light glowing, to wait. Three keys were in his pocket, and two ledgers in his lap. His own breath, in and out, in and out, was the only sound he heard for most of an hour, but he didn't move from behind that desk. Questions screamed in his brain. Fury roiled in his heart, disquieted by the halting effort to pray for courage that he was doing the right thing finally. But he held perfectly still, waiting.

At last he heard footsteps in the hall, and the door opened.

"What the devil are you doing, Matthew?"

"Sit down, Judd."

"Get out from behind my desk." Judd came toward him.

Matthew stood up. "Sit down, Judd—over there."

Matthew's full height was six foot four, and eventually his shoulders had broadened. He was not afraid.

"You're going to tell me the truth," Matthew said. "All of it."

"I don't know what you're talking about." Judd sat down in a chair generally meant for the guests in his office.

Matthew raised the two ledgers in one hand. "I have all the keys, Judd."

"You have no right." Judd's face flashed red and his hands went to the arms of the chair.

"Don't get up," Matthew said. "How many children? Let's start there."

Judd pushed out breath. "You don't want to do this."

"I'm a grown man, Judd. I can decide what I want to do. How many children?"

"Why does it matter to you?"

"Do you even know?"

Judd paused. "I would have to check the records."

"Hundreds?"

Judd was silent.

"Thousands? Thousands of children, Judd?" Matthew sank back into the chair behind the desk. "This whole enterprise, all the 'capital' that you raised, is built on selling children?"

"You make it sound like such nasty business."

"It is nasty business, Judd. People's *children*. You were stealing people's children and selling them."

"Don't say that."

"It's true, isn't it?"

"I told you a long time ago that occasionally I help with some adoptions so children can have the loving homes they deserve."

"That's the lie you like to tell yourself—and Mama. You've been telling yourself the story so long that you want to believe it because it would fit into this nice life you've built. But it's not true. Even Mama knows that's not true."

"These children need good homes, Matthew. I help make sure they get them. Solid homes with loving parents who can give them everything they need. There is nothing unsavory about it."

"Except the part where you take them from parents who want them."

"You don't know that."

"Don't I? Mrs. Liston that day in the clinic?"

"She was unstable even before she had a baby."

Bile rose in the back of Matthew's throat. "I'm inclined to believe her at the moment. That nurse who gave a baby to a man and didn't care about dropping his blanket? I was only four, but I knew something was wrong."

"If you have such a sharp memory, then you know good and well I was in a sales meeting when that happened."

"But you were in some other meetings right before that. Who knows what you arranged?"

"I don't run this business, Matthew. I am a way station."

"Then you are a very well paid way station, from the looks of these ledgers."

"The activity comes with certain risks, so yes, it commands a certain level of compensation."

"I don't believe you, Judd. How can I be certain you are not directing this whole business—where the children come from and where they go?"

"Because I'm telling you."

"And you have such a long record of telling me the truth—even about myself."

"I did that for your mother. It wasn't even supposed to be you."

"What does that mean?"

"She saw you and misunderstood."

Matthew's stomach clenched. He had to choose one path of questions at a time.

"If you are not directing this. . .you are in a position that you could bring it down?"

"Yes. But not without being implicated." Judd got up, planted his hands on the desk, and leaned forward to glare at Matthew. "And even you would not do that to your mother—or to this town. Do you really want to undo all the good the company has brought to Maple Turn?"

Matthew reached under the desk for Judd's wastebasket and vomited the dinner he'd shared with Jane. He would never eat crab legs again.

Shaking, he fumbled in his pocket for a handkerchief to wipe his mouth.

"Did you steal me yourself, or did you get someone else to do it?" he asked. A woman with a baby in a buggy in a store turns her head for just a moment, and when she looks back, the baby is gone. Was that it?

"I promised your mother I would never tell her—or you."

"Don't I have a right to know? I'm not a child any longer." A baby left in the care of someone the parents trusted, but gone when they returned. Was that it?

Judd put his hands in his trouser pockets and shook his head. "I gave her my word. You saw what happened to her a few years ago when you disobeyed me and started asking questions. I won't do that to her again."

"I want to know, and you are going to tell me." Matthew swallowed back the bile rising from his stomach. A young father uncertain how to care for his infant son who is sick takes him to a clinic, relieved to hand him to a nurse, and never sees him again. Was that it?

They glared at each other.

"Is my file in that cabinet?" Matthew said. Maybe he was listed under another name. Were the names he saw birth names or adopted names—or something transitory?

"No."

"I want it. I want to see it for myself."

Judd pressed his lips in and out before exhaling. "I will do this. I will leave everything I know about you—which is very little, so don't get your hopes up—in a sealed envelope with the lawyers with instructions that you are not to receive it or unseal it while your mother is alive. I don't want you looking for your other family. It would break her heart."

"Judd, she could live a long time still. I hope she will live a long time."

"So do I, but that's the best I will offer you."

Matthew stood up and stared into Judd's brooding eyes. "I'm keeping the keys, and you stop. It all stops. Whatever you have going in the places you travel to, it stops."

"That will affect the business here, Matthew."

"I'll take that chance."

"It's not your responsibility."

"It is now, because you will announce a planned transition of leadership to be accomplished over the next two months."

Judd scoffed. "You're too young, and I'm in good health. The company is barely a dozen years old. No one will believe that."

"You have a way of making anyone believe what you want them to believe. Give any reason you like or none at all. If you don't announce the transition of leadership, I leave the business and I tell Jane why. You can say whatever you want to Mama, but Jane will know the truth. If anything happens to Jane, Jackson will get a sealed envelope. I know how to talk to lawyers too."

"What kind of monster do you think I am? Nothing will happen to Jane. I have never hurt anyone. I told you. I'm helping people. Parents with loving hearts get children to dote on, and the children get better lives than the ones they were born into. The children are well looked after at every step. Besides, your mother adores Jane. I wouldn't do that to Alyce."

"I'm counting on that. But my offer doesn't change."

Matthew allowed himself only controlled, shallow breaths as he listened to Judd's breathing grow labored. Panicked. Unbelieving.

"You can't be serious," Judd said.

"I've never been more serious."

They glowered at each other. Matthew willed his eyes not to blink.

"Fine. I will stop." Judd shifted. "You have my word. You can have full access to the books. I will make you a junior partner. There's no need for you to take over the company."

Matthew shook his head.

"If I do this, Matthew, there could be trouble. You don't know these people."

"Then figure it out and make it go away. You must have as much on them as they have on you. You keep impeccable records."

"You're being naive."

"This is the deal, Judd. Take it or leave it. And don't think that you can just change the locks or get a different room in another location or start a new set of doctored books. I'll be watching things at home. If I even suspect you have a personal windfall in retirement, all promises are null."

"You leave me little choice."

"You made your choices long ago."

"The truth shall make you free." Matthew never felt more trapped. Could he really put this in a box and carry on with his life? Like Judd? He hated himself.

CHAPTER TWENTY-SIX

O kay," Kris said. "You win."

"Look. Here's Lindy now." Jillian put a hand on Kris's arm. "The shop will be in good hands."

Lindy entered and stamped snow off her feet. "Maybe we should catch the fresh stuff while it's coming down next time and advertise snow cones."

"Initiative," Kris said. "I like it." She got up and followed Lindy toward the counter.

"I need to steal Kris away for a while," Jillian said. "You can handle things here, right?"

Lindy spread her arms wide. "You're going to trust me with this mob on my own? Absolutely."

"Initiative and reliability," Jillian said. "The whole package. Come on, Kris."

Lindy disappeared into the kitchen.

"You don't need me," Kris said. "If I'd been able to stop Tucker from skiing Hidden Run, I would have done it by now."

"I disagree. You tried. My dad tried. I certainly said all the wrong things every time I opened my mouth around him."

"That's not true."

"You know it is," Jillian said, "but my point is we were all trying and didn't get through to him. Maybe Laurie Beth can help."

"Makes sense. So rotate me out and her in."

"If you're making me team captain, then I'm not cutting anybody from Team Tucker."

"Nia sent you to make sure I didn't show up with Tucker without warning, and you did your job."

"I'm sorry he hurt you, Kris."

"Don't be. I'm the one who got so caught up that I almost let him make me someone I'm not."

"I wonder if there's something making Tucker someone he's not too," Jillian said. "Maybe that's why Team Tucker isn't finished yet."

"That ridiculous backpack," Kris muttered.

Jillian waited.

"Do you suppose he walked into a bank and withdrew all that cash at one time? It's a lot to get from ATMs, even if you push your daily limits."

The wheels were churning.

"It's like he can't get rid of his money fast enough." Kris looked up. "And it doesn't matter, because he doesn't care if he hurts himself. Maybe it would have if I'd gone with him. I should have gone with him. Why did I suddenly get sensible? What if he's gone to break something? I could have used the time driving up there to get sensible."

"Stop it, Kris. But get your jacket," Jillian said. "And boots."

Back at the Inn a few minutes later, they climbed the steps to the veranda that wrapped the house and pushed through the heavy front door and into the roomy hall at the foot of the broad oak staircase. Jillian had no time to enjoy her favorite spot in the Inn and the temptation to slide into the library, her favorite room. Instead, she turned into the parlor, where Laurie Beth sprang from the sofa.

"Did you find him?"

"I'm sorry, no," Jillian said. "Uncle Patrick, what are you doing here?"

"I sensed some urgency about the situation when you left the house. Maybe I can help."

This can't have been the day her father had in mind when he invited his estranged brother to spend the day in Canyon Mines.

"Kris, this is my uncle Patrick," Jillian said, "and this is Laurie Beth."

"Nice to meet you," Laurie Beth muttered, glancing at her phone.

"Still no word from Tucker?" Jillian said.

"Nothing. Do you think he's off skiing somewhere?"

"I'm afraid so." Jillian caught Nolan's eye.

"Then I guess I just have to wait for him to come back," Laurie Beth said.

"Actually," Nolan said, "we should go look for him. Isn't that right, Jillian?"

"Yes, it's absolutely right."

"I don't understand." Laurie Beth used both hands to smooth back her straight, long, dark hair. "Wouldn't it be hard to find him? Aren't there a lot of ski resorts around here? Nolan was just telling me Tucker has been taking a lot of day trips to do the double blacks, sometimes with a friend he met here in town."

"That's all true," Kris said, "but he came by my ice cream parlor this morning. I know for sure he was going to ski alone today. And where."

Jillian pressed her lips together. This was not the time to tell Laurie Beth that the friend her fiancée has been skiing with, and generally gallivanting around Canyon Mines with, was the attractive owner of the local ice cream parlor.

"Well, where is he skiing then?" Laurie Beth asked.

"Nearby." Kris flicked her eyes toward Nolan. "Hidden Run."

"Aren't we at Hidden Run?"

"We named the Inn for a lost ski resort," Nia said. "Sort of a local legend."

"But it's a real place?"

"Possibly on private property," Nia said. "We're not entirely sure."

"That doesn't sound like Tucker," Laurie Beth said. "He has never trespassed in his life."

"That's it." Nolan reached for his jacket. "We have to go right now."

"My rental is a Tahoe," Patrick said. "Room for everyone."

"The maps," Nia said.

"Maps?" Laurie Beth echoed.

"He pores over them at breakfast and in the evenings in the library," Nia said. "He's been looking for the exact location."

"I want to see them."

"They're in his room," Nia said. "But that's private space."

"I'm going to marry him. I thought we didn't keep secrets—until this."

Nia pressed her lips together. "I'm probably crossing a line, because I'm really good at doing that, but I may or may not wander past the reception desk over there, and I may or may not happen to drop a key on it in about one minute."

"Hurry up!" Laurie Beth said.

The whole operation took under four minutes, and Laurie Beth was back in the parlor and tossed the key to Nia. "There are no maps in that room."

"He's got them then," Nolan said.

"You all go," Nia said. "I'll stay here in case he shows up."

Around the room, jacket zippers scraped up.

Kris said, "The new snow overnight made him even more excited to ski fresh powder where no one else has been for so many decades."

"Is this Hidden Run dangerous?" Laurie Beth asked. "Or is it just trespassing?"

Jillian and Nolan locked eyes.

"Dangerous," Nolan said. "We've been trying to persuade him not to do it."

"Then why would he insist?"

"Is it out of character?" Jillian asked.

"He likes a challenge, but he's not stupid." Laurie Beth charged for the door.

In Patrick's Tahoe, Kris said, "We'd better swing by my place and pick up those backcountry skis he bought me. We might need them."

Jillian's heart lurched.

"He bought you *skis*?" Squeezed in between Kris and Jillian, Laurie Beth's head rotated to stare at Kris.

"I didn't ask for them," Kris said. "He wanted me to ski Hidden Run with him. I never said I would."

"You're the friend he's been skiing with."

Jillian winced. It would have been nice to have time for a quick strategy session with her father and Kris before bits of information leaked out in hurtful ways.

"Then we should get my skis too," Nolan said. "And my copy of the topography map. Just in case."

In case of what? Jillian refused to picture her father going down Hidden Run on his dated equipment and middle-aged knees.

"Laurie Beth," Jillian said, "can I ask a question?"

"If it will help Tucker, of course."

"Does he normally carry around large amounts of cash?"

Laurie Beth scoffed. "I tease him all the time about using plastic to pay for something that costs two dollars. And besides, other than the fact that he likes to ski for a couple of days now and then, he's sort of a miser. Wild spending is not his thing."

Kris and Jillian exchanged a glance.

"What?" Laurie Beth said.

"We've seen a different side of Tucker," Kris said.

"He's been using a lot of cash while he's here, that's all," Jillian said.

Laurie Beth eyed Kris. "Enough to buy expensive new skis?"

"Really," Kris said, "I did not ask for them! But if he's on that hill, it could be a good thing I have them."

"All right." Laurie Beth folded her arms in her lap. "For Tucker's sake, I'll believe you."

"Directions, please," Patrick said.

Kris told Patrick how to find her home. They loaded her skis through the back of the vehicle, the ends coming over the seat between Kris and Laurie Beth. A few minutes later, Nolan's sliced between Laurie Beth and Jillian on the other side.

"Sorry," Patrick said, "I didn't know I was going to need a hitch or a ski rack."

"No problem." Jillian gripped her dad's skis with one hand. "We don't have far to go, right, Dad?"

"It's snowing again," Nolan said. "I grabbed a couple of flares, just in case."

Just in case. Jillian was tired of that phrase.

Kris held her skis in place with one hand and now rubbed an eye with the other. "If he wasn't already on Hidden Run, he will be now. He loves to ski when it's snowing."

Laurie Beth turned to her. "That's right, he does. I never understood it. It makes it harder to see."

"Adds to the thrill, he says."

"That's exactly what he says."

Kris and Laurie Beth looked at each other, some understanding passing between them.

"Are we positive we shouldn't look somewhere else first?" Nolan asked.

"Yes," Kris said. "He was headed to Hidden Run, and that was a couple of hours ago."

"He can't drive all the way up," Nolan said. "He'll have to climb."

"Then we might catch him," Laurie Beth said.

"He's got a huge head start," Kris said. "Keep trying to call him,

Laurie Beth. You're the one he's most likely to answer."

"Not you?"

Kris shook her head. "You have nothing to worry about."

Nolan unfolded his topography map and handed Jillian a road map. "We just have to match the current road to the best approach of our best guess for where the Hidden Run hill is."

"Tell me you've been thinking about this," Jillian said.

"I have. I'm pretty sure I've got it marked correctly on both maps. But I was thinking as a driver, not as a backcountry skier."

"Well, we don't have one of those."

"No, but we have Kris." Nolan looked over his shoulder. "What kind of terrain would he be looking for to climb up there? Surely not the steep side he'll ski down."

All eyes turned to Kris. Her face blanched.

"Think, Kris," Laurie Beth said. "This is the part that you know."

Kris licked her lips. "No, not the steep side. He'll try to drive as far as possible, of course, but he'll be looking for flat spaces for at least some of the time."

"Like cross-country skiing," Nolan said.

Kris nodded. "He wouldn't want to get up there and be exhausted. Some climbing, some flat spaces. Maybe a back side where the slope is gentler."

"Like switchbacking up a mountain," Nolan said.

"Sort of. Yes. And he's going to want to get high, to get all the lift he can out of the initial push-off. He's not going to go to all the effort to get up there and not have that moment of exhilaration."

"You really do know him," Laurie Beth said.

"You're the one who's going to make him see sense," Kris said.

"Trade maps, Jilly." Nolan shoved the topographical map to the back seat and took the road map. "Start studying the topography, Kris. Get your bearings. Just in case."

Jillian put one hand to her forehead. Enough with those three little words!

Nolan gave directions. Patrick drove. Kris and Jillian gripped the skis. Laurie Beth fingered the phone in her lap. They navigated out of town on the old highway heading west. The snowfall thickened, and Jillian was grateful for the heavy vehicle.

"Turn here, and you'll have to slow down," Nolan said after a few minutes. "If I'm right about how the topography matches the roads, we won't be able to go very far up, but there's a place where hikers leave cars in the summer. I never realized it was so close to Hidden Run."

The Tahoe ground forward and maintained purchase on the incline.

Kris leaned forward a couple of minutes later. "There's his truck."

Jillian's stomach sank. Her brain knew Kris would be right about where Tucker was headed, but her heart nevertheless had hoped she'd be wrong and they'd simply be ruling out Hidden Run.

Patrick eased in alongside the gray pickup, and Nolan leaped out of his side of the car.

"He's not in the truck," he said.

The others exited the Tahoe.

"How much farther to the top?" Patrick asked.

Looking at the topography map, Nolan said, "Quite a ways. It's steep in places. He could still be climbing."

"He has skins on his skis," Kris said, "for climbing. It won't take him as long as you think."

"Tucker, you idiot." Laurie Beth trudged through the snow toward his truck and pulled at the driver door. "It's unlocked. Don't know why it matters, but it is."

"Did he leave anything?" Jillian asked.

Laurie Beth groaned and leaned into the cab. "Just his helmet."

"He didn't take his helmet?" Kris said. "I've never seen him ski without it."

"Me neither," Laurie Beth said. "He's very safety conscious even on easy hills."

"This one is full of trees," Nolan said.

Silence fanned across the group.

"You can say it," Laurie Beth said. "The biggest benefit of a helmet is reducing head injuries when a skier hits a tree."

Nolan nodded.

"Open the back, please, Patrick," Kris said. "I'm going after him."

"We all are," Nolan said.

Patrick unlocked the rear of the Tahoe.

"It's the ultimate high to climb as high as you can get." Sitting under the open hatch, Kris tugged off her snow boots and began putting on her ski boots. "Tucker has been researching every detail about Hidden Run. He wanted to get even higher than two thousand feet vertical. Skiing down without his helmet—well, it would be quite a rush."

"What is he trying to prove?" Laurie Beth put a hand against her forehead as she strayed from Tucker's truck. "This is not Tucker. I don't understand."

Jillian stepped closer to the truck and looked inside. The backpack was there. She reached in and retrieved it.

"It's empty." She held it up for the others to see.

"What's that doing here?" Laurie Beth asked.

"You recognize it?" Jillian said.

"He's had it since he was a kid. His Grandpa Matt's friend Jackson gave it to him. But he never uses it now. It's very sentimental. It would be like a grown man carrying around a teddy bear."

"He's hardly let it out of his sight since he came to Canyon Mines," Jillian said.

Kris clomped over to take the limp bag from Jillian and unzipped it. "It's gone, all right."

"What's gone?" Laurie Beth asked.

"The sealed envelope," Kris said.

"The one his Grandpa Matt left him," Nolan said.

Laurie Beth looked up the mountain. Jillian followed her gaze through the gray sky and snowflakes dampening everyone's outerwear. Nolan was at the back of the Tahoe now, pulling his skis out.

"So a sealed envelope from Grandpa Matt has something to do with why Tucker wants to be an idiot on this mountain," Laurie Beth said. "And you've all been trying to figure out why. Am I up to speed now?"

"Pretty much," Jillian said.

"Then the only thing I want to say is thank you, and I don't care how much money he spent buying fancy skis for a woman he just met."

"Then you'll be glad to know he bought me the fancy climbing skins too," Kris said. "I can still see his tracks, but not for long. I'm going to climb as fast as I can. You all keep up the best you can."

CHAPTER TWENTY-SEVEN

Kris's skis and bindings were made for backcountry climbing, and she was half Nolan's age, so he didn't try to match her pace. On an uphill climb, even cross-country skis would have been more efficient than what Nolan had on his feet, but he persisted. In some stretches, he made a V formation in the snow with his skis, stabbing his poles into the snowpack and moving forward one foot at a time. In others, sidestepping up the incline seemed to work better. In stretches of flat surface, he could ski more smoothly. With each exhaling effort, he also offered a breath prayer for the real reason he hoped his skis would not be needed—gingerly navigating down the more treacherous slope in search of an injured Tucker.

Patrick surprised him. He'd always had big feet, and they came in handy now as he walked ahead of Jillian and Laurie Beth and dragged his boots just enough to clear a path that made their progress easier.

"I don't see Kris anymore." Laurie Beth's breath came heavy.

The terrain was not a direct upward incline. Kris occasionally dipped out of sight or went behind a cluster of trees.

"She's there," Nolan said. "Do you need to stop and catch your breath?"

Laurie Beth shook her head. "I can't. Not with Tucker up there." But she bent over, hands on knees.

"You haven't had time to adjust to the altitude." Canyon Mines was a good seven thousand feet higher than St. Louis. Under normal circumstances, Laurie Beth should have had a day or two to adjust before attempting this level of exertion. They hadn't even grabbed water bottles.

"Eat some snow," Jillian said. "Hydration is number one up here."

Laurie Beth made a face but complied.

"Go on, Dad," Jillian said. "I'll stay with her until she's ready."

"Yes," Patrick said. "Someone has to stay with Kris's tracks."

"We should stay together," Nolan said.

"Kris is already on her own," Jillian said. "Someone should try to have eyes on her."

"I'm sorry," Laurie Beth said. "I think I'm going to be okay."

Jillian took off a glove and pushed up the cuff of Laurie Beth's jacket to put a finger on her wrist. "Pretty fast pulse still. Please go, Dad. For Kris and Tucker."

"I'm so sorry," Laurie Beth said.

"It's all right," Nolan said. "You just need some time." A fallen log for her to sit on would have been handy, but any in the vicinity were long buried under the snowpack.

"Eat more snow," Jillian urged. "Dad, what are you doing still here?"

"Patrick," he said.

"I've got this," Patrick said.

Nolan pulled a flare out of his jacket. "At least keep this. Just in case."

"Dad, please," Jillian said. "You have the other one, right?"

"Yes."

"Well, Kris doesn't have one. And neither does Tucker. So go."

Nolan set his skis and poles and pushed upward, searching for a glimpse of purple. The new snow had let up during the moments they'd stopped for Laurie Beth. Visibility in the sky was still a dingy gray, but Kris's path on the ground was clear enough to follow, and even traces of Tucker's that she had let be her guide.

As Nolan climbed, so did his heart rate. His mind's eye saw the careful draftsman's lettering of the topography map indicating the elevation rises between the lines curving around the mountain. Laurie Beth would insist on pressing ahead, unaware of what the impact of the altitude could be. Jillian and Patrick would have to pace her and take advantage of the flat stretches to let her heart rate adjust. Nolan pushed his own speed enough to catch glimpses of Kris's purple jacket against the white expanses, while balancing his concern with being able to look back at the trio of colors advancing more slowly behind him.

The moment of decision came though. Nolan could see neither Kris ahead nor Jillian and the others behind him. He paused, catching his breath and considering options. The path Tucker and Kris had skied remained visible, and he was adding his tracks as well. He dug for his phone and tried calling Jillian but got no answer. Exhaling, he chose not to read too much into the lack of response. She could be in a spot where her phone wasn't picking up a signal. Between the layers of winter gear and the wind, she might not have heard the phone. Her hands might have been busy helping Laurie Beth. Nolan left a message and chose to continue upward. Now he made an extra effort to dig the edges of his skis into the snow and leave deeper tracks.

He finally crested and caught up with the vision of purple planted uncomfortably close to the edge of the mountain.

But Kris was facing away from the view and into Tucker's face. She'd gotten there in time.

"You brought reinforcements, I see," Tucker said.

On more level terrain, Nolan glided closer. Tucker was ready, the skins off his skis, goggles on, fists gripping his poles. Nolan had never been this high up on this mountain, so far above the innocuous spring and summer hiking options. It was a sheer, pristine drop. A skier pushing off from this spot would have immediate high, long lift. It would require incredible aim to land in the narrow path between the trees. Nolan's stomach dropped just thinking of the sensation. He slid into position beside Kris. Tucker would have to get past the two of them now in order to do anything rash, and Nolan didn't believe he would risk sending them sliding down the mountain.

"Look at the state o' you." Nolan gasped for breath. "We're going to have more company in a few minutes. Wish I had thought to bring the party snacks."

"A thermos of hot chocolate would be nice right about now," Kris said. "That's your department."

"You guys are a riot," Tucker said. "I'm impressed you got up here, Nolan."

"Hey, you were the one with the great remedial tips about how to climb efficiently." Nolan lifted his phone, searching for the bars that showed he had a signal. "Oh good. Service."

He removed a glove and thumbed a text message. AT THE TOP. KRIS FOUND TUCKER. COMING? The message was taking a long time to go through.

"Why can't you just let me have this one last ski?" Tucker picked up a pole and jammed it again into the snowpack, but not in a way that threatened imminent departure. Nevertheless, Nolan held his position.

"Because we'd like you to have many more years of exciting but slightly more sensible skiing," Nolan said.

"Like with a helmet," Kris said.

Tucker glared.

"There's a fallen log right over there," Nolan said. "Why don't we get out of our bindings, clear it off, and sit?" Finally, the message showed it was delivered.

"I didn't climb all the way up here just for the vistas." Tucker adjusted both his gloves.

Nolan's phone pinged with a message from Jillian. COMING. LB BETTER ENOUGH TO KEEP GOING. P IS A HUMAN SNOWPLOW.

"I will kick those poles out from under you with these new fancy skis if I have to," Kris said. "You need to wait."

"What for?" Tucker said.

"You just do."

"That's no logic."

"We have a surprise for you," Nolan said.

"Maybe another day."

"It would be a shame to miss her."

"Her?"

"Let's sit, Tucker."

"I prefer to remain ready to ski, thank you."

Nolan's phone pinged again. I SEE YOU. ALMOST THERE.

Patrick plowed across the flat space just then. Nolan eased out his breath. Jillian and Laurie Beth could not be far behind.

"Meet my brother," Nolan said. "Patrick."

Tucker leaned away from his poles. "The one your grandfather liked best?"

"Guilty as charged." Patrick grinned. "Somebody had to be the favorite."

"I get it," Tucker said. "I'm in that club. Hey, what are you doing up here with no skis?"

"Chasing my little brother, who for some reason is chasing you."

"He shouldn't have bothered." Tucker looked at Nolan. "This is not a 'her.' "

"That part of the surprise is still coming." Nolan glanced at the ridge. Two hooded heads crested. "Here we go."

Tucker turned only his head, his skis still aimed for the hill. "Laurie Beth! What are you doing here?"

"I should write a song," Laurie Beth said. "Fly anywhere, climb any mountain, just to reach you."

"Are you all right?" Tucker asked.

"The locals tell me I'm having trouble with the altitude, and I tend to believe them." Laurie Beth trudged closer to him, breathing hard. "Maybe that will be a good bridge in my love ballad."

Tucker's eyes went from Laurie Beth to Kris, clouding with confusion.

"Yes, I've met your ski partner," Laurie Beth said. "We've all been worried about you. Especially me. It's not like you to be so out of touch."

"I'm sorry for not calling," Tucker said, "but as you can see, I'm fine."

"You're not fine," Kris said.

"What she said," Laurie Beth added.

Tucker's exhale swirled in the cold air around his face.

"We're here to help," Nolan said.

"You can't help me ski with your old equipment," Tucker said. "Kris could come."

"You know that's not what they mean," Laurie Beth said.

"As the nonskier in the bunch," Jillian said, "please let me say that they just want to help you *not* ski for all the right reasons."

Tucker pulled his poles out of the snow to reposition them. "It's my decision. It's terrific to have a cheering section when I take off, but you need to move out of the way."

"We're not moving," Kris said. "We'll cheer when you climb down the safe path with us, back to the cars."

"Now you're getting bossy. That's not like you."

"You have people who care about you," Nolan said. "Whatever you're facing, remember that. Your mother, your family. Laurie Beth tracked you down and came all this way. We've only known you a few days, but we care."

"You don't understand."

"We want to. As exciting as Hidden Run sounds, it's not worth it. You can't see the rocks it's littered with even if you find a path through the trees. The run is literally hidden."

"I've been staring at it. Planning my route. That's the only reason I was still here. Where I could push off, where I'd likely land, calculating speed based on the height of the lift, where I'd have to adjust in the air, and how fast I'd have to find the clear space through. I can do it."

"What about the boulders you can't see?" Kris said. "There's a lot of fresh powder hiding obstacles."

"That's why I have backcountry skis," Tucker said.

"And the reason you left your helmet behind to ski a heavily wooded rugged run?"

Tucker's response was to pull the goggles off the top of his head and position them over his eyes.

"What about me, Tucker?" Laurie Beth wanted to know. "We made promises to each other when we got engaged."

He hesitated, his jawline softening.

Laurie Beth moved from beside him to in front of him, straddling his skis. With her right hand she removed the goggles from his face and with her left she stroked his cheek. Then she kissed him unabashedly, lingering, unselfconsciously.

"Why didn't I try that?" Kris muttered.

Nolan laughed softly. "Because you don't have that rock on your finger."

When Laurie Beth stepped back, Tucker's composure was less adamant, but his feet had not moved.

"Where's the envelope, Tucker?" Kris asked.

"And why does she know about the envelope and I don't?" Laurie Beth said.

"I'll explain that later." Tucker unzipped his jacket a few inches, exposing the envelope trapped between layers of clothing.

"Have you opened it?" Kris asked.

"Nope." Tucker zipped his jacket, sealing the packet away again.

"You've been carrying it around ever since you got to Canyon Mines."

"I know. Grandpa Matt left me that. . .that. . .ridiculous letter. And this. I just wanted to do this one thing first."

"Whatever is in there," Jillian said, "must really scare you."

"Whatever is in there," Laurie Beth said, "we'll face it together. You and me. Just like we promised. We've always said we were already completely committed, heart-to-heart, just waiting for our wedding day."

"See," Nolan said. "You are not alone. Love upholds you."

"This is not fair," Tucker said. "Five against one."

"We are Team Tucker," Jillian said, "and we don't give up. And I talked to Jackson today. He wants to see you."

"Jackson?" Tucker's eyes flickered.

"Yep."

"You leave me no option then."

Tucker's feet moved at last. He picked up one ski and repositioned it in the laborious way required for taking steps with legs attached to six-foot appendages. Laurie Beth stepped out of the way, back from the edge as Tucker seemed to be swinging his feet around. The tension in Nolan's muscles eased. Beside him, Kris repositioned her poles to allow Tucker some space.

Nolan didn't see Patrick coming, but suddenly he was there, knocking the poles out of Tucker's hands and sending his feet flying.

"Uncle Patrick!" Jillian rushed toward Tucker, now flat on his back.

"What in the world?" Nolan said.

Patrick was half astride Tucker, wrestling for control of the poles.

"I can't believe you were going to do that!" Laurie Beth dropped to her knees beside Tucker.

"Do what?" Nolan snatched the poles from Patrick for safekeeping.

"We fell for it, Nolan," Kris said. "He had Laurie Beth out of the way, and we were just about to give him all the clearance he needed to glide right around us and take off."

Laurie Beth dug the heels of her hands into her eyes. "Whatever pain is inside you is huge, Tucker, but it's not so huge that it scares me away. So get used to it. You're stuck with me."

Nolan handed his poles and Tucker's to Jillian. "Maybe these will help you and Laurie Beth on the climb down. Patrick and I will take Tucker." The two of them lifted him to his feet and steadied him between them. "And if it's all the same to you, ski man, I'll drive back into town, so hand over the keys right now."

CHAPTER TWENTY-EIGHT

Maple Turn, Missouri, 1989

Alyce walked with her arm slung casually through Matthew's, not because she needed his support but because she still enjoyed letting everyone know he was her son. With pride beaming in her face, an expression Matthew knew meant all was well, she walked erect down the hall from the dining room to her apartment.

"That's my good Mattie," she said.

"Did you get enough to eat?"

She ducked her glance. "They are always feeding us around here. Haven't you noticed that? Someone will be along soon enough to knock on my door and see if I want to come out for an afternoon smoothie."

"Well, Mama, you do like smoothies."

She smiled. "I can't argue with you there. Occasionally they even get imaginative with the fruits they put in them."

They reached her apartment, and Alyce turned the key in the lock.

"Do you need anything before I go?" Matthew asked.

"Not a thing. You get back to work," she said. "I'm going to put my feet up with a book for a few minutes."

This was code for taking a nap in the recliner in her living room. As long as she didn't go into the bedroom and get under the blankets, Alyce didn't consider it sleeping, but whoever knocked on her door in a couple of hours was likely to find that she'd dozed off with the book in her lap. She was eighty-five years old. If she wanted an after-lunch nap, there was no reason she shouldn't have one.

"Tell Jane I found a new quilt block pattern in a magazine in the common room," Alyce said. "I clipped it for the next time I see her."

"I don't think you're supposed to clip things out of magazines in the common room, Mama."

She waved him off. "People do it all the time. No one cares."

"I'll tell her." Matthew leaned down and kissed her cheek. "Enjoy your book. I'll bring groceries on Saturday."

"Don't forget creamer. I like the vanilla-flavored one."

"I'll remember."

"That's my good Mattie."

Alyce withdrew into the apartment, and Matthew turned to stride toward the main entrance.

Judd had been gone ten years, lost within moments to a massive heart attack after dinner at the age of eighty-one. After a brief transition period at Ryder Manufacturing, during which he publicly handed the reins over to his son, in retirement Judd had paid close attention to Alyce. For twenty years, he tended closely to her and made her exquisitely happy. Matthew could not deny those two decades were perhaps the most content of his mother's life. Judd was always there, always attentive, always companionable. No more trips. No more wondering. She sensed the shift and was relieved at long last.

But Alyce never truly adapted to anyone else's presence in the big house after Gertrude left. It was her idea to move. She didn't want to be next to Ryder Manufacturing without Judd. She would always be lonely without Judd, but she wanted to live somewhere else. Alyce even chose the place. Maple Turn wasn't large enough to support an assisted living community, so it was a bit of a drive to visit, but Matthew saw her a couple of times a week and made sure she got to church every Sunday and out to lunch with her old friends a couple of times a month. As long as she had a routine, she did well. Even a decade later, her own health showed no serious sign of physical or further mental decline. She seemed as settled as someone could be after losing a beloved lifelong partner.

Matthew got in his car and aimed it toward Ryder Manufacturing. His mother was right that he had to return to work. The pace never let up, but at least he had the next twenty-five minutes to himself before plunging back into the pile of reports on his desk and the little pink slips of phone messages that no doubt stacked up during a two-hour absence to have lunch with his mother.

Alyce had tried to give the big house to Matthew and Jane, but he hadn't wanted it. The house was Judd's, and it came with too many ghosts.

Jane hadn't understood, and he didn't explain—couldn't explain—why he wouldn't live in that house again. It was perhaps the biggest quarrel of their marriage, but he'd sold the house and deposited the funds to support his mother's care. Then he'd mollified Jane by also moving their family, with three children, to a larger home than where they'd started out. The youngest, Debra, still kept a bedroom at home, though she rarely was there while she finished college, and Matthew didn't expect she would be around much longer. Stephen had already moved to Iowa. Nannette, the eldest, was the one who was sticking around.

He had his life with Jane after all, though he had trapped himself into playing out a lie all this time. He'd kept his promise not to look into his own past, even apart from any information that might be in a sealed envelope left with the lawyers that he didn't have access to until Alyce passed away—if Judd had kept his word and left an envelope. Matthew and Jane had their children, and now they had Nannette's son, their own grandson. For the sake of the life in front of him, it was easier and easier to push his questions to the back of his mind.

Most of the time.

He'd never told Jane, and keeping a secret from her was a seeping wound that never healed.

Back at Ryder, Matthew walked into the office suite and held out his hand, knowing that Rachel, his secretary, would hand him messages as he passed. She'd been with him for years, and they had a practiced rhythm.

"How was the food?" she said.

He gave her a wry smile that said he wished he'd had time to stop for a decent hot dog on the way back. She would have scolded him if she detected the scent of fast food on his breath though. Rachel and Jane were colluding to reform his eating habits. After all, they thought his father died from a heart attack and maybe he'd inherited heart disease.

"The business journal called again," Rachel said.

"I'll call them."

In his office, Matthew dropped the stack of pink message slips on his teak desk without flipping through them. Already his head was back in the quarterly production report he needed to analyze before tomorrow's meeting.

After Judd's retirement, Matthew had been tempted to remodel the entire suite of offices and eradicate any evidence of access to the private storage room through a private hall by simply sealing it off once and for all. But someday, when Alyce was gone, he might want to follow the trail of answers, and going into that room might be necessary. In the meantime, as much as he hated Judd's office, he couldn't let anyone else have it because of that doorway. So he'd settled for moving out the heavy cherry-wood furniture and bringing in an entirely new look with the teak. He made sure to place a tall bookcase so it blocked the door from his view completely. Only one person ever asked about it, and Matthew simply said he didn't intend to use his father's old storeroom, so it was a waste of space not to put something on that wall.

That was that.

Jane had been nagging him for years to redecorate again—thirty years was a long time with the same furniture—but for now, Matthew left well enough alone.

But he had rebricked the back of the building and in the process sealed off the exterior entrance to the room. It was the only true argument he'd ever had with the affable, ever-grinning Jackson, who'd never gotten his chance to pick the lock on that door. He'd left Ryder Manufacturing over that disagreement and opened his own locksmith business. For a while, the quarrel put some distance in their relationship, but ultimately Jackson's change in employment saved their friendship for the long haul. It was better if he wasn't in the building, presuming access to Matthew's new office once the outside door was gone. Questions about where the door led fell out of bounds once and for all.

Matthew took out the green pen he always used to mark up reports, straightened his bifocals on his face so they didn't catch the glare from the light, and dug in. He worked with the door open, the office sounds fading into a white noise that helped him concentrate better than complete silence would have. Page after page, he circled the numbers with the most significance and underlined the ones he wanted to get more information about. In the margins, he jotted notes about the machines that seemed to be most productive and which operators were on the shifts that turned out the highest number of products and those who lagged behind targets.

"Grandpa Matt!"

At the chirpy voice, Matthew immediately dropped his pen and lifted his eyes, a grin cracking his face. He pushed his chair back from his desk just in time to receive the hurtling little boy into his lap.

"Tucker! What brings you here?"

"I came to run the factory!"

"Taking over my job already?"

Tucker giggled. "You know what I mean. I want to run in the factory by the machines like we always do."

Matthew rubbed his six-year-old grandson's back. "Right now the machines are operating, so it's not safe for you to be in the factory. But if you're still here when the shift ends, we'll do the safety check together, and if it's all clear, then you can run. How does that sound?"

"Not as good as running now, but I guess it's okay."

"Where's your mother?"

Tucker rolled his eyes. "She never keeps up. You know how that is."

Matthew laughed. "Your mother is a very efficient person. I don't know how I'd get things done around here without her."

"That's certainly good to hear." Nannette's voice came from the doorway. "The little rascal got away when I stopped to answer someone's question."

"At least you knew where he was headed," Matthew said.

"Always headed for Grandpa Matt," Nannette said. "I just picked him up from school. The sitter has an appointment and Mom is busy. He's supposed to play quietly in my office for a couple of hours."

"He can always hang out here."

"You indulge him too much."

"That's a grandpa's job." Tucker nestled under Matthew's chin.

When Nannette married at only twenty years old, Matthew and Jane hadn't wanted to flat-out say it was a mistake, but she hadn't known John Kintzler very long, and she dropped out of college with stars in her eyes in order to marry him. By the time they came home from their honeymoon, Tucker was on the way. And by the time Tucker was two years old, Nannette didn't even know where John was. She still didn't four years later. But she'd had the good sense to admit she needed help, and of course Matthew and Jane had taken mother and child back into their home. Nannette returned to school, got a degree, and joined Ryder Manufacturing. In Matthew's opinion, although her responsibilities were very junior at the moment, she had natural aptitude for finance and she could someday be at the helm of the company. Maybe Tucker would be as well—if he wanted to be. For Matthew there was little choice, but Tucker might choose to, or another grandchild still to be born to Nannette or Stephen or Debra might choose.

Ryder Manufacturing was on solid ground, despite Matthew's rejection of Judd's funding strategies. When he took over, Matthew's first priority was to bear down to make sure the company would still succeed and serve the town well as a reliable employer without Judd's unsavory methods. The outrageous growth of its first decade had slowed, of course, but it had still grown at sustainable rates. In the nights when thoughts of the cash influxes from the early days sickened Matthew into wakefulness, he determined to slog through all the more. Too many people in Maple Turn depended on Ryder Manufacturing now. He could hardly put them all out of work to assuage his guilt over something he had no part in doing.

And no matter how sick it made him, he could not expose his mother to shame.

"Grandpa Matt, you're not listening." Tucker put his hand on Matthew's face and turned it toward him.

"You caught me," Matthew said. "Tell me again."

Tucker dipped his head in an impish grin, and the light went on in his eyes. "It's about Aubree. She got into so much trouble with Mrs. Ojed again today."

"And did you have anything to do with this trouble?"

Tucker drew an indignant breath. "No, Grandpa Matt! Sometimes you are impossible!"

Matthew laughed. Could any man ask for a more delightful grandson?

His breath caught. A father, grandfather, and great-grandfather never got to know Tucker existed because they never saw Matthew grow up. Surely they would have delighted in Tucker had they not been cheated of the chance to know him.

Matthew deftly zippered that wound closed again, as he had learned long ago to do.

CHAPTER TWENTY-NINE

Nolan felt his age in every muscle of his body the next morning. Even all his remedial recreational refreshment excursions with Tucker hadn't conditioned his body to climb so high up on Hidden Run and then reverse the path in a measured manner that made sure Tucker didn't elude the guard Nolan and Patrick formed around him.

Tucker hadn't yielded any more information about his grandfather's letter or the envelope on the way down. During the ride returning to town, he only wanted to hold Laurie Beth's hand, and back at the Inn, Tucker shooed Nolan, Patrick, Kris, and Jillian away. He was exhausted, he said, and he only wanted to talk to Laurie Beth.

Who could argue with that? The woman who wore his ring had tracked him down and come all the way from St. Louis to make sure he was all right. She was entitled to the story. Nolan made sure Laurie Beth had custody of the key to Tucker's rental truck, lest he get any ideas, and Nia promised to make sure they were amply fed without hovering.

Kris went back to Ore the Mountain long enough to satisfy herself that everything was buttoned down for the night. Theoretically Patrick, Nolan, and Jillian could have salvaged a few hours of their reunion day. The truth was they were all exhausted. Patrick opted to stay the night. Hot showers, dry clothes, and food delivered from Burgers 'n' More helped some, but the only topic on their minds was Tucker and what could possibly be in that envelope. Their speculations came up empty.

Nolan was determined Patrick would have some approximation of an Irish breakfast before he left for his meetings in Denver, so battling screaming muscles, he rummaged in the kitchen. He came up with a can of baked beans and an apple and green pepper he could dice into them. So far so good.

He turned on the oven, in the belief that there were tomatoes somewhere that he could roast.

He was certain he still had a few slices of thick bacon in the refrigerator.

Eggs, of course.

Bangers and mash would have been nice, but that was not to be.

Nolan pushed the power buttons on all of Jillian's fancy coffee machines. They might as well have them all on standby.

His shoulders protested. His calves howled. One hip screamed every time he shifted his weight. Somehow Nolan put the meal together anyway. By the time Patrick came downstairs, Nolan was taking the roasted tomatoes and baked beans out of the oven, the bacon was ready for a final turn, and the last skillet was hot and waiting for the eggs to fry.

"What, no black pudding?" Patrick said.

Nolan chuckled. "No one in town sells the pig's blood sausage, and even if they did, Jillian wouldn't allow it in the house."

"What kind of an Irish girl is she?"

"One who remembers her Italian mother never liked that stuff."

"Bella." The humor dropped out of Patrick's voice. "Another casualty of our wasted years. I should have known her better."

Jillian entered the room. "I need coffee."

"You mean you need something that is an adulterated imitation of coffee." Nolan popped four slices of bread into the toaster. "Patrick and I will have the real thing."

"Whatever." Jillian took three mugs out of the cupboard, fiddled with the machines, and produced aromatic beverages in time to set them on the kitchen nook table as Nolan placed the plates. Nolan smelled cinnamon in today's caffeinated concoction.

"Sort of feels like we pushed the PAUSE button for twenty-four hours," Jillian said after the blessing. "Here we are again."

"Only this time Patrick has to leave," Nolan said, "instead of having the whole day to spend with us."

"I did spend a day with you," Patrick said. "Fresh air. Mountain views. Skis."

"But we didn't really get to talk." Jillian lifted her mug. "About. Things."

"About what happened." Nolan pushed his fork into a runny fried egg. It was time. He wanted to do this while Patrick was there to see him tell his daughter the truth. "I was in my first semester of law school and had just met your mother—old enough to know what I was doing even if at the time I let myself believe it wasn't intentional. Pop Paddy only had one possession that came from Ireland."

"The painting," Jillian said. "Uncle Seamus has it in his den."

"That's right," Nolan said. "I couldn't keep it, not after the way I came to have it."

Jillian's eyes widened.

"We all liked to hear Paddy tell stories about Ireland," Nolan said, "stories that his father told him about growing up in Ireland before he came here to work the mines. His father's best friend made that painting for him and gave it to him just before he got on the boat so he would never forget the old country. They knew they would never see each other again. That little painting meant more to Paddy's father than anything else he owned. That's why it meant so much to Paddy. I suppose that's why I wanted it too."

"I don't understand." Jillian had stopped eating. "Then why does Uncle Seamus have it?"

"Paddy had always promised that picture to Patrick. We all knew it—Seamus and I and the other cousins." Nolan glanced at Patrick, whose features were crunched and still. "But I was admiring it that day and saying there would never be another family heirloom like it. And then he asked if I would like to have it."

"And you said yes," Jillian said.

Nolan nodded. "I never should have. It was my fault. I shouldn't have put him in that position. I let him wrap it up for me in a wool scarf and put it in a canvas bag, and I walked out of his house like it was a trophy. When Patrick found out. . .well. . .gloating only made things worse. He was mad as a box of frogs."

On the table, Patrick's hands fisted. "I should have lit into your father, but I went after Pop Paddy instead. I charged over and shouted things no grown man should ever say to his elderly grandfather."

"You were hurt," Nolan said, "because of me."

"You weren't there." Patrick's eyes dropped to his lap. "You didn't hear. I might as well have knocked him down and kicked him in the teeth."

"Patrick."

"Don't, Nolan. It's the truth. After that, I had to leave. I couldn't face him again."

"I should have given you the painting. I should have stopped you. I should have gone with you to Pop Paddy to make things right."

Patrick shook his head. "What you did was wrong, Nolan, but you are not responsible for what I did that was wrong."

"Uncle Patrick," Jillian said, "why didn't you come back? When tempers weren't so high."

Patrick's voice hitched. "Shame is a powerful force. I hope you never have to feel the way I do."

Silence cloaked the room.

"Patrick," Nolan said, "if I could take back what I did, I would—a thousand times over."

"My shame is my own," Patrick said. "I could have come back and boxed your head and gotten that out of my system. But I could never take back the way I spoke to Pop Paddy."

"He would have forgiven you." All these years. Wasted in mute, taciturn pain. Nolan never knew Patrick felt this way. Even when they'd circled each other during Patrick's infrequent visits with the wider family, Nolan never picked up signals that Patrick's anger was with himself. Nolan's own shame was too thick a veil to see through.

"I couldn't forgive myself," Patrick said. "And then he died while I was off berating myself, too ashamed to come home."

"All this time you've carried this weight." Jillian's voice cradled tenderness.

"I didn't know how to make it right. How could it ever be right for anyone after Pop Paddy died?"

"And you and Dad?" Jillian's voice went breathy. "My whole life and then some."

"I'm sorry for that too," Patrick said. "I wish I'd known you."

"I'm still here." Jillian glanced at Nolan. "You still can."

"Then we'll fix it," Patrick said. "I'm working on amends all around. I'm not very good at it. Just ask Seamus and Nana and Big Seamus. But I know it's time to try."

Nolan pushed beans around his plate. "You're not the only one, Patrick."

"I told you, Nolan. I've stopped hiding behind blaming you."

"But I've been keeping this from Jillian her whole life," Nolan said.

"I told myself I wanted to protect her from the hurt of the past, but I was protecting myself. If I told her the truth, I'd have to let her see my own sense of responsibility."

"Dad." Jillian shifted her eyes to his.

"I know. You're not a child."

She nodded. "I'm a genealogist. Finding the hurt of the past, along with the joy, is kind of my thing. And healing it in family mediation is yours."

"You are not wrong." Nolan's voice seized. "I tell people all the time it's never too late to understand the truth better, even if it doesn't change the circumstances."

"Wow." Patrick leaned back in his chair. "Where did you learn that?"

Nolan met his brother's eyes, the third pair of green orbs in the room. "Bella used to say it when I felt stuck."

"Someday I want you to tell me all about your wife," Patrick said. "I'll bring Grace. You can tell us both."

"Paddy would have liked that."

"I'm going to hold you to it," Jillian said.

Patrick shifted in his chair. "Speaking of grandfathers, I can't stick around to help, but the two of you have to straighten out your friend Tucker. He didn't say vile things to his grandfather like I did, but something happened at the end to ruin their relationship just the same, and you can't let him leave it like that. It'll eat him up like it did me—and you, Nolan."

Nolan nodded. "You're right. Something spoiled it at the end. Something about their last conversation—and then the letter he mentioned and that envelope he's afraid to open. But he loved his grandfather. Maybe there's still time to help him understand the truth better even if it doesn't change the circumstances."

Patrick slapped the table. "There you go."

Beside his plate, Nolan's phone vibrated with a text. "Speaking of Tucker, he wants to bring Laurie Beth and come over."

CHAPTER THIRTY

Maple Turn, Missouri, 2018

How is she doing?" Matthew caught the eye of Sheila, the caregiver he knew would give him the most truthful report.

"The music therapist was here this morning for the group time," Sheila said. "She seemed to really like that. She always does."

"Does she still sing along?"

"Better than most in the group. Especially the old hymns."

"Is she eating?"

Sheila half-smiled. "Meat and dessert."

Matthew nodded. It had been that way for years. For someone who had pestered him about his eating habits for so many years, Jane would no longer abide eating anything she wasn't truly interested in.

He'd kept her at home as long as he could, even hiring a rotating crew of home health workers when he couldn't manage everything on his own. If Jane started to fall, he wouldn't be able to stop her. More likely they would both fall. He could hardly turn his back long enough to fix her a simple microwave meal before she would be into something that could be harmful. There weren't enough high shelves in the house to put everything out of reach, and Jane would just climb for them anyway. Debra had said she would quit her job, move home, and look after both of them, but Matthew refused the offer. Debra didn't know what she would be getting into. That was two years ago, and it was the right decision. Jane's dementia was so advanced even then that she barely noticed that Matthew moved her into a care facility where there were people to look after her around the clock and it was impossible for her to get out of the building and wander the neighborhood in her nightgown and slippers, oblivious to traffic.

Matthew was eighty-six now but still had a driver's license, which he used primarily to go see Jane.

"Where is she now?" he asked Sheila.

"Try as we might, we can't keep her out here in the afternoons any-more. It's not good enough to doze off in the chair like she used to. She insists on lying down."

"She always hated napping."

"The disease changes everything."

"In her room then."

Sheila nodded.

Matthew traipsed down the hall and let himself into Jane's room, grateful that she was there rather than in one of the public areas. If tears broke out of him, he'd rather be in the room.

He had spilled tears often enough for what had become of Jane. Those tears he could spill with his children or Tucker or many friends who knew and loved her.

But these tears—these were for the words he had never spoken to her, the truth he had never told to the one person who mattered most.

Now she would never understand.

And now it was too late for him as well. Too late for truth. Too late for apologies.

Matthew pulled a chair up to her bedside and picked up Jane's hand. She didn't stir. He stroked her hand and then her cheek. She gave no sign of response but only kept breathing deeply and rhythmically.

"Jane, sweetheart," Matthew said, "I'm here."

Only breathing.

Most days she woke for him, even if she didn't recognize him. Some days it was better if he saw her in the common areas so she didn't wonder why there was a man in her room, or some days she might look at him with a prolonged expression while she tried to sort out how she knew him. She might pretend that she remembered him. He might remind her.

"I'm Matthew, your husband."

"I knew that."

But she didn't.

He could tell her now, but she would never keep facts straight from fiction, and there was no predicting what she might say to someone, what isolated bit of conversation she would remember and repeat. That would set off a storm if the wrong person decided there was fact mixed in with what sounded like outrageous fiction. The days of trusted confidence were past.

Two to four months, six at the outside, the doctors told him about his own condition. He didn't have much time. Pancreatic cancer. Not likely a treatable form, and definitely not a treatable location.

Why would he tell her now when he had spared her for more than sixty years? She could not absolve him of anything. She could not redeem any of the stolen lives. Speaking aloud the hideous words to this tender soul would change nothing. If anything, Jane had redeemed him a long time ago with her faith in a good God and resilience to have a good future after her own loss. And they did have a good future. Wasn't that what mattered? He stopped Judd, and they had a good future. Alyce did too—better than if Matthew had left town and let Judd continue.

After Alyce died—not until she was ninety-eight—Matthew unsealed his envelope, which had come to him yellowed and brittle from the hands of an entirely different generation at the law firm where Judd had first left it. At least Judd had told the truth about leaving the envelope. Matthew had his information, scant as it was. But it had not come to him until he was seventy years old, and by then he had let it be.

He couldn't quite imagine saying to Jane and his grown children and their children, "I just found out I was adopted." That wasn't true.

Neither could he say, "I promised to keep my adoption a secret for the last forty-five years because of a hideous family secret you will all wish you didn't know."

No. He'd let it be.

But the room. The way it shredded him. Gnawed at him all the more once Alyce was gone and there was nothing to protect her from. The more hideous secret was that he'd lived another sixteen years and never done anything with it or the information it contained. He'd had his good future, but what about all those other people whose love and futures were stolen? The impossible scale of redemption, of putting everything right, snuck up on him like scattered moments of grief all his life and made him understand his mother's decision simply not to know all those years ago.

The problem with a secret is that the truth of it did not die with the last person who knew it. And as long as that room, with the old files, still stood, the secret lived. As long as anyone who lived anywhere in the country had a whisper of memory of any of those children, the secret lived. The evil lived. The lies lived. The empty cradles lived.

Jane was not going to wake up this afternoon. Matthew kissed her forehead and drove home. He found a padded manila envelope, set out three smaller envelopes, and arranged three keys. Then he began to write.

Dear Tucker...

CHAPTER THIRTY-ONE

I wish you didn't have to go." Jillian kissed her uncle's cheek at the front door.

"Next time I want to hear all about your work." Patrick squeezed her hand. "From what Seamus and Gwen say, it sounds fascinating."

"Next time. I like the sound of that." Patrick had never said those words to her before in her twenty-eight years. No one ever knew when—or if—he'd ever be present at a family event. "And if you don't bring Grace and Brinlee, I shall storm the gates of Seattle."

Patrick laughed. "And I like the sound of that. But I know they'd both love to come for a good long visit with everyone here, and I owe it to them. I've still got some explaining to do to Brinlee, but I'll work on that."

As her father clasped his arms around his brother, something Jillian had never witnessed before, he squeezed his eyes closed. Tears leaked out the corner crevices nevertheless, and Jillian's chest clenched. She sniffed back the sudden drip in her nose.

"Give me a good report to Big Seamus," Nolan said.

"Ma is the one who matters most," Patrick said. "You know that."

Jillian laughed. "All the cousins know Nana is the one!"

A timer went off on Patrick's wrist, and he tapped his watch. "I had to set an alarm. I knew we would stand here and get stuck at this part."

"Get to your meeting," Nolan said, "but call me later. I promise, no more dodging your calls."

"I guess I won't have to break your kneecaps after all."

Jillian and Nolan walked Patrick outside and shivered on the porch as they watched him get in his rental car and pull away. Then Jillian swatted her dad's shoulder.

"See? Isn't this better than declining his calls?"

"So much!" Nolan said. "In penance, I shall go on snow shoveling duty for the rest of the month."

"Right. You watched the forecast last night, didn't you? Warming trend right around the corner is what I heard."

"Might be." Nolan pivoted back into the house. "We've got guests coming."

Jillian followed her father. "I predict Laurie Beth is someone who can appreciate a fine latte when one is placed in her hands."

"At the very least, she'll say she does."

Jillian stuck out her tongue. "I want to show you something serious—about Tucker." She ducked into her office for a folder and pulled out a paper to hand Nolan.

"A vintage retirement press release?" he said.

"Essentially. Over sixty years ago. It's Matthew's father—adoptive father, that is. I got it from a library in St. Louis."

"It's so short."

"And to the point, don't you think?"

"Terse, even."

"Where are the accolades for a man who built a company from the ground up?"

"I looked up Judd's death record," Jillian said. "He didn't die for another twenty years after the date on this release. Why would he suddenly announce retirement and hand his company over to a son who was barely twenty-five when he wasn't particularly in poor health?"

"Interesting question indeed."

"I don't think Tucker knows about this."

"Seems doubtful. But you'll have a chance to tell him soon enough."

Jillian went into her office for the file she had on the Ryder family, which seemed to grow by the day but raised more questions than it answered. The family tree she'd assembled for Tucker had only one branch she could trust—his grandmother Jane's. She knew nothing of the Kintzlers, and news of Matthew's adoption meant questions about his biological family were unanswered—if he was even asking them. The abrupt retirement of Judd. Jackson's reference to Alyce's mental health. The mysterious locked door that nearly ruptured a lifelong friendship. Matthew's wrestling with truth and family. How much of this did Tucker even know?

The breakfast mess in the kitchen would have to wait. Jillian would find the largest clean mugs for her caffeinated creations, and they could sit either in the dining room or living room with Tucker and Laurie Beth. She had supplies lined up just in time when the doorbell sounded, and she turned the machines back on while Nolan went to the door.

Jillian followed him, ready to brightly offer refreshments.

The pair's faces reminded Jillian immediately that they could use fortification, but *bright* was the wrong tone. She hadn't quite made the emotional shift from elation at resolution between her uncle and father to the complexity of what lay ahead now. Nolan took the guests' jackets and gestured toward the sofa, and Jillian offered hot beverages, which they seemed grateful for. She'd been right about Laurie Beth's preference for a latte over black coffee, but it wasn't the time to gloat.

In the kitchen, with her machines grinding beans and whirring to steam and froth milk, Jillian didn't try to hear conversation from the other room. The few bits that wafted in were muted. When Jillian carried in a tray of four generous steaming mugs to distribute, Tucker and Laurie Beth sat on the sofa with strained, exhausted faces but with hands clasped and shoulders leaning in against each other. Whatever familiarity she thought she'd seen between Tucker and Kris faded in comparison. She could easily believe they had been up all night talking, Tucker unburdening himself finally to the person who knew him best, and deciding what to do.

And now they had presented themselves to Nolan and Jillian for help. Jillian sat on the edge of the ottoman, tucked her folder of papers into the purple chair behind her, and picked up her own latte, ready to listen.

"It's hard to know where to start," Tucker said.

Laurie Beth reached out a hand to calm his jiggling knee.

"Take your time," Nolan said.

Jillian raised her mug and sipped coffee laced with Irish Cream syrup, letting the warmth sliding down her gullet occupy her mouth and mind and still her tongue while Tucker's face roiled with uncertainty.

"He had cancer," he finally said. "He didn't tell any of us just how bad it was or what decisions he'd made about not fighting it when the odds were stacked so high against him until there wasn't much time left. I spent time with him, of course, but he waited until the very end, when we were alone one night to say something. It happened one night when the hospice chaplain came to visit. Looking back, I think he made sure the chaplain was coming. Maybe he even called her. The others stepped out, and he asked me to stay. It was so. . .calculated. . .carefully timed, even as sick as he was. Down to the minute."

"Maliciously?" Nolan asked.

Tucker exhaled. "I hope not. But it didn't feel like love. It undid everything."

Laurie Beth reached around and rubbed Tucker's back. "Tell them what he said. Just the way you told me. That's why we're here."

Tucker nodded. "He said it was all a lie, everything the family was built on. Any chance of being happy depended on getting out from under the hideous burden of being afraid of the truth."

"That's a strong phrase," Nolan said.

"I thought he was delirious or something. I didn't feel any burden. What was he talking about? He was in pain, and he wouldn't let them give him morphine until he talked to me, but I thought the disease had gotten to him anyway. Maybe it had moved to his brain. It didn't make any sense."

"And now?" Jillian said.

"The last thing he said was 'Find the letter,' " Tucker said. "Then my mom and her brother and sister came back in. He accepted the morphine, and he died the next morning without being fully conscious again. I never got to ask a single question."

"But you found the letter," Nolan said.

"It wasn't easy," Tucker said. "I almost didn't bother looking at all. I mean, he could have been hallucinating, and I could have been looking for months. Years. For something that might not even exist."

"But you weren't. You found it." Jillian set her mug on a side table, taking no risk of distraction.

"Not for several months. The family funeral. The public memorial. All the condolences. Settling the estate. Getting back to work where the whole company was mourning someone they loved. I felt like I had to be a steadying presence. And he didn't even tell me where to look for the letter. My mother was on her own for so long. She divorced my father for abandonment when I was little. Eventually she heard that he'd died, so at least she knew that much. She ran the company for a while, and she did a good job. Grandpa Matt always said she did. But she met someone and remarried and moved to Europe a couple of years ago. She didn't stay around long after the funeral and the memorial service. My uncle doesn't live in the area either. My aunt spends a lot of time looking after my grandmother, who has dementia. It fell to me to go through a lot of my grandfather's things when I had time. There didn't seem to be a big rush."

"And there it was," Jillian said.

"In a box of old puzzles we used to do together, as if he knew I would be the only one who would care about anything in that particular box. I don't know why he even still had them."

"Sounds like he was a sharp tack even at the end."

"Like I said. Calculated." Tucker opened a palm, and Laurie Beth pulled an ordinary white letter envelope from her handbag and handed it to him. "Maybe I should just read it to you."

"Do you mind if share a few things first? They might help fill in some backdrop." Jillian opened her folder and handed the old press release to Tucker. "Have you ever seen this?"

He scanned it. "Never! Judd retired and appointed Grandpa Matt president of the company. I knew that, but I never realized he was so young. He never wanted to talk about Judd. But considering the letter he left me, it's starting to make sense."

"Your grandfather's favorite Bible verse was John 8:32, right?"

Tucker shrugged. "He never said. How did you know that?"

Jillian handed Tucker the copy of the business journal interview. "You were only a little boy when this came out. I do a lot of reading between the lines in my work. He seemed to struggle to say—or not say—something in this interview about your family. He was wrestling with some piece of truth about your family history right at the core of his being."

Tucker covered his eyes. "If only you knew."

"It had something to do with your great-grandmother Alyce's mental health?"

He moved his hand away from his face. "Why would you say that?"

"Does it?"

He exhaled heavily. "If she knew what my grandfather told me, it could explain a lot. She was already ancient when I knew her as a little boy, but my mother always described her as fragile. She said Grandpa Matt treated her like glass."

"But you don't know why?"

"I'm sure my mother never did. Something happened when Grandpa Matt was young that he never wanted to talk about. He always told my mother that Great-grandma Alyce was entitled to her privacy and not to ask questions."

"Something about a lock and a bricked wall?"

"Wow." Tucker's jaw dropped.

"Talk to Jackson when you get home."

"I told you she was good," Nolan said.

"I haven't figured out what the brick wall has to do with anything—yet," Jillian said, "but maybe between us we have enough pieces to put the picture together."

"Read the letter," Laurie Beth said.

Tucker took a deep breath and began.

Dear Tucker,

I could write many sentimental things about how I feel about you, but I believe I've told you those things often enough while I was still with you. These words are much harder to say.

I have failed in courage every day for seventy years and now bequeath my cowardice to you to redeem. That's not fair. I know that. But I have no choice. You are my only hope for expiation. I will write words here that I have never spoken aloud to anyone, not even your grandmother, whom I loved more than my own breath.

I was not born a Ryder. I know little of where I came from. I do know that my adoption was not a voluntary surrender. And I do know that Judd Ryder was involved with untold numbers of involuntary adoptions—children coerced or outright stolen from parents who loved them and placed for profit in homes that could pay considerable sums. These payments funded the early days of Ryder Manufacturing, until I could ensure they stopped. At least I had the courage to do that much. However, I lacked the fortitude to set right what was so egregiously wrong because of what the man who called himself my father had done on the very premises of the company he founded.

So many children, Tucker. So many families. Yet I did nothing. Am I not complicit in this cruel brokenness across generations? Was I entitled to the sweet life I had with your grandma Jane and your mother and aunt and uncle and grandchildren in my old age when so many others lived out their lives with heartbreak and I might have done something to ease their sorrow?

I could tell you that the reasons are complicated, but in the end, I made the choices I did for benefit that only I will appreciate. It was done for love. I will assure you of that. But it was also at the sacrifice of so many. Hundreds? Thousands? I do not even know. It's all in the room. To get rid of that room would be to erase the lives of all those people, and I just couldn't do it.

I cannot tell you what to do, Tucker. I will only tell you that I have left a sealed packet in the safe at my attorney's office. They will not seek you out. You must go to them. Opening the packet will require great courage. Living with what you see will require even more—and acting on it most of all.

Please, Tucker. Pick up the envelope. You will see for yourself what I am talking about. Then you can decide. May God forgive me.

Your loving grandfather,
Matthew Ryder

Tucker folded the creased and tattered letter.

"A baby-snatching ring?" The wheels of Jillian's mind chugged, trying to make sense of what she had heard. Stolen babies were not entirely unheard of in genealogical circles, and of course everyone in the business knew of figures like Georgia Tann in Memphis, who used a network of social workers, nurses, and judges for a lucrative baby-selling business for decades, including to Hollywood celebrities, or of the networks in Spain or Mexico that took children from unmarried mothers against their will. Even in the United States, every now and then a newspaper article surfaced about a mother and child reunited after decades apart, inevitably replete with quotes from other mothers who believed their children were out there somewhere even though they were told they were dead. But Jillian had never known anyone personally affected by the nefarious activity.

"I think your great-grandma Alyce did know what Judd was doing,"

Jillian said. "And where Matthew came from. That's what made her fragile and why she needed protecting. And Matthew chose to protect her."

"But did she help?" Tucker asked. "Was she in on it?"

"We may never know."

"The room," Nolan said, "do you know what he's talking about?"

Tucker shook his head. "It sounds like he's saying it's in the company building, but I honestly don't know where it could be."

"It's what he argued with Jackson about," Jillian said. "I'd stake my reputation on it."

"Before today I didn't know they ever argued," Tucker said.

"What about the sealed packet? Did you open that last night?"

Laurie Beth spoke up. "I wanted to. Tucker wanted to wait and do it now." She pulled the packet from her bag.

"The answer may be in there." Jillian slid to the edge of her ottoman perch. "Are you ready now, Tucker?"

"It's time." Tucker took the envelope from Laurie Beth and tugged at its seal. He reached inside. "It's like Russian nesting dolls. More envelopes."

Nolan shifted a stack of magazines on the coffee table, and Tucker set down three envelopes in the cleared space. One obviously was another letter in a plain white envelope. The second was larger with more definition. Jillian speculated a stack of five-by-seven photographs. The third was small and clunked slightly when it hit the table.

Tucker picked up the letter. "I guess we start here." He broke the seal with one swipe of a finger.

Dear Tucker,

Thank you. Thank you for being curious or brave enough to come at least this far. The road ahead is rocky, but I know how strong and fearless you are, and I have never seen you shrink from a challenge in your life.

There is a reason why I was stubborn about maintaining a figure-head office even after I passed the reins to your mother and she to you. I was aware of all the mutterings about the waste of space and how shabby the furnishings had become. I hope you are reading this letter because you chose to pick up the packet from the attorney and not because you tried to remodel the office and found the note I taped behind the bookcase imploring you to reconsider my wishes.

Move the large bookcase on the right end of the shelving wall and you will find a door. Go through that door into the small hallway behind it, and you'll see another door. I long ago sealed the direct access to this room from the outside. There were many questions at the time, which I refused to answer. I paid for the work with my personal funds, including bricking over the back of the building, so few people even remember the door was ever there. Jackson will remember, but even he never knew what was in the room. He pestered me about it constantly when we were young, only stopping after I bricked off the outside entrance so he couldn't pick the lock behind my back.

This is the room Judd used. Old man that I am, I emptied that bookcase, moved it, and went through that door to take the photos you'll find with this letter. The keys you need are also here.

Everything is there, Tucker. Judd was nothing if not fastidious. He was not about to be short-changed for his share of this horrid affair. He knew where the children came from and how much money was due him for the service he was providing. Names. Places. It's all there. If anyone had ever tried to cheat him, he had leverage for revenge. And after I ensured he stopped, I'm certain others knew he had what he needed to make sure no one would punish him for quitting. You are far more resourceful than I ever was. I beg God to show you what to do and give you the courage to do it.

I do love you, Tucker. I'm sorry that my final legacy to you is unresolved guilt, a cry for help. But it is not for myself that I cry. When you see the room, you will understand that.

Your grandfather,
Matthew Ryder

Born Dennis Mullins, 1932, St. Louis, Missouri, to Alfred and Rebecca Mullins, wearing a blue knit one-piece gown and matching hat when taken.

"And ye shall know the truth, and the truth shall make you free." (John 8:32)

Jillian gasped.

Tucker's eyes lifted to hers. "He knew who his birth parents were!"

Jillian nodded. "And where. That information opens up all sorts of possibilities."

There would be an original birth certificate, even in the absence of a legal amended document. If Matthew was stolen and not abandoned or otherwise legally surrendered, someone would have had to go to great lengths to also steal and destroy evidence of a signed birth certificate. Perhaps it would have been just as easy to manufacture a second one without destroying the first. It could still exist. A year. A city. Names of parents. It was a lot to go on.

Tucker pulled the smallest envelope toward him and dumped out a set of keys. "I found these in my grandfather's desk once when I was very little. I was just playing, pretending I was the boss, like I sometimes did. He came in from a meeting and yelled at me. *Yelled* at me. He never did that."

"I guess now you understand his reaction."

Tucker nodded and blew out his breath. "That just leaves looking at the pictures." He broke the final seal.

An old wooden four-drawer file cabinet filled with files. Handwritten financial records. Bunks. Clothing. Bedding. Twin sinks. Cracked tile.

"It's like looking at a museum exhibit." Laurie Beth's blue eyes were wide, unblinking.

"I can't believe Grandpa Matt went in there to take these photos," Tucker said. "My mother would have had his head if she knew he was moving furniture on his own when he was so sick. Or even at his age."

"He knew he was out of time," Jillian said.

Laurie Beth reached for Tucker's hand. "Jillian, can you help find Matthew's birth family?"

"Please," Tucker said.

"He did leave some good leads," Jillian said. Between social media and ancestry search sites, along with public records, it could be fast, but Jillian didn't want to get Tucker's hopes up.

Nolan set down the last of the photos. "And the rest of it?"

Tucker wiped one hand across his eyes. "It's so much to absorb. I have to think."

"All the money you've been spending and leaving around town,"

Nolan said, "it was because of your grandfather's letter?"

"It's filthy." Tucker clenched his fists. "How my great-grandfather got it and used it to build Ryder Manufacturing in the first place—how was I supposed to want to have anything to do with that money?"

Jillian picked up a photo of a bunk with a child's blanket still neatly folded at the foot. "And now that you know more about what your grandfather wanted?"

Tucker shook his head and could only repeat, "I have to think."

CHAPTER THIRTY-TWO

Normally Nolan was the one pulling Jillian away from slaving at her computer on Saturdays, but the unexpected events had chewed up so much of the week that he could see the virtue of trying at least to organize the wreckage of his work schedule and find a reset point for when Monday rolled in. His email inbox was out of control, and the pile of reading he'd brought home from his office in Denver languished untouched. In sweatpants, a long-sleeved T-shirt, and his gray-and-red plaid flannel robe, he was doing triage in his home office before the wintry dawn cast pink and golden hues over the mountains.

He liked the placid time, the only sounds the muffled depressions his fingers made on keys, the rustle of papers he flipped, the slurp of black coffee between his lips, the squeak of his desk chair as he rotated or leaned back, the furnace as it cycled on to warm the house to a daytime temperature. Even as he worked, it was good to feel present to the task before him. Nolan drained his coffee mug about the time he had his inbox down to the last two dozen unread messages.

What was that noise? It wasn't a house sound or anything he was doing. He held still, his head cocked to one side to listen.

There it was again. Knocking. Softly.

It was crazy early in the morning though. A few diehards might be out for a run, even before sunrise and even in the cold, but it would still be a couple of hours before Canyon Mines would come to life.

Yet the sound was there. A branch perhaps? The wind had kicked up overnight. Something might have broken and could be rubbing a window downstairs. Nolan would have a look once daylight was on his side.

The knocking subsided. He clicked open another email. Then a second and a third. The end was in sight. He could have some more coffee, maybe a bit of breakfast, settle in for a reading session, and still have most of the day free.

And the crash came.

Nolan jumped out of his chair.

In the hall, Jillian was rubbing sleep out of her eyes. "What in the world?"

"I'll investigate," Nolan said. "Let me get something on my feet."

Jillian followed him to his bedroom. "An animal?"

"Maybe." Nolan slid his feet into comfortable Saturday loafers and tied his robe closed. "Sounded like it was on the porch."

"Could be gone by now." Jillian followed him down the stairs.

"Stay right there," Nolan said when they reached the bottom.

"I'm not afraid of an animal, Dad."

This is what he got for raising such an independent child. She never obeyed anymore.

"I don't hear anything," Jillian said.

Nolan flipped the light switch beside the front door, and the porch outside lit up.

Something rustled.

With one knee in the sofa, Jillian leaned over it and pushed a curtain aside to peer out. "It's Tucker!"

Nolan turned the dead bolt and opened the door.

Tucker stopped midmotion and stared up at him, one of the porch wicker chairs in his hands.

"I'm sorry," Tucker said. "I was trying to wait for daylight, but I got impatient and knocked lightly just in case you were up. Then I accidentally tipped over the metal end table and tripped over a chair in the process."

Jillian's hand was on Nolan's shoulder. "You've been sitting out here in the dark? For how long?"

"Long time."

"Come in," Nolan said. "We're up now, and you must be half frozen. Jillian, make him something hot to drink."

"Finally, somebody appreciates my talents." Jillian went through the kitchen door. Nolan was fairly certain she would take the opportunity to dash up the back stairs and change into something slightly more socially presentable than the old high school track sweats she slept in.

"You don't have to worry." Tucker shirked out of his jacket. "Today

I'm going to pack up my skis to ship home. I won't be doing anything else ludicrous while I'm in Canyon Mines."

"I'll be honest and say I'm glad to hear that," Nolan said.

"Laurie Beth and I talked all day after we left here, and I was up all night—even before I acted like a prowler on your porch. I guess I should be glad none of the neighbors called the police."

"Sound sleepers. But it doesn't sound like you've slept much the past couple of nights."

"I can't get those pictures out of my head. I think I have every detail memorized."

"It's a lot to take in."

"Great-grandma Alyce. I was nine when she died. So I have some memories of her. She was always really old, but I thought she was sweet. How could she have anything to do with stealing babies? With stealing Grandpa Matt?"

"I'm sure you have a lot of questions you wish you could ask," Nolan said. "Maybe your grandfather had some answers, but I suspect he lived with many unanswered questions as well."

"I wish I could know what he meant by making choices for benefit that only he would appreciate," Tucker said. "But in the end, it comes down to whether I trust who my grandfather was, even if I don't know all the answers."

"And do you?"

Tucker nodded.

Jillian returned, wearing a pair of jeans and a hoodie and carrying a tray with coffee for all three of them.

"Thanks, Jillian." Tucker gripped the large mug she handed him. "Have I mentioned I think you make fantastic coffee? Just the right amount of steamed milk. I've never seen the point of putting cold milk into a hot beverage."

Jillian laughed. "We are entirely simpatico on that point. Now what have I missed?"

"I think Tucker has come to some decisions," Nolan said. "Am I right?"

"You are," Tucker said. "But I need your help. Both of you."

"That's all we've wanted to do."

"What happened to all those families is terrible. My great-grandparents are gone. Anybody of their age bracket would be as well.

There's probably no one left to bring to justice legally."

"Doubtful," Nolan said.

"But if it's true that Judd used dirty money—probably laundering it on top of the ugly way he got it—to build Ryder Manufacturing, maybe it's not too late to find a way to use the money in some way to help families find some truth. What if I could find a way to clean that money after all this time?"

"I'm with you so far," Nolan said.

"Me too," Jillian said.

"Good." Tucker drank more coffee. "I think I just might thaw out after all."

"What exactly do you want us to do?" Jillian said.

"For starters, I want a real family tree. No more secrets. I'm going to have to tell my family what Grandpa Matt has told me. They're going to be just as shocked as I am, of course. But they're also going to be just as curious about the way he signed that second letter."

"Born Dennis Mullins, 1932," Jillian said.

Tucker nodded. "He had his birth parents' names. Surely that's something to start with."

"It is."

"So you'll try?"

"I will."

Tucker exhaled. "That's the easy part."

"There's more?"

"The room. The files."

"I don't understand." Jillian scrunched her face.

"I do," Nolan said. "The drawers are full of files. Whatever information is in them is the only starting point anyone has for reconnecting what was broken in all those families."

"Exactly," Tucker said. "I want to pack it all up and make sure you get it, Jillian. Or you should come to Maple Turn and see for yourself if there's anything there worth bringing back. I'll put you on retainer to try to use any information at all to piece together the broken family lines."

"That could be a massive job—and time-consuming."

"I know. But you must know some other genealogists you could subcontract."

"Yes, plenty. But we'd hit a lot of dead ends. The information is old, and under the circumstances it's sure to be incomplete or cryptic or even some kind of code."

"That may all be true. So just focus on the leads that are not dead ends. Will you do it?"

"Wow." Jillian ran her hands through her hair. "I can try. Once we see the actual files, I'll have a better idea if anything is feasible."

"Fair enough." Tucker turned to Nolan. "Will you help with legalities?"

"What legalities do you have in mind?"

"This might be a hard sell with my family, but I want to divest myself of my share of the ownership in Ryder Manufacturing and use the money to begin a foundation. I can't speak for anyone else, because there are other heirs who own parts of the company. I can't force them to give up a good chunk of their net worth. I also can't just close the place down, because a lot of people in town depend on Ryder for employment, and we have to keep the pensions funded and all that sort of thing. And I won't risk selling it either, and have some corporate owner decide in a year or two that it's not profitable enough to keep open. But I can work on changing the financial structuring—at least my share in it. I can do what seems reasonable to take back out whatever ill-gotten money went into the business in the first place, with interest. Maybe I can find some way to buy out the others or convince them to contribute to the foundation. It would take some time, and I'll have to get some serious financial advice, but that's the general direction."

"A foundation," Nolan said. "I like it."

"To reunite families," Tucker said. "Pay for DNA testing. Travel expenses for face-to-face meetings of descendants. Help with medical expenses for any elderly stolen babies still alive. Others could be sick like my grandfather was. There might even still be a few parents, although that would be a stretch. We could find some descendants to serve on the board and help figure out what we should be doing."

"You'll want to protect yourself and the company from legal liability."

"That's why I need lawyers," Tucker said.

"I have a couple law school classmates who are practicing in Missouri now. I can at least put you in touch."

"I want you involved in some way," Tucker said. "I trust you."

"I can be an adviser," Nolan said, "but you need people licensed with the bar in Missouri."

"We'll work it out then." Tucker stood. "That's really all I came for."

"Do you want breakfast?" Nolan said.

Tucker shook his head. "I'm staying at a bed-and-breakfast, remember? It's Saturday."

"Nia's french toast cream cheese casserole," Jillian said.

"Right. And I don't want to miss Laurie Beth's face when she tastes it for the first time."

Nolan walked Tucker to the door. Once it was closed, he turned to Jillian. "I'm sorry for how he toyed with Kris, but he seems genuinely bound to Laurie Beth."

"I agree on both counts." Jillian gathered the empty mugs. "Do you think any of this can really be done?"

"Maybe, maybe not. Matthew probably knew it was a long shot after all these years. But perhaps he also knew Tucker is a long-shot kind of guy, among all the members of his family."

"If it turns out the files have any decent leads, I can call Eloise, Sally, Charlotte, and Elsa."

"That was fast thinking."

"They are the most dogged, determined genealogists I know."

"Besides you."

"Besides me." Jillian brandished a grin.

"I need breakfast," Nolan said, "unless we're going to crash Nia's dining room."

"She'd kick you out. She's full up this weekend."

"Fine. I'll make us some ordinary french toast then."

Nolan hardly had the bread out and the eggs and milk whisked together before Jillian came out of her office with her laptop.

"Look," she said.

Nolan squinted. "What am I looking at?"

"Census record for Alfred and Rebecca Mullins in 1930."

"That was fast!"

"I got lucky. They could have been anywhere, or at least in any county in Missouri, before Matthew was born. But they were right there in

St. Louis all this time."

"Oh my. And this place where Tucker lives? Maple Turn?"

"Not more than thirty miles."

Nolan set down his spatula, stabbed with fresh heartache. "Very daring. To take a child and keep him so close. Suppose he grew up looking just like his birth father and was recognized. If Judd and Alyce wanted a child for themselves, why not keep one from farther away?"

Jillian shrugged. "Perhaps there were special circumstances?"

"More unanswered questions."

"They had other children, Dad. Older children who were born before 1930 and are listed in the census. Three girls."

"Still alive?"

"That's what I'll have to find out. They'd all be in their nineties. But they could be alive."

CHAPTER THIRTY-THREE

Nia and Leo must have risked leaving their brand-new employee in charge of the inn for a couple of hours, because they were both in church on Sunday morning. Jillian sat wedged between Nia and her father, doing her best to pay attention to the morning's order of service. Instrumentation relied on an accomplished pianist, a couple of guitars, a bass player, and rotating other musicians. Today there was a flute and violin, which Jillian especially liked. Musical selections blended hymns and contemporary choices in an effort to have something for everyone. Prayers and scripture readings were interspersed with the music as the service moved toward the sermon.

Nia leaned over and whispered, "That's the second time your phone has vibrated."

"I didn't hear it." Jillian reached into the purse she only carried on Sundays and special occasions, and pulled the phone from a side pouch. Sure enough, a tiny icon showed two missed calls. If the caller hadn't even left a voice mail, how urgent could it be? Jillian tucked the phone back in place.

The music ended, and the children's sermon began. Twenty kids under the age of ten ran, paraded, or straggled to the front of the sanctuary to see what interactive lesson a children's ministry leader had in store this week. Sometimes this was Jillian's favorite part of the service, and she was sure she wasn't alone.

Five minutes later, her phone was at it again.

On the other side of Nia, Leo leaned forward and pushed his glasses on top of his head as he stared at Jillian. She grabbed her phone and swiftly declined the call. This time she also fiddled with other settings so her phone wouldn't audibly vibrate.

The children were dismissed from their message, and the congregation stood to sing a short song before settling in for the main sermon. Ten minutes in, the phone flashed signals of an incoming call despite being silenced.

"Why did you do that?" Nolan whispered.

"I didn't realize I had." Jillian grabbed the phone again. At least the song covered the commotion.

"Maybe you'd better just take the call," Nia muttered.

"Please," Nolan mumbled.

Jillian snatched her purse, excused herself past the others in the pew, and hustled out to the narthex. By then the call had expired—again without a voice mail. Jillian looked at her recent call history. All four calls during the worship service came from the same unfamiliar number. Her phone was sure to ring again if she didn't try to reach the caller now.

She tapped the number to call it back.

"This is Jillian Parisi-Duffy," she said when a woman answered. "I've received several calls from this number in the last few minutes."

"Thanks for calling back. I tried to leave a message, but your voice mail box is full. I thought if I kept calling you might pick up."

"I'm sorry. I wasn't aware. I'll take care of that. May I ask who's calling?"

"My name is Flor Childers. I understand you're looking for me on a personal matter."

Flor Childers. Jillian's brain indexed the lists of names she'd pored over the day before in various birth, death, and marriage records. Flor. Flora.

Flora, youngest child of Teresa Mullins Watts. She hadn't yet connected the name Childers to the thread. It must be a married name. Male lines with the family name would have been so much easier to track, but the Mullins family had three daughters, all born before 1930. If they'd married in the midcentury, it would have been long before women keeping their own names was in vogue, so it was unlikely there were any Mullinses to track directly through that name. Mullins was hardly a distinctive name anyway. She'd spent hours combing records, trying to find connections in and around St. Louis that might be right, knowing all along that the odds were that most of the family had dispersed from the region.

"Hello? Are you there?" Flor said.

"Yes!" Jillian said. "Sorry. I'm just so surprised to hear from you."

"I don't usually return messages that come to me through the hospital. If this is about a patient, I probably cannot help you directly."

"No, it's something else. Was your mother Teresa Mullins?"

"That's right. How did you find me? And why were you even looking for me?"

Jillian wandered away from the speakers that carried the pastor's voice into the narthex and sank into a high-backed upholstered chair. "I'm a genealogist. It's a long story."

Flor was silent for a few seconds and then said, "A genealogist. Do you find lost family members and things like that?"

"Yes. I do."

Jillian heard the breath leave Flor's chest.

"Is this about Dennis?" Flor said.

Jillian's heart pounded. "Yes."

Three heavy breaths. "You'd better tell me then. The family has been waiting a long time for a call like this. I never imagined I'd be the one. Not after all these years."

For once in her life, Jillian was glad she had a purse. Somewhere in its caverns were a pen and a small notebook, and if she could remember to write things down during this conversation, she wouldn't have to trust her memory later while relating what she learned to Tucker and Laurie Beth.

She told what she knew, which was far less than what she learned. Still, she knew that the notes she scribbled were only the beginning.

"I have to go to work," Flor finally said. "I had no idea what I was getting into when I called or I would have made arrangements, but I'm the charge nurse and they need me."

"I'll email you about setting up a time to Skype." Jillian flipped her notebook closed just as the sanctuary doors opened and the first worshippers exited.

"At the very first opportunity," Flor said.

Nia, Leo, and Nolan set their sights on her. Jillian put her things away in the unfamiliar bag that had rescued her with its supplies.

"I found someone!" she said.

Her father's eyes widened.

"Since yesterday?" Nia said. "I didn't even know you were that good."

"Neither did I." Jillian stood and straightened her shirt. "I made a lot of wild guesses yesterday and threw a lot of stuff at the wall to see what might stick. Honestly, I didn't think anything would—not this fast. Cold calls hardly ever pay off so quickly."

"Well done!" Nolan said. "I suspect your wild guesses were actually years of practiced intuition."

"With a little help from the Holy Spirit," Jillian said. "Tucker really needs this. Where is he today?"

"Not skiing," Nia said, "but he and Laurie Beth went for a long drive. Meandering, they called it. She's in love with our mountains."

"Who can blame her?" Nolan said.

"We gave them a key," Leo said. "They might not be back until very late."

"Then I'll have to call." Jillian reached for her phone. "This can't wait."

Nolan put a hand on her arm. "It'll have to wait. They need this time together. Let them soak up some Colorado beauty and have this day together before they go back to what they have to deal with."

Jillian met his gaze and drew a deep breath. "Okay, but first thing tomorrow."

"Come for breakfast," Nia said.

"I will. But don't tell him! I want to do it."

Nia turned up her palms. "What would I tell him? You haven't even told me."

Nolan, of course, pumped her for information over homemade tomato soup and four-cheese grilled sandwiches at the granite breakfast bar at home. The news caused him to let loose with the "Se Il Mio Nome Saper Voi Bramate" aria from Rossini's *Barber of Seville*. He hadn't sung that one in years, but he still knew the words. This father of hers was full of surprises. It was an appropriate choice for the engaged couple who would hear the news tomorrow. *A heart I give to you, a loving soul, that loyally and constantly for you only sighs like this from dawn till the end of day.*

Jillian was at the Inn at Hidden Run before Tucker and Laurie Beth came downstairs in the morning—even before Nia finished putting out the breakfast buffet for the handful of guests who hadn't checked out by Sunday afternoon. Nia always gave herself an easy morning on Mondays after going full-tilt on the weekends, so the menu featured assorted pastries from Ben's Bakery, whole fruit to reduce both effort and waste, and scrambled eggs, which Joelle had been trained to make with a dash of water—no milk—and Nia's signature splash of vanilla. Although the long dining room table wouldn't be full, Nia had gone to extra lengths to set a separate small table in one corner of the dining room with three places—and the good china and crystal.

"Nia," Jillian said, "it's lovely."

"It's a celebration," Nia said. "I know just how you all like your eggs, so I'll make them myself."

"Then I guess I'll wait."

"Well, there you have it."

Jillian chose a chair, tapped her toes, fiddled with her phone, reviewed the notes she'd scribbled, went over the family tree she'd been able to fill in so far—especially after talking to Flor—and generally tried not to disturb the splendor of Nia's table with her impatience.

Tucker and Laurie Beth entered the dining room together, the last of the guests to come downstairs. Their mountain meandering must have kept them out late enough to use Leo's key the night before. The guests at the main table buzzed with their own conversation as the pair came in hand in hand.

"Jillian!" Laurie Beth cried. "What's all this?"

"Come sit down," Jillian said. "I have news."

Tucker held Laurie Beth's chair, something Jillian couldn't remember seeing him do for Kris, now that she thought about it. They took the cloth napkins and spread them in their laps.

"This is a fancy table for breakfast," Tucker said.

"This is a fancy day," Jillian said. "I spoke to someone yesterday who is very eager to meet you."

"Who?"

"Already?" Laurie Beth said.

"Let me back up just a little. Your grandfather had three older sisters, all born in the late 1920s."

"Are any of them still alive?" Hope suffused Tucker's face.

"I'm afraid not," Jillian said, "but they all had children and grandchildren. There's quite a bountiful family. I spoke to a woman name Flora Childers, who is Matthew's niece."

"My mother's cousin," Tucker said. "She always wished she had cousins on Grandpa Matt's side."

"She has quite a few, actually. Between the three sisters, Flor says there were eleven grandchildren."

"And Grandpa Matt had three. That's fourteen cousins."

"And two generations after that." Jillian pulled a sheet of paper from a folder. "This may be the fastest family tree I've ever put together. All the birth dates are not there, but Flor gave me everyone's names. Tucker, someday I'd love to help you with the Kintzler question too, but right now we have the answers about your grandfather's biological family."

"Never in my wildest dreams did I imagine you'd do this so fast."

"Neither did I. But sometimes it just takes breaking through one wall. I'm glad it happened that way—for you. You can go home with some answers, at least." Perhaps this start would give him hope for what was to come. And sustenance for the journey.

"Where does Flor live?"

"Springfield, Missouri. She said quite a few of the family still live in various parts of Missouri or southern Illinois. You can meet them in person if you want to. In the meantime, she'd like to get some of them together for a Skype call. Would you like to do that?"

"How soon?" Tucker nearly jumped out of his chair.

"Flor is available tomorrow morning."

"Then so am I."

Nia swooped in balancing three plates. "Celebration eggs all around!"

"I'm Skyping my long-lost cousins tomorrow." Tucker beamed.

"Well, there you have it."

They set up to Skype the next day in Jillian's office, where it was quieter than the Inn and where Tucker could take advantage of the large monitor to see all the faces on the screen.

"I let Flor know the call would come from your Skype ID." Jillian tapped the back of her chair, inviting Tucker to sit. "Laurie Beth and I will sit right across the desk if you need anything."

Nolan cleared his throat in the doorway.

"And of course my dad is hovering, as he likes to do."

"You didn't think I would miss this, did you?" Nolan said.

"Just don't sing in the middle of it." Jillian shook her finger at him.

He wagged his errant eyebrow.

Jillian's office had needed a thorough cleaning, and this was just the occasion to motivate her last night. The desk was clutter-free, the shelves dusted, and the keyboard devoid of food crumbs.

Tucker sat in Jillian's chair, and Laurie Beth leaned over for a kiss before taking a seat beside Jillian across the desk. They both watched the concentration in Tucker's face as he logged into Skype and initiated a call to Flor's ID.

A few seconds later a voice said, "Hello? Is that Tucker?"

His breath caught and his eyes darted around the screen. "It is. Wow." He raised a finger to count heads on the screen. "Twelve of you."

"I'm Flor. I spoke to your friend Jillian. Everybody wanted to be here, but this is all that could manage their schedules."

"It's quite a turnout on such short notice." Tucker's Adam's apple seemed to get stuck. "I'm touched. I don't know what to say."

"He looks like Gramps, don't you think?" another voice said.

Laurie Beth raised a hand to cover her mouth. Jillian gripped her other hand.

"That's my sister Taryn," Flor said. "And yes, you do look a bit like our grandfather."

"Alfred," Tucker said.

"That's right. I see it most around the eyes."

Flor made introductions of representatives from three generations.

"People always said I looked like my grandfather." Tucker lifted his phone. "I have a photo here, one of my favorites."

"That's Dennis?" Flor said.

Tucker nodded. "He was Matthew to us, but at the end he knew he was Dennis. That's how we found you."

"I have some pictures too."

Tucker hunched toward the screen. It was all Jillian could do to stay in her chair and not go around the desk to gawk at what someone in Missouri was holding up for Tucker to view. Matthew's parents. His sisters as they grew through the years. Masses of cousins through the generations.

"I want you to know something," Flor said at the end of the photo narration. "I thought a lot about this since Sunday, and I think it's important. Our grandparents never gave up on Dennis. Never. He was always loved, even in absence. They were never afraid or ashamed to speak his name. Our mother continued the traditions. We remembered his birthday every year growing up, because we knew he was out there somewhere, and we prayed for his safety and happiness."

"Even when our parents were gone," Taryn said, "we girls still prayed for Dennis. He was always our uncle, our mother's brother."

"He never knew," Tucker said. "But I'm sure he wondered. I only wish I could tell him now."

"It's too late to tell him," Flor said, "but we can tell you what happened—if you want to know, the way our mother told us."

"Yes!" Tucker's voice cracked and his face pinched, but he nodded.

"They were all little when it happened. They lived not too far from the church, only a few blocks, and he was such a good baby that Grams thought it would be all right to take him to a ladies' meeting when he was three weeks old. She was ready to get out of the house, I think. That's what Mother always said. It was only for an hour or so. On the way home, there was a young woman carrying packages, and she stumbled and dropped them. Of course Grams wanted to help, so she took her hands off the pram just for a bit to help pick them up. It can't have been more than half a minute in broad daylight. She realized later it was an intentional diversion, but in those few seconds, the baby was gone from the pram."

Tucker squeezed his eyes between thumb and forefinger, heaving breath.

"Our oldest aunt," Flor continued, "claimed there was someone else no one else saw. A man in a dark suit. He must have taken Dennis. They couldn't see where he could have disappeared to so quickly. Maybe an alley or into a doorway. No one else on the street just then remembered seeing him, and the word of a five-year-old didn't count for anything."

"So fast!" Tucker said. "They must have been lying in wait, looking for someone with a baby who was vulnerable, susceptible."

"Grams was so sure the new baby was going to be a boy after three girls that she knitted a blue gown and cap and had it ready three months before Dennis was born. Gramps was so pleased to have a son. After they lost Dennis, Grams and Gramps never wanted another baby. It was bad enough they lost him, but the accusations were awful."

"Accusations?" Tucker said.

"That they were unfit parents or they wouldn't have lost him. That Grams was neglectful. That maybe the girls should have been taken into care for their own good. That perhaps they had even killed him and made up the story. But none of that was true. It was a happy home. They all said so."

Laurie Beth's tears splashed across flushed cheeks. Tucker's breath caught with every rise of his chest.

"I can't tell you what this means to me," he said. "I want to meet you all when I get home."

"We'll organize a proper family reunion in your honor," Flor said. "You'll fit right in. You'll see. Bring anyone else who wants to come."

Tucker's eyes raised above the monitor to hold Laurie Beth's. "I'll start with the woman who will be the mother of my own children."

It took another five minutes and a dozen more promises for Flor and Tucker to bring themselves to end the call. As soon as they did, Laurie Beth shot out of her chair and into Tucker's arms.

Nolan came out of the shadows and slung an arm around Jillian.

"I just did something Grandpa Matt would have loved to do." Tucker's throaty voice was barely audible. "And when I get back to Missouri, I will do something else he always wanted to do. I may never fully understand his reasons for not doing it, but I shouldn't have doubted him. He wanted to, and it tore him apart that he couldn't. People always say, 'Peace to his memory.' I'm going to make sure that means something."

Laurie Beth stroked his cheek. "Let's go home and get to work. Tomorrow."

CHAPTER THIRTY-FOUR

Keep up, old man." Jillian zipped her perfectly warm jacket up to her chin and pulled her blue knit cap snug around her ears. "I don't intend to miss saying goodbye because of a slowpoke."

"They're not going to leave without saying goodbye to us."

"They do have a plane to catch."

"There will be other planes."

"I'm leaving." Jillian went out the back door.

"Hey! Wait for me."

The door closed behind Jillian. Nolan was still getting his arms into his jacket as she set her stride. Crunching over snow in boots would be slower than a spring walk, but she wanted to burn off built-up nervous energy. Events of the last week were simultaneously exhausting, exhilarating, breathtaking, daring, distracting, mind-boggling.

So many words.

"How are you doing, Silly Jilly?" Nolan caught up and fell in step.

"Well, Dad, a little like I'm going down Hidden Run blind. Stolen babies! I was incredibly blessed to find Matthew's family in one day because I had the name of his parents and a good guess of where they lived, but it won't be like that with all the others."

"I know."

"Judd Ryder would have had good reason to protect himself with the way he kept his records, not look out for the kids."

"Again, right."

"But we can't just walk away from Tucker, not after all this."

"I know that too."

"So we're going to do it, aren't we, Dad?"

"Yes, we are. To the best we can, Jilly, to the best we can."

Jillian looped an arm through her dad's. "Have I mentioned lately how awesome I think you are?"

"Nope. Only how slow you think I am."

"Well, work on that." Jillian stepped off the sidewalk into a mound of snow and kicked up a flurry of white toward her father.

"Hey!"

Jillian stayed ahead of her father for the remaining blocks to the bed-and-breakfast, determined not to let him know how much effort it took. She hadn't had a good run since cold weather set in. He was a year-round power walker and, of late, a skier, and his skills stood up well to her youth.

It felt good to laugh as they tumbled up the steps to the Inn and through the front door.

Nia looked up from behind the reception desk in the parlor. "What's gotten into you two?"

"Oh, just the usual," Nolan said.

"That's what scares me." Nia threw her long dark braid over her shoulder. "They're in the dining room. I suspect Laurie Beth might be loading up her carry-on with extra scones and thinks I haven't noticed."

"I knew I liked her." Jillian passed the pile of luggage in the hall signaling the imminent departure.

"You made it!" Tucker's grin matched his relaxed shoulders, and he and Nolan exchanged a slap-style handshake.

"We just wanted to say again that we are all in with you," Jillian said. "Whatever we can do to help, we'll try, or we'll find the right people."

"I know it's all an incredible long shot." Tucker's features sobered. "Getting the best advice I can is the first step, and we'll figure it out from there."

"That's exactly the spirit," Nolan said.

They all turned their heads toward a knock. Kristina stood at the entrance to the dining room.

"Kris!" Jillian pivoted and closed the few yards between them. They stepped into the hall.

"I heard Tucker was leaving today," Kris said softly.

"Small town."

"Yep. Do you think it would be all right if I talked to him?"

Jillian glanced over her shoulder at Tucker and Laurie Beth. "Actually, I think it would be good for him." *And you.*

Jillian stepped back into the dining room and caught Tucker's eye and beckoned with a couple of fingers. He looked past her at Kris, leaned over to whisper something in Laurie Beth's ear before kissing her cheek, and then came toward the hall.

"I'll. . .let you two. . .whatever." Jillian got out of the way. From the far end of the dining room, Laurie Beth's wide blue eyes watched, and Jillian went to her.

"It's okay," Laurie Beth said.

"I'm glad to hear you say that." Jillian gave Laurie Beth's shoulder a squeeze. "He loves you."

"I know. I feel bad for Kris. So does Tucker. I hope he's apologizing."

"So he told you?"

"Everything. He just didn't know what to say to Kris—and everything else has been so overwhelming. But I think he would have called or written to her eventually."

"He's a good man, Laurie Beth."

"Of course he is. He just lost his way for a few days while he was here. It can happen to any of us. That's why we all need each other."

"And you are a wise woman."

Tucker and Kris embraced. Kris wiped her eyes, turned, and left without seeking out Jillian. Perhaps later she would want to tell Jillian about her final conversation with Tucker. If so, Jillian would listen. If not, Jillian would be still and present for her friend.

Nolan unfolded a half sheet of paper and had it ready when Tucker returned.

"Here's contact information for two attorneys I've known for thirty years," Nolan said. "They went into practice together after law school. You should hear from them soon, but if you don't, feel free to reach out."

"This is great." Tucker read the names before refolding the paper and stowing it in his wallet. "Thank you for talking to them."

"Expect that this could take some time," Nolan said. "Be patient. Remember that you are the client. Your attorneys will want to protect Ryder Manufacturing, protect your family, protect you, set up the foundation properly. We won't really know the extent of things until you see the files for yourself and get some help interpreting them. There could be hundreds of people affected—even thousands. Some limitations will have to apply for the restitution you can offer."

"I understand."

"It's not an area of law I claim expertise in. Even my law school class-mates are likely to seek other expert counsel, considering the unique and complex circumstances."

"Of course."

"And there will be publicity. Once the nature of the foundation becomes known, it will be difficult to contain the story."

Tucker blinked. "I hadn't really thought about that."

"You'll figure it out. Just get help at every turn."

"I will." Tucker reached for Laurie Beth's hand. "The most important thing is that I have what my grandfather never got. Truth. Information. Faces. No more lies—or untold truths—in the family. No more secret rooms."

" 'And ye shall know the truth,' " Jillian said, " 'and the truth shall make you free.' "

"I think that's what Grandpa Matt wanted most of all. To be free and stand in the truth. It makes me sad that I'll never know for sure what held him back."

"He'd be so proud of you now," Laurie Beth said.

Nia came in. "Not that I don't love having you here, but don't you two have a plane to catch?"

Tucker grabbed his jacket. "Absolutely! Are you ready, my beautiful bride-to-be?"

"The wedding!" Jillian said.

"Watch your mail," Laurie Beth said. "It's still a few months off, but you are definitely on the list!"

"Too bad you aren't staying just a little longer," Nia said. "Veronica and Luke's winter party theme is right up your alley."

Jillian and Nolan stared at her.

"You know the theme?" Jillian said.

"Uh-oh." Nia clamped her hand over her mouth.

"You can't take it back now," Jillian said.

"I found out by accident. But Marilyn said it was Tucker's idea to do something with those old photos of Veronica's grandfather's cousin and the old ski resorts. She's going to start by displaying them at the party for her ski theme. Then they're going to use your postcard idea and sell them around town."

"Those boxes came from Veronica's family?" Jillian's mouth hung open in disbelief.

"Some third cousin or something," Nia said, "who lives higher up in the mountains."

Tucker laughed. "Then I guess my work in Canyon Mines is finished."

In a cyclonic burst of activity, Tucker loaded luggage into his rental truck, and he and Laurie Beth headed toward Denver.

"I don't know about you," Nolan said, "but I have a hankering for some ice cream."

Jillian smiled. How Kris was feeling was on her dad's mind as well. "Well, we are halfway there. Might as well."

"Then let's go."

"But no singing."

AUTHOR'S NOTE

While I was growing up, my grandmother's sister was one of my favorite parts of visiting my grandparents. Aunt Lennie was a ball of spunk and personality, and she'd pile us into her boat of a car and take us down to the main street of the small town where my mother grew up for dime store shopping and drugstore treats. I don't remember how old I was before I realized the sisters also had a brother. I don't recall ever meeting him. A shroud hung over the reasons why. When I was older and understood more, I could also see the shame factor at play.

Even a little closer to my story, after both of my parents were gone, my siblings had opportunity to talk about pieces of what we didn't know or understand very well about our own loving father. Something similar happened when my father-in-law died, and his sisters shared details of a defining season of his young adulthood that his children had never known. The silences and gaps were best explained by shades of shame and pieces of the past that parents don't always feel their children need to know.

As a parent, I understand that.

Yet as any person who has experienced shame knows—which is all of us—shame is a powerful shaper of our personal stories and certainly has the potential to shape the generations as well, even when shame is undeserved. It separates branches of the family. It shuts down conversation. It leaves questions unanswered. It reframes the narrative to something more bearable even if less truthful.

The silences and gaps in our generational stories may also remind us that we don't always understand the reasons for the choices others make—and we may never. Our responsibility is to wrestle through our obligations to be truthful with ourselves first of all and in that truth find the courage to frame our choices in love.

Matthew Tucker and his adoptive parents are fictional, but the pain Matthew experienced—and Judd inflicted—reflects true facts and a true range of emotions associated with them, including shame. Perhaps the most famous baby snatcher in American history was Georgia Tann, a Tennessee social worker who took advantage of the lack of regulation around adoption in the early decades of the twentieth century and began selling children stolen from poor families for large sums of money to wealthy adoptive parents. Her clients included Hollywood legends, such as Lana Turner, June Allyson, and Joan Crawford. Most clients had no idea that the children she placed had not been voluntarily surrendered by their birth parents. In fact, Tann had a network of doctors, nurses, social workers, and judges who handled every phase of finding children—sometimes literally from the sidewalk—transporting them, falsifying documents, moving them between locations, placing them in homes, collecting fees, and legalizing the adoptions without ever verifying where the children came from or the status of the birth parents. Tann's network was shut down in the mid-1940s, though she died of cancer before facing legal consequences.

Periodically, other stories emerge. I chose to set my story in the St. Louis area after reading about a woman who gave birth at a hospital in St. Louis and was told her infant had died, but she never saw the child and never received a death certificate. Fifty years later, DNA testing confirmed her child was still alive and had been adopted. This opened up a series of similar stories from other low-income women who gave birth at the same hospital, which had been closed for years by then. International examples occur as well. In a network in Spain, families paid a priest or nun installments on illegal adoption fees for children who never knew they were stolen and adopted, often offspring of young, unmarried mothers considered unfit by the Roman Catholic Church. Even some adoptions of these children that were technically legal had been coerced.

For so many families, adoption is a gift. That it should ever be a stolen gift is a travesty. No matter how our families are formed, may we treasure the life they give us and seek to honor them with righteousness and truth rather than be swallowed in shame.

Olivia Newport
2019

CHAPTER ONE

Jillian supposed she should be grateful he hadn't gagged and blindfolded her when he intruded into her home office, snatched her, and stuffed her in the truck. She'd already been out for a morning run and wasn't planning to spend all of Saturday afternoon working. Tidying up was all she had in mind. And then he burst in, and now she was strapped into the front seat without her phone as the truck rolled out of town.

She gripped the passenger door armrest. He clicked the power button to lock all the doors.

"Dad. You can tell me where we're going." Jillian cocked her head toward her father. "I'm hardly going to leap out of a moving vehicle on the highway."

"Why do you demand to know every detail about everything?"

From behind the steering wheel of his pickup, which he'd been driving so long he talked about it like an old friend, Nolan grinned at Jillian with green eyes that mirrored hers. Spring mountain sunlight bounced off his pupils, and he reached in the console for his dark glasses and set them on his face. In his midfifties, he still had a fit, youthful figure. Rediscovering skiing over the winter, after a long hiatus, had suited him.

"And why do you insist on doing everything by the seat of your pants?" Jillian raised both hands to draw her long, dark waves under control behind her neck. He hadn't given her a chance to grab a band or clip before leaving the house, a circumstance she was likely to regret if there was any wind once they were out of the truck at their mystery destination.

Her retort was halfhearted. Who could complain about a Saturday afternoon drive on a day like this? The rainy mid-April week seemed to be behind them, the bounty from the sky having nourished the earth and coaxed forth undulating ripe, burgeoning greens of the season. They were barely out of Canyon Mines, so the mountains still cradled them, and light radiated like a mammoth burning flare across the view. Immaculate snow lingered on the shoulders of the Rockies, and the vistas, as they did on so many days when she paused from her work to raise her eyes to the dazzling Colorado terrain, tugged at her spirit.

"I promise you'll like it," Nolan said. "You have to admit I know you well."

"The people stipulate to that point, Your Honor."

"Someday I might give up lawyering and become a judge, and you'll really have to use that title with me."

"And I would do so proudly," Jillian said. "Now let's see. Heading east. Probably Denver." Unless they would turn north to her Duffy grandparents' home once they got to I-25.

"Maybe, maybe not."

"So it is Denver."

"You think you're so smart."

"I am smart."

"The court stipulates to that point."

"What's going on in Denver that we need to go today?"

"A museum. You like museums. And you've never been to this one."

"Why not? Did I have a deprived childhood?"

"Hardly. I always let you bring home souvenirs, and you'll get a doozy today."

"Okay, you've got me curious."

"Good. You need to get out more."

"We're both going to St. Louis in a few weeks for Tucker and Laurie Beth's wedding," she pointed out.

"And we'll have a spectacular time," Nolan said, "but we have our own great city right here with history and culture and all the good stuff. You liked it when you went to college."

"I still do. I just haven't had a lot of reason to come down."

"Well, today you do." Nolan merged into a faster lane and accelerated.

"I have a feeling there's a story here," Jillian said.

With her dad, there was always a story. People liked to talk to Nolan. He was one of those people who made friends wherever he went and stuck in people's minds. In his work as a family law attorney and legal mediator, he met a lot of people other than his clients, but he could still drop into a random coffee shop or a hardware store and come out having met four new people—and probably would talk with them long enough to find a common connection with at least one. Shops, parties, sporting events, business meetings. People remembered Nolan Duffy. He thrived on it. Not Jillian. She inherited some sort of recessive introvert gene—and another one for preferring a well-ordered life.

"The curator called me," Nolan said.

"And how do you know a museum curator?"

He shrugged. "We had coffee once."

That meant Nolan had chatted with the curator in the line ordering coffee or something else equally ordinary and forgettable to most people.

"And?" Jillian said.

"And he has a situation he thinks may require legal attention. Or at least he'd like a legal opinion about the advisability of legal representation around matters of liability and financial consequence."

"Now that's legal speak if ever I've heard it."

"Do not mock my profession, young lady."

"Never!" Jillian laughed. "What does this have to do with me? Or a souvenir? Is this all just an excuse to get me out of the house?"

"What if it is? It's a fine day for a drive, and I enjoy your company."

"You don't have to charm me. I already love you."

"Oh, right."

"It's Saturday. And you'll be in Denver on Monday. Why the special trip?"

"Because I wanted to bring you along, obviously."

"Dad."

Nolan checked his mirrors and changed lanes again. They clearly were headed to Denver now.

"Here's what I know," he said. "It's not much. Years ago—decades, I think—the museum received a trunk that was abandoned at Union Station."

"Decades?"

He nodded. "The curator is relatively recent, but the museum is about fifty years old. He's not at all sure of the story, but from what he can tell, the trunk arrived at Union Station over a hundred years ago and somehow was separated from its owner."

"Surely the railroad would have had a procedure for unclaimed luggage."

"We don't know what happened, Jilly."

"How did the museum get the trunk?"

"I don't know that either. He didn't say. I'm not sure he knows. It's not a large museum. It's one of those places where a historic home in a notable neighborhood has been converted to a museum, and gradually they collect pieces that might have been authentic to the period. My guess is that they ended up with the trunk that way."

"Union Station wouldn't just give away lost luggage."

"Not at the time, no. Perhaps never, officially. But at some point, someone took possession of it. Maybe after a while someone just thought it was in the way. Rich, the curator, discovered it just a few days ago while he was overseeing an effort to clean out and organize some overcrowded storage space in the house's basement. There's no record of the item being logged into the collection of the museum, yet there it is."

"Very irregular."

"Yep."

"Somebody must have had it in between. Whoever's hands it ended up in after Union Station got tired of it and dumped it on the museum because the thrift store didn't want it. It's probably been painted and full of junk while somebody used it as a coffee table after finding it at a flea market."

"Nope. It's the real deal. Rich brought in a locksmith to pick the locks as carefully as possible to preserve the integrity of the trunk," Nolan said.

Jillian's jaw dropped. "You mean it hadn't been opened before this? In a hundred years?"

"As I understand it, that seems to be the case."

"They didn't find a body, did they?"

Nolan laughed. "I'm pretty sure Rich would have recognized that as a legal matter without requiring my opinion."

"Then?"

"The usual personal items," Nolan said, "along with a considerable stack of business records from a company in Ohio. Financial records."

"Enter the legal questions."

"Maybe or maybe not."

"It is a curious question why someone travels from Ohio to Colorado with a trunk full of business financial records and then abandons them."

Nolan wiggled one eyebrow. "See? Isn't this better than cleaning your office?"

"Just tidying." Jillian turned up her palms. "But my piles can wait."

"As a historian, Rich is intrigued. But he is also concerned about the museum having custody of these records. He's wondering whether there might be legal liability without due provenance of the alleged donation. And then there's also the issue of the financial documents—what they might mean for whoever could have benefited by how the matters they represent were or were not resolved."

"But you said it was over a hundred years ago," Jillian said. "Can you really figure that out now?"

Nolan nodded. "These are all questions I'd have to look into. My instinct is that Rich wants to dot every i and cross every t but that there won't be any legality to pursue."

"But you don't know for sure."

"Not until we see what he has."

They weren't far from Denver now. In a few minutes, Nolan exited the highway and began a series of turns along surface streets taking them through downtown.

"What's this place called?" Jillian asked.

"Owens House Museum."

"Never heard of it."

"Me neither, until I met Rich. But from what I understand, it's just a turn-of-the-century house."

"Denver has a lot of those."

"That they do."

Nolan pulled up in front of the house and put the truck in Park. Jillian considered the structure as they got out.

"Considering what this neighborhood was like a hundred years ago," she said, "this house is fairly modest."

"I agree," Nolan said. "No wonder I couldn't place it. It must have been an ordinary family's home, not the mansion of a silver mine millionaire."

"I wonder how it came to be a museum then."

"I'm sure Rich will tell you if you want to ask."

Jillian pivoted in a circle. "And how did it survive all the demolition and modernizing in the immediate neighborhood?"

"You have an inquisitive mind," Nolan said. "Now let's go see a man about a trunk."

Side by side, they proceeded past the sign that welcomed visitors to the Owens House Museum and up the wide walk at a pace that allowed absorbing the details. The sandstone house, built in the Queen Anne style popular in the last two decades of the nineteenth century, was a simple two-story home in contrast to some of the three- and four-story homes of the era popular among Denver's wealthiest. With a downtown location, it likely never had much of a lawn, but the carriage house set back from the street suggested that it supported at least one pair of horses with space for a full-sized carriage, a service cart, and living quarters for liverymen above. The house itself boasted the requisite rounded tower, steeply pitched roof, twin chimneys, and generous windows of Queen Anne architecture.

"This house could be in Canyon Mines," Jillian said.

"It's certainly the right era." They went up the front steps, and Nolan pushed the front door open. A young man at a welcome desk looked up expectantly, and Nolan asked for the curator.

"They've done an amazing job with the restoration," Jillian said while they waited. "The woodwork is gorgeous. Nia and Leo would love to see this. Even Veronica and Luke." The Dunstons had undertaken an ambitious renovation of a sprawling Victorian home and opened a bed and breakfast in Canyon Mines, and the O'Reillys ran the Victorium Emporium because Veronica was enthralled with all things Victorian.

"I'm sure they have some brochures you could take to Nia," Nolan said. "Here's Rich now."

"Thank you for coming." Rich offered a handshake.

"This is my daughter, Jillian Parisi-Duffy."

"I'm glad to meet you," Jillian said. "Your museum is very inviting."

"We have the standard drawing room, music room, dining room, and kitchen on the ground floor," Rich said, "and offices in the back. Bedrooms and attic upstairs. And of course the basement, which is what has brought you here today."

"Are we going downstairs?" Nolan asked.

Rich shook his head. "I have the piece in my office. We've taken the liberty of cleaning it up a little bit."

Nolan rubbed his palms together. "Then let's have a look at it."

They followed Rich through the house, bypassing a tour in progress and slipping past a red-lettered No ENTRANCE sign to an area behind the kitchen that originally might have been a back porch and was enclosed at a later stage. Rich opened the door to his unassuming office. Centered in the space between the door and his desk stood a steamer trunk whose grand presence beckoned to the most profound calling of Jillian's work. Her breath stopped, and the pulse at her temples magnified.

"Can I touch it?" she blurted out.

Nolan smiled.

Rich nodded. "The gloves are on the desk."

"Of course." Jillian donned the pair of white gloves that would keep her oils off the antique piece and ran her hands around the upright form of the wardrobe style steamer. "Did my dad tell you what I do for a living?"

"Genealogist. I can imagine you have special appreciation for what you're looking at and the story it might tell in the hands of the family."

"I don't usually get to look at the past quite so directly," Jillian said. "It's stunning."

The stenciled blue beryl and muted gold canvas was far more captivating than the brown or green metal trunk Jillian had mentally prepared for. This was sheer enchantment, artistry created and selected with care. And monogrammed. Someone's story.

"It doesn't have many stickers," Jillian observed.

"I noticed that too," Rich said. "It might have been used for regional rail travel, but it was a steamer trunk only in name. This trunk was never on the water. I would stake my reputation on it."

"But my dad said you think it came from Ohio. Colorado is not regional to Ohio."

"Perhaps we should have a look at the papers you mentioned," Nolan said. "Are they still in the trunk?"

"Yes," Rich said. "It seemed the safest place to leave them."

"May I?" Jillian couldn't help herself. Although the steamer had been opened at least once—and occasioned Rich's call to her father—*she* hadn't opened it. The moment would be exquisite, a first look not just at census records or overlooked birth certificates or a chain of addresses tracking an individual's movements from fifty years ago, but at abandoned personal possessions that had been sealed away for over a century until a locksmith's delicate touch unlocked them two days ago.

But why?

ABOUT THE AUTHOR

Olivia Newport's novels blend the truths of where we find ourselves now with insights into what carried us in the past. Enjoying life with her husband and nearby grown children, she chases joy in stunning Colorado at the foot of Pikes Peak.